# Dan's Hauntastic Haunts Investigates: Goodman Dairy

## Hauntastic Haunts Book 1

### Alex Silver

*Alex Silver*

# Copyright

This is a work of fiction. Names, characters, places, and incidents either are the product of the author's imagination or are used fictitiously. Any resemblance to actual persons, living or dead, events, or locales is entirely coincidental. All products/brands names mentioned herein are registered trademarks of their respective holders/companies.

Copyright © 2020 by Alex Silver

ISBN (ebook): 978-1-9995310-6-5
ISBN (paperback): 978-1-7773563-0-9

# Dedication

To O and R, you're my inspiration.

# ONE
## *Dan*

Dan Collins, ghost hunter, was trending on social media. This was it. The moment I'd been living for since I started my vlog channel. My moment to shine. Too bad that instead of incontrovertible proof that ghosts walk among us, I'd become an overnight vlogging sensation because I fell. Through—not down—the rotted out steps of the old deserted building I was investigating. Over a quarter of a million views and everyone was yukking it up because I almost broke my neck.

At least I had good insurance, the ambulance trip and treatment for my broken leg were both covered. And my phone survived the fall, even if some of my ghost hunting equipment did not.

The footage captured the characteristic lens flare of a ghost in the corner of the frame right before I took my plunge back to the ground floor.

No one cared about that. No, all they saw was my expression of shocked horror as the ground gave way under me. My arms windmilling, my expensive gear smashing down the stairs and then I fell out of frame.

People posted reaction videos to my video. Kids reenacted my facial expression at the moment the ghost touched me. None of them seemed to notice the evidence of a spirit pushing me onto the rotten stairs. Only my most devoted subscribers pointed out the other presence in the frame.

The social media frenzy took off with me stuck in a hospital bed with nothing but my phone for company. Stacy quit once it was clear I would not die. She claimed she hadn't signed on to risk her neck as my personal assistant. In all honesty, I couldn't blame her. This wasn't the first time I'd ended up with injuries while capturing footage.

It wouldn't be the last time. Not that it was my fault. It was just that hauntings drove the living away. So they showed up in places that were falling apart.

By the time they generated enough buzz as urban legends to reach my ears and became accessible to the public, haunted places got rundown.

It also wasn't the first time I'd lost an assistant to my injury prone nature. Stacy had lasted for almost a year. Zack, the assistant before her, quit after a couple months. Others had come and gone too. Martha, my first hire, quit after our first haunting.

Martha preceded me into the building to film my entrance. Her first step into a spider web had resulted in her screaming at coming face to face with the web's occupant and then running back out of the building. Martha hadn't been my best hiring decision ever, but I was still new to figuring out the whole employer thing.

My vlog, which I started after high school, took off enough to consider supporting myself with it when I was a community college freshman. I developed a loyal core of followers. And I put out quality content.

My brand started as more of a 'dare me to stay overnight in the spookiest spots on earth' gimmick. But after my experiences road tripping to various spooky spots all around the Northeastern US, I'd started to believe in ghosts. How could I doubt, after all the weird stuff that happened?

My subscribers agreed. Ghosts were real, and we were on a quest to prove it. I started getting gifts of ghost hunting gear and researching it more myself.

A good quarter of my webisodes were just talking about the ways we could measure paranormal activity. On my site fans discussed what would constitute incontrovertible proof of a haunting these days. In an age with digital media being what it was, skeptics could refute any evidence we found.

The other half of my video archives were the hauntings. Like the Old Miller House. Where I fell.

I sighed and refreshed my landing page. The view counts had ticked past three hundred thousand now.

I got an email notification. Since my video took off, my fan-mail had increased on a massive scale. I considered ignoring it. I used the term 'fan' in a loose sense, most of the people writing to me after the accident thought I was a joke.

But the preview in the notification for this message showed it was from my insurance carrier. They had denied my latest claim. *Not again, ugh.*

It probably said something about me that I had my favorite insurance agent's extension saved to my speed dial. Heck, it said something that I even *had* a favorite insurance agent.

Stacy said it wasn't normal. She joked that I should add a channel to my vlog rating the nation's ERs since I spent so much time in them. Setting bones and getting stitches.

I suspected she was right about the not normal part. But my job could be dangerous. It wasn't like haunted sites were famous for their impeccable maintenance. I dialed Chad's direct line. He picked up on the third ring with his usual professional greeting.

"Chorus Insurance, Chad speaking, how may I help you this evening?"

"Hey, Chad, it's me again, your favorite customer."

There was a beat of silence.

"Mr. Collins?" Chad said.

"Ding, ding, ding, we have a winner!" I crowed.

Chad sighed into the phone. Well, that was a break from the cool professionalism, progress on my campaign to wear him down from a call center bot.

"What can I do for you this time, Mr. Collins?"

"You can start by calling me Daniel, come on, Chad, we're best buds at this point."

I imagined Chad pinching the bridge of his nose. It was a gesture my dad used to do a lot with me when I strained his patience, so that was where the mental image came from.

Not that I'd ever seen Chad to compare him to my father, but from his voice I imagined he was a hot older guy. Maybe a bit of a nerdy professor vibe going. Salt and pepper hair, clean shaven. A person who wore chinos and pressed dress shirts and thought hipsters ate too much avocado toast. A real stickler for the rules. Real dad-like.

"Mr. Collins, can I just have the claim number you are calling about?"

"See? This is the reason I always turn to you in my hour of need, Chad, you're just so efficient." I rattled off the claim number from the email.

"It says here that your claim got rejected because you are being dropped as a Chorus Insurance client."

"That can't be right, I always pay my premiums on time." I did too. The first thing I paid for each month was my insurance. I'd used it enough that I wasn't about to mess around with it getting canceled.

"The note says you are a high liability patient and Chorus Insurance can no longer meet your healthcare needs."

"Chad, buddy, come on. There must be some way you can help me."

"I can ask my manager about getting you signed up for a high risk policy." Chad sounded doubtful. "The premiums are higher. You would have a larger deductible and the coverage isn't as comprehensive as your current policy, but it would at least keep you covered."

"If that's the best you can do."

"Let me speak to my supervisor and get back to you. And I'll resubmit the current claim, since your old policy still covered you when it came through. As you said, you do always pay your premiums on time."

"That would be great, thanks. I knew I could count on you!"

Chad gave me a canned response to the effect that I should have a great day and hung up on me.

A few hours later an email arrived saying they had approved the claim. Once again, I thanked my lucky stars that Zack had taken down Chad's phone extension when we were dealing with the claims for my first concussion last year.

A direct line to Chad cut my call wait times down to nothing. He might sound like a crusty old guy, but he always came through for me. Even when I called on a Saturday evening.

# TWO
## *Chad*

D aniel Collins would be the death of me. In the insurance industry, I rarely talked to the same customers all that often. Not unless they were dealing with something catastrophic like a cancer diagnosis or something terminal.

Chorus was a large enough company, I didn't get to develop relationships with most of the patients. Sure I dealt with people from doctor's offices and pharmacies on a regular basis, and established working relationships with plenty of them. But no one seemed as accident prone as Daniel.

The kid was an idiot, if a lovable one. *Kid, right*, he was a year older than me. But he acted like a kid. A big reckless kid who did not understand the consequences to his actions.

I'd seen his latest stunt on his vlog when it went viral last night. I mean, I would have seen it anyway since I was a subscriber. But the viral video hit my social media before I checked for his weekly update.

The guy needed all the help he could get, so I figured a monthly sub to his channel was the least I could do for him. The rational part of me knew I shouldn't think about him at all. He was a client. A frequent client.

One who forced me to find every loophole in the system to get his ridiculous claims covered. Not that I owed him anything. But my entire purpose in working at Chorus Insurance was to make sure other families didn't go through the same uncaring crap mine dealt with to get their claims covered.

Without insurance Daniel would be up to his eyeballs in debt for just one of his many forays to the emergency department. Let alone the over a dozen trips in the year since I'd first gotten a call from him to complain about a rejected claim.

Well, the first time I'd spoken to his assistant. I snorted, remembering my incredulity that Daniel had an assistant making his calls for him. I thought it must be a pretense, to make him feel like a real star instead of a two-bit vlogger.

The situation piqued my curiosity. I shouldn't have looked him up, but I had typed his name into the search bar, and there he was.

Six feet of athletic hunk creeping through what he claimed was a haunted forest. The first video gave a *Blair Witch Project* vibe, the video a clear amateur effort. But the camera work had improved in the later ones.

Dan had hit his stride as a paranormal investigations persona. His videos were good. He had a magnetic personality that drew me in from the first webisode.

The ghosts were a load of malarkey. But the guy was a natural showman and his videos kept me engaged. I had a soft spot for the ones where he responded to fans live.

The way he interacted with people, open and at ease with himself. His charisma captivated me. I might have a bit of an unrequited crush on the guy. Or I was just a giant sucker.

Here I was spending hours trying to finagle a way for the adrenaline junkie social media personality to keep his primo policy. Despite the latest projections from our actuarial department labeling him a high risk.

He *was* high risk, but he hadn't violated the terms of his policy. It seemed wrong to cancel it. Once again Daniel had me tilting at windmills for him.

I at least got the claim for the ambulance ride and ER visit for his broken leg approved. I checked the claim still being processed for his inpatient hospital stay and flagged it to my attention to make sure it got approved too.

That only left the policy issue. Since I worked the evening shift, there weren't any supervisors to bring it up with tonight. They had left a couple hours into my shift.

I made a note in Daniel's file and sent a message to the day shift supervisor who would be most sympathetic to the request. I used the subject line 'urgent customer service matter' and I wrote a quick note requesting a moment to discuss the matter at the start of my shift tomorrow. Then I donned my headset and returned to the phone lines.

# THREE
## *Dan*

The problem with being a social media hit was going viral came with an expiry date. My fifteen minutes of fame ended before my doctors signed off on my discharge papers. Let alone before I achieved full mobility again.

When it all blew over, I still wasn't a household name. At least I picked up some new subscribers to my channel. Loads of my videos got a boost in their view and like counts. I had hundreds of new comments to moderate on my website.

The viral video generated plenty of buzz. Shame I was too overwhelmed at the moment to take full advantage of that fact. Modding the forum on my website was part of Stacy's job, except that Stacy had quit.

So I had to take on all her responsibilities, including lining up a new site for next month's Hauntastic Haunts webisodes. The one Stacy had arranged for August would be difficult to navigate with my broken leg.

My top priority once I got released was finding a new assistant. Preferably one who cared about the paranormal as much as I did. Or at least wouldn't freak out at the first cold spot or disembodied voice.

It would be killer if one of my longtime fans took the job. They would know my brand and be able to hit the ground running. My wish list sounded like a pipe-dream.

Another pro of hiring a fan was that they might be less likely to expect another viral video of me injuring myself. It shouldn't have come as a shock that my most watched videos

14

were now all the ones where I got injured. To be fair, there were a number of them.

Some enterprising individual had spliced together a greatest hits reel of all the injuries I'd caught on tape over the years. I reported the content as my IP, sent a cease and desist I kept handy, and then cut together my own version as a blooper reel set to funny music.

I had purchased a license for some generic mood music on the cheap from a friend who liked to compose in her spare time. The blooper video didn't quite achieve viral success, but it did well enough. Better than the paranormal investigation 101 series I posted on occasion as bonus content.

That was a depressing thought. People would rather tune in to watch me get hurt than to see the ghosts I was trying to help. When I got into the paranormal aspects of hauntings, it occurred to me that most ghosts were looking for a resolution.

I figured showcasing their stories might help them find rest. If people learned what happened to ghosts in life, then it might help their spirits find peace in death. A way to crowdfund a happy ending for the ghosts I encountered. That was how I saw it, anyway.

My video release schedule adhered to a pattern. The first Saturday of the month was the site reveal and gear review. I did it as an unboxing deal.

I reviewed the new tech at the new site, double unboxing, mind-blown. That had been Zack's idea. I followed the unboxing up with a haunting profile of the site for the month on the second Saturday. I talked about who the ghosts in question were. Any relevant historical details. That was where the crowdsourcing came in, my fans liked to do their own amateur sleuthing. It got them invested in the hauntings.

Then, if it was a month with five Saturdays I devoted two weeks to the actual investigation, otherwise I just did one.

Either way, I spent the first three weeks of the month on site, giving me a week or two to travel between sites.

My busy schedule was why I lived out of Vanessa, my converted van. Easier than paying rent on a place I never saw.

It wasn't the worst way to live. I preferred it to being stuck in one place. Stacy hadn't been a fan of the close quarters. I suspected the nomadic lifestyle more than anything had been her reason for tendering her resignation.

The last Saturday of the month I uploaded a wrap up for the investigation. We talked about the ghosts we'd encountered and brainstormed ways to put them to rest. Sometimes, I felt like we put the hauntings to rest. Other times we couldn't.

Not that I was an expert on communicating with ghosts, I never claimed to be a medium. I was just an average guy using modern science to track the paranormal and try to be a good Samaritan for ghosts.

Sure, it sounded cheesy, but I brought in enough money to support myself and pay my assistant as long as I was frugal about it. And when I helped a spirit, well, that was all the reward I needed.

That and I lived for new subs. My view count and my likes were the difference between continuing to do what I loved for a living and giving it all up for a steady paycheck.

I shuddered at the thought of going to a cubicle farm and turning into someone like my dad. Or Chad the insurance agent. Someone who spoke in a customer service voice and couldn't loosen up if my life depended on it.

Lucky for me, I could film the "Old Miller House" wrap up vid from my hospital bed. It would boost my credibility and perhaps gain sympathy donations from my regulars. I should do a live Q&A from the hospital too.

That was the marketing stuff that Stacy had excelled at. She'd posted a promise to do a live video in the update to the site, assuring my patrons I wasn't dead before ditching me here.

For all that we'd parted ways, Stacy had been good at the job. I would miss her. But I had too much to do to dwell on her departure.

I posted a notification to all my patrons that I would go live to answer their questions about the Miller House haunting at six. Then I set up my phone to film the wrap up episode in the meantime.

I had filmed most of what I wanted to say plus extra material to make the editing process more smooth by the time the Q&A rolled around. I still wanted more footage from the site, but that would have to wait until the hospital released me.

I went live at six on the dot and there were already two dozen patrons signed in. Not a bad turnout for the short notice. Though it was better when Stacy announced a live feed in advance.

File that under things to delegate to my new assistant. I greeted my fans and gave them a quick update on my health.

"Hey, everyone! It's me, Dan." I waved, then I panned the camera around the room. "As you can see, I'm still in the hospital."

A wave of messages wishing me a speedy recovery and expressing their sympathies scrolled by, replacing a bunch of generic greetings.

"So, I figured since I'm a captive audience at the moment I'd take a moment to catch up with my most loyal viewers, you all."

I responded to a few of my most devoted followers as they commented. Then my elusive top tier patron, RedHerring99, popped into the message stream.

RedHerring99: Glad to see you recovering.

"Aw, thanks, Red. Thank you all for your well wishes. So they've got me comfortable for now. The staff here at Saint Vincent's have been treating me fantastic. My recovery is going well. They had me walking with crutches earlier. They say I should be mobile again soon. So, hit me up with your questions about the show."

RadRaf: What are you working on next?

BriBri: Are you going back to the Miller House?

"Okay, so, Raf, glad you asked. I just finished filming part of the wrap up vid for the Miller House. Unfortunately, BriBri, after the incident, they won't allow anyone back inside the property as the city has condemned it as unsafe. I hope to get more footage of the exterior once I blow this popsicle stand. So, stay tuned for the wrap up video next week and the big reveal of August's site going live in two weeks."

Collins4life: Where is Stacy?

GhastLee: Do you have your next haunting picked yet?

"Collins4life, Stace has been a great asset, huh? I know I appreciated her help, but we have parted ways. So I need to hire a new assistant. Before the accident, I had a few options in contention for the August haunting. My doctors are telling me I need to avoid abandoned buildings until my leg is healed. I'll have to look for more accessible sites for the next couple months. And as always, I've got something big coming up for the October haunting."

I ignored the handful of comments about Stacy's appearance. She was an attractive girl, but Zack had been more appealing to my personal tastes. Not that I would make a move with my employee. That would cross a line.

Considering that we bunked together and lived in each other's pockets, the arrangement would be inappropriate for anything other than a working relationship. So, yeah, Stace may have been smoking hot. And Zack might have starred in several of my fantasies, but they were off limits.

I ignored the questions about my dating life. It was DOA anyway. I never stayed in one place longer than the month it took to film a haunting, dating would be a fruitless effort.

Funny how that only bothered me recently. I shoved the thought aside and focused on my fans. I was only twenty-eight, I had plenty of time to worry about dating when I wasn't living out my dreams on the open road.

RadRaf: Check out the old Cedar Creek asylum here in Michigan.

Drew: Hauntoween is gonna be lit!

I chuckled. "Yeah, Drew, it will be hauntastic. I'll add that to my research list, thanks, Raf. Getting back the PA thing, if joining me on the road interests any of you, or you know someone who would like the PA gig, shoot me an email." I reminded them of my email address.

RadRaf: If I were a few decades younger I'd take you up on that.

"Thanks, Raf." I chuckled. He wasn't the biggest donor, but he was consistent and he was among the most vocal of my supporters.

Redherring99: How do you find assistants willing to gallivant around the country with you?

"Well, Red, that's one perk of the job. We travel the country on my dime, right? I'd say that's living the dream. I found Stace through a mutual friend. Zack and I attended college together. The others I found on Craigslist. I know, glamorous, right?"

RadRaf: You be careful meeting internet strangers.

Drew: Wish my mom would let me do something like that.

Christie: Were you and Stacy dating?

BriBri: Did you break up, is that why she left?

I suppressed a sigh, ignoring those questions didn't make them go away. The chat box had too many comments along those lines to ignore now.

I resigned myself to coming out again for the new subscribers. Not my favorite part of being an out social media personality, but it came with the territory.

"Raf, thanks for your concern, I do my best to stay safe about it. I run a background check before I hire anyone. Drew, hit me up if you're ever able to join me on the road." I skimmed the comment feed. "Um, since I'm seeing lots of speculation and comments, Stace and I were never an item. I'm not seeing anyone to be honest with you all. Right now my focus is on the channel and trying to put lingering spirits to rest."

I'd done this before, but I had a bunch of new subs after the Miller house. BriBri had no excuse, she was a longtime fan. Maybe she just forgot.

No sense putting off the inevitable. I braced myself for the reactions and came out to my patrons, yet again. "Besides, as my longtime patrons know—I'm gay. Stacy isn't my type."

Drew: Love you, Dan.

RadRaf sent a heart emoji. My longtime patrons spammed the channel with hearts, messages of support, and pride flag emojis. BriBri made a comment about sexuality being fluid, skirting the line between supportive and hoping that I would change my mind.

She liked to flirt with me though. So it might be more wishful thinking than an actual belief the right girl could turn my head.

Christie and a handful of others left the chat. I expected a few unsubscribes. That could have gone worse.

At least they didn't stick around to harass me. Or recruit their friends to join in a hate campaign. I'd dealt with instances of that early in my vlogging career.

"Aw, thanks for the love, everyone. I have the best patrons."

RedHerring99: Solidarity, man.

Whoa. Hold the phone. The elusive Red was gay too? I was reading too much into it. He was more likely just an ally.

For all I knew Red wasn't even a guy. What if Red was a lesbian? Solidarity could mean anything.

Not that it mattered. I just appreciated the support, financial and otherwise, I got from my number one patron.

"Thanks, Red. Okay, so, back to the Q&A, right?"

Drew: How did you know for sure you were gay?

"Drew, buddy, I'd prefer to keep the questions related to the channel. I'm not here to talk about my sexuality. If you're questioning your sexuality or looking for mentorship or something you can email me. I would love to point you to local resources or provide a listening ear one-on-one. This isn't the forum for that."

Drew: Sorry, I'll message you.

"No problem. I need to wrap this up soon. Does anyone else have questions for me before I sign off?"

BriBri: Are any of the sites you're considering in the Midwest again?

RadRaf: Are you attending the fan expo in Detroit this year?

Drew: Has that medium you mentioned in the video two weeks ago been in touch again?

"I am considering several sites all across the country for future filming. As you know, I don't reveal my selected sites until the unboxing video drops.

"A big part of that is the liability involved. As the Miller House proved, this can be a dangerous profession. I'd hate for any of you to put yourselves in danger scoping out our filming sites in advance.

"As to cons, we'll see. This leg will put a crimp in my filming schedule so I might have to scrap my con appearances for the time being. The situation is fluid. And, no, I haven't heard from Madame Karen again since my last video dropped. I'll share it on the site if I do.

"Keep an eye out for a short bonus video I'm planning on doing to review some new gear in the next week. So, I think I'll leave it there for tonight. Thanks for tuning in and asking questions, I couldn't keep Hauntastic Haunts going without you, have a hauntastic evening!"

I ended the livestream. A few more messages rolled by, people saying goodbye. Some thanking me for being available to my fans. A scattering of last minute well wishes over my leg.

I logged out and put my phone aside in favor of my meal tray.

That went well. And the new patrons my viral status had attracted hadn't derailed the group. That aspect surpassed expectations too. Now I just needed to find an assistant and a couple hauntings that took place at sites I could explore with a cast and crutches.

# FOUR

## *Chad*

Daniel was looking for a new assistant. I closed the tab from his live feed. The dashboard clock confirmed that my lunch hour was fast approaching its end.

I typed out a quick message from my RedHerring99 email account. Before I could overthink it, I hit send and hurried from my car back to my cubicle.

Six was not the most convenient time for a Q&A since it was only a couple hours into my shift tonight. But it was Dan, so I'd finagled my break to align with the time for the livestream.

I was glad I caught it too. It was nice to see visual evidence he was on the road to recovery and in good spirits.

I was glad to be a supportive presence in the chat when he had to come out, yet again, to allay suspicions about his relationship with Stacy. She was his PA for Pete's sake. People were always looking for the next scandal I supposed.

I clocked back into work with moments to spare. A yellow post-it note adorned my monitor. I recognized the writing on it. Harold, the evening manager, demanded my presence in his office. It was five of seven. He would leave for the night soon.

With a resigned sigh, I strode to his office.

"You wanted to see me, sir?" I asked from the open door to his domain.

Harold glanced up from his desk. "Brewer, yeah, you're fired."

"What?"

"Last night you put through a claim for a policy on hold pending review. That goes against regulations. It wasn't the first time you've pulled something like that. You're still on probation from the last incident, so you're fired."

I blinked at him. "You mean the claim for Daniel Collins' broken leg? He paid his policy in full. The claim was legit, how is that against protocol?"

"His file is pending review. Standard procedure is not to pay claims until that process resolves. Regardless of the outcome, you stepped over the line. This isn't the first time I've talked to you about it either. Three strikes, you're out—pack your things, Brewer."

My mouth went dry. But what else could I say? "Don't I at least get severance pay?"

"Two weeks pay, so that's two more paychecks for you. HR will mail you the relevant documents, including information on your insurance policy and how you can continue to pay for it out of pocket. If you have questions, you can refer them to Lucy in HR. You have half an hour to clear out your cubicle and exit the premises, am I clear?"

"Yeah, crystal clear," I said. No point arguing. I didn't leave many personal effects at work, anyway. Within five minutes I had taken down the pictures of my nieces and colorful art I'd tacked to the cubicle walls. I gathered up the few knickknacks from the desk along with a well-used stress ball. The stash of good pens I bought for myself since the company only sprung for cheapo ones completed my collection.

As I was turning to leave, my desk phone rang. I should have ignored it. I wasn't on the clock, heck, as of tonight I wasn't on the payroll. But a glance at the caller ID showed a familiar number.

Daniel.

"Chorus Insurance, Chad speaking, how can I help you this evening?" I said as I dropped into my chair, the familiar phrase rolling off my tongue.

"Chad, buddy, pal. So, I just got an official email saying Chorus is dropping me from the premium plan and offering me a high risk policy at double my prior rate—what gives?"

"I'm sorry to hear that, Mr. Collins. Unfortunately, I am no longer an employee at Chorus Insurance, effective about five minutes ago, so I can't help you."

A beat of silence.

"Uh, if you aren't working for Chorus anymore, why are you still answering your work phone?" Daniel asked.

I sighed, my answer would go straight to his head and inflate his ego. "I saw that it was your number calling."

"Yes! I knew it! We are friends, ha! So, Chad, should I take the new policy, fight them, or what?"

"In my professional opinion?" I asked.

"As my friend," Daniel said.

"You should take the policy for now to avoid having a gap in coverage and then you need to find a policy through another insurer that covers your needs. I can help you with that, if you want to send me an email later." I gave him my personal address. Not the RedHerring99 one, that would be as much as admitting I'd internet stalked him.

"Thanks, you don't know how much I will miss you. You make me feel like I have a direct line to the insurance gods."

I laughed. "Well, apparently I had the same delusion. Turns out I can't right the world's wrongs for you."

"Oh, shit, am I the reason you lost your job?"

"No, of course not," I fibbed, he was one of the patients I'd stuck my neck out for, but not the only one. "Just moving on to bigger and better things, it's been a pleasure meeting your insurance needs, Mr. Collins. Message me and I'll send that email your way when I get home."

"Great, I'll look forward to hearing from you. Later." Daniel sounded relieved.

"Goodbye." I didn't bother with the signature BS sign-off about we at Chorus Insurance wishing health and happiness to you and yours. I hung up the receiver for the final time, gathered my meager belongings and left without a backward glance.

# FIVE

## *Dan*

My emails weren't all bad. The bump in volume to my fan mail from the viral video was tapering off. I received a few negative messages out of the live chat. Christie among them, asking for a refund on her two dollar pledge for the month. I offered to refund her through PayPal.

Messages of support and encouragement from my regulars balanced those negative messages. RadRaf sent me a digital gift card for a coffee and told me how much it meant to him that the younger generation could be out and proud.

Drew came out to me. He thanked me for being a role model he looked up to. That alone was priceless.

We'd talked a little before, but I made a mental note to message the kid more often. Drew was one of my younger subs, and he seemed lonely. Like he needed all the support I had to offer.

Overall, the good outweighed the bad in my inbox. Sure I had the irritating notice of policy termination from Chorus Insurance, but Chad would help me figure out that whole mess.

I got a handful of replies to the hiring call for a PA from my livestream too. That helped brighten my mood. The sooner I hired a replacement, the better.

Unfortunately, none of the candidates seemed like a good fit for the position. My fans didn't seem to understand how much actual work the job involved.

I doubted BriBri would do well with the tiny bathroom in my converted van when we were on location. The amount she hit on me online was enough to make her an automatic no, anyway.

Drew was still a teenager, or I might consider him. I suspected he might have a slight crush, though, so maybe not. I sent him information on PFLAG and the Trevor Project along with an encouraging note about his home situation.

RedHerring99 sent me an email too. Just a few lines encouraging me to keep being unashamed to be myself and wishing me luck in finding a replacement PA. I shot back a quick response thanking them for their continued support.

Then I opened the email from Chad. He encouraged me to accept the policy changes for now so I'd have gap coverage through the fall. Then I should find a new policy in November during open enrollment season.

He included loads of technical jargon and suggested companies that offered policies that might meet my needs. The TL; DR matched what he told me on the phone. I would miss having him as a resource.

I sent a reply thanking him for the advice. On an impulse, I added in a casual mention that I was hiring a new PA, if he was looking for work. I needed someone detail-oriented like him for the role.

I attached the google doc with the job description before I overthought the offer. It was stupid to consider it. He was an office worker, a stereotypical professional. Used to set hours and being beholden to the man.

Chad wasn't just going to uproot his life to follow me around the country. I highlighted the job offer, considered deleting it. Paused with my finger over the key.

Then I moved the cursor to the send button and imagined the email whisking off into cyberspace. It would find Chad, a middle-aged balding family man. Someone who would laugh in my face if I made him such an offer in person.

But what if?

What if he wasn't the person I imagined when I heard his voice over the phone? What if he was as helpful and organized as he appeared? What would it be like to have someone with Chad's quiet competence at my side?

Someone reliable and devoted to his work. Someone who didn't give an inch when I was at my most trying. It was worth a shot. I hit send.

# SIX

## *C*had

I didn't expect the offer from Daniel. Maybe I should have. Did he feel guilty about costing me my job? Was the offer of the PA gig penance?

My problem was, the offer was tempting. I didn't believe in ghosts, but it was clear Daniel did.

He wanted to help people and his social media presence brought together a bunch of like-minded people who just wanted to help restless souls. I could think of worse life missions.

He had attached a link to a google doc with the full job description. I clicked the link, double checking it opened through my professional account and not the RedHerring99 one that I used for social media.

Most of the information fit what I knew of Daniel and his Haunted Holdings company. The job included near constant travel. We would live out of his converted van.

The schematic attached to the job description said it had two bunks, so I would at least have some personal space. I paused at that.

If we were sharing such tight quarters, I should out myself to him. All things considered, I doubted it would pose a problem, but better to find out before I gave my landlord notice.

The thing was, if he had an issue with me, then I'd rather not hear it. Rather not give up the fantasy of him as someone I admired. Still, nothing ventured, nothing gained.

The ghost hunting stuff was fine. I excelled at doing research, so that would be a good fit. Helping Daniel with tracking down local history wherever we went sounded simple enough. I was no camera expert, but he had the knowledge to teach me those skills.

I had no problem handling making calls and scheduling appointments and viewings and getting filming permits for the historical sites he used for his show. Easy work.

It only paid minimum wage, but it came with free housing. Daniel was offering a chance to see the country. I even got a travel companion I genuinely liked, at least from our interactions so far.

This would be strictly professional. No fanboying all over him. No revealing I was a fan. Let alone that I was Dan's elusive superfan, RedHerring99.

Red would have to go into hiding. I'd need to be careful not to reveal that identity to him. Shouldn't be a problem. Though if I was working with him for live events, then Red might become conspicuous by his absence.

That was a concern for another day.

I needed a job. This one looked interesting. The pay wasn't great, but not having to pay rent should offset that.

I had enough health industry experience to figure out getting my testosterone filled while on the road. Most states didn't require a prescription for buying syringes and needles. And I could order a three-month supply through my mail order pharmacy. I just needed to stay on top of updating my mailing address. Easy peasy.

First things first though. I needed to be sure Daniel would be all right hiring a trans guy. And that he wouldn't require me to disclose that to his fans.

I doubted he would force me to out myself, but I would have to be careful about where I stored my T. Only film with a shirt on to hide my surgical scars.

Not that they were super obvious, faded by the years and covered in ink. Nor was Daniel one for topless filming. But it wouldn't hurt to remember the practical details if I didn't want to share my business with the world.

Unless I decided to join him in being out to the fans. I'd need to think about it. Dan's fans were an accepting group, so maybe I could at least share with the livestream patrons. I was getting ahead of myself.

Still, it was workable. Before I second-guessed or talked myself out of applying, I shot back a response. I kept it brief—I was interested in the position and he could call me to discuss it further.

It was getting late, so I didn't expect a response right away. A moment later, my ringtone startled the wits out of me. I almost fumbled the call straight to voicemail.

"Hello?" I squeaked.

"Chad? Huh, you sound different when you aren't in drone mode. Who knew?" Daniel's familiar voice greeted me.

"Daniel, hey," I greeted him again, trying not to sound quite so squeaky. "Thanks for getting back to me so fast."

"Oh, it's Daniel now, is it?" He sounded amused.

"Sure, I'm not at work, and you don't strike me as a stickler for formality," I explained.

"I'm not. You had me convinced that *you* were, though. Just a work persona then?"

"In part, sure. Like you, the Dan you present in front of the camera is a persona, right?"

"Okay, sure. And way to blow away my preconceived notions. Next you'll tell me you aren't a middle-aged dad who is only entertaining my offer because he's going through a midlife crisis," Daniel teased.

"Close," I shot back, "I'm a recent-ish college grad looking for my next adventure."

"No shit?"

"I mean, it took me a couple extra years to get through my program, so I'm twenty-seven, but yeah, graduated two years ago. Worked my way through school at Chorus Insurance."

"Ready to move on to better things? Sounds good. Okay, my man, why do you want the job?"

"You seem like a decent guy." I shrugged, not sure how to explain my impulse to see where this job offer might lead. "And I suspect you need someone around to keep you from breaking your neck on location. For serious, dude, in all my years at Chorus you're the only healthy twenty-something who needed a service rep's name on speed dial."

He gave a self-conscious chuckle.

"What?" I asked, suspicious.

"Nothing." Daniel chuckled again. "It's just that your work number is on my speed dial, no joke."

"Well, if you give me the job we should update that to my cell, huh?"

"Do you want the job?" He sounded incredulous.

"Yes, it sounds like an adventure. There's just one thing."

"Okay, shoot."

"I'm trans," I blurted before I could chicken out. "I'm not sure about advertising it in the videos, at least not right away. But I figure if we are living out of your van you will figure it out and I'd rather be upfront about it. Is that a problem?"

"Phew, for a minute there I thought you were going to confess you don't believe in ghosts," Daniel joked, his voice warm and accepting. "In all seriousness, though, I don't see why it would be. I mean, unless it would be too hard to get your HRT? Are you on hormones? Quinn was. They were one of my earlier assistants. They were great, but getting prescriptions filled when we were in a different state every month was a pain in the ass for them."

I breathed a sigh of relief. I'd seen the videos with Quinn in them. Duh, I should have known Daniel wouldn't be a bigot. Okay then.

"Lucky for me, I have a bit of experience working with the medical system. I go through a mail order pharmacy, so I can just change the address as needed, no worries. I'll figure out the details. Um, but since you brought it up, I actually am a skeptic. Still want me?"

"Sure," Daniel said, "I'm up for the challenge of working with a doubter. Give it a few months and we'll see if we can't convince you to believe."

"We'll see about that. So, do we schedule a formal interview next?" I asked.

"No need. The job is yours, if you want it. I know you're a hard worker and you go to bat for your clients. You're upfront with me, what more do I need to know?"

"That we'll be compatible, since the work is like a never ending road trip?" I suggested.

"Half the adventure is getting acquainted." He laughed. "So, when can you start?"

"When do you need me? I have to give notice on my apartment, but otherwise there isn't much to handle on my end."

There wasn't either. My unit came furnished, and I'd learned to travel light over the years. Between moving in with Kay and college. I figured I could pack most of my stuff into the battered old pair of suitcases jammed in the back of my closet.

Clothes, my e-reader, a laptop and a few mementos too precious to leave behind, that was pretty much everything. Anything I couldn't bring I could leave at Kay's place on my way out of town.

"Well, I'm still in New Hampshire after the Miller House debacle. Doc says they're releasing me Tuesday morning. If you can get here, for your first official act as my PA you can retrieve my van, Vanessa, and drive her to the hospital to collect me. I'll ask Stace to overnight the keys to you if you message me your mailing address."

Tuesday morning. It was Sunday night, that only gave me twenty-four hours to pack, and wrap up all the loose ends of my life. Doable. A change would do me good.

"Can do," I agreed. "Anything I should do to prepare?"

"Check out the channel. There's a link in the job description I sent you. No need to watch everything. I've got a few years worth of footage uploaded, but watch enough to familiarize yourself with what we do."

Easiest homework ever. I'd already watched every webisode of his show on the net. Including the ones on Patreon exclusive to his patrons

"Roger that," I said.

"Great. Pleasure talking to you, Chad. I'll be in touch. Oh, and welcome to the Hauntastic Haunts family."

"Thanks." I grinned. "I'll email you my address for the keys. See you Tuesday."

# SEVEN

## *Dan*

I was antsy to leave the hospital by the time I got discharged on Tuesday morning. I had a new assistant to meet, a wrap-up video to finish shooting and a site to figure out for next month's haunting. It should be a helluva day.

Stacy came through on the key delivery at least. Chad had messaged me about an hour ago that he was at the Miller place and heading to the hospital with Vanessa, as promised.

I had my fingers crossed that one glance at my home and production lab on wheels wouldn't scare him away.

He claimed to have watched some of my videos though, so he'd seen Vanessa on my channel. Still, seeing her in person was different. Drove home that I lived and worked in a six by twelve room and expected him to do likewise.

I loved Vanessa. I converted her myself with help from my uncle and a college buddy. We'd scavenged discount stores to get good deals on high end looking lightweight finishes.

Uncle Kurt constructed the custom interior with me. I needed it to look decent for filming. The result had an Ikea Chic esthetic.

Vanessa boasted full insulation, wiring with solar power, and a 40 gallon freshwater tank. It held enough to last two weeks. An equally large gray water tank and fan for air circulation rounded out my utilities.

I had a functional kitchenette on the right wall complete with a propane stove and oven combo and an isotherm fridge and freezer combo inset under the bunks. I could store a week's worth of food on the road.

We had a nice standard size sink and a pull out cutting board that added counter-space. Overhead cabinets stored dry goods and kitchen gear. Cabinets on the bottom stored cleaning supplies.

A bathroom complete with a shower stall and porta potty toilet occupied the space behind the driver's seat. The passenger seat swiveled to face the back and provide extra seating. I'd installed a storage unit over the seats. A curtain separated the cab from the living space when we parked.

I'd initially had what amounted to a king-size bed in the back, but when I'd first hired a PA I'd converted it into two bunks. It was as simple as cutting into the foam mattress to accommodate a removable partition between the two halves. Each half had a light, an electrical outlet, and a narrow window for ventilation. Overhead cabinets for clothes and personal gear completed the two bunks.

We had additional storage accessible from the rear, under the bed platform. That's where I kept my ghost hunting gear, less delicate filming equipment like tripods and lighting kit, minus the bulbs which I stored up front, and a handheld vacuum.

The left wall between the bed and the shower housed my production gear. My good cameras and lenses had their own padded cabinet.

I mounted two large monitors to the wall above the narrow swivel-top desk for video editing and filming live streams and any segments I didn't need to film on location.

The desk doubled as a dining table, and could swivel out to accommodate up to four people. I had enough room for two chairs. I'd mounted a curtain between the bunk space and the living quarters that doubled as a backdrop for filming.

A signal booster for my cell ensured we could stay connected to social media even when our film sites were out in the middle of nowhere. It was a sweet setup, and it was mine all mine.

Investing in Vanessa made it possible for me to support myself and pay an employee with my earnings since I didn't have overhead costs for housing and office space.

Solar power met my energy needs, another bill I didn't have to worry about. I had to be careful when I was running both computer monitors for video editing, though.

Vanessa was my dream home, but she was still a van and I could understand how my dream might be someone else's nightmare. And living cheek to jowl with a stranger took some adjusting. Stacy never loved the arrangement.

Zack and I had a blast with it while it lasted. Chad was right, my life was like an unending awesome road trip. I hoped he would enjoy that as much as I did. Hiring new PAs was a pain.

When Chad arrived at the hospital, he sent me a text. I replied with my room number. A few impatient moments later, a guy who looked nothing like I had pictured stood in my doorway.

He wasn't a middle-aged balding dad type at all. Chad was almost twinkish. Slim, average height, shaggy blond hair left intentionally mussed, clean-shaven cheeks and a wary expression. At least Vanessa hadn't scared him away.

"Chad, right?" I asked when he hesitated at the threshold.

"Yeah, hey, it's nice to meet you in person."

"Same to you. Now what do you say you bust me out of here and we blow this popsicle stand?"

"Sure, I'll go check with the nurse and see about getting you released," Chad said with a flush. *Odd. Oh well,* at least he was taking the initiative right out of the gate. Just what I needed in an assistant.

It wasn't long before Chad returned with a pair of nurses pushing a wheelchair. I stifled a groan of protest. I'd been in enough hospitals not to fight against their discharge policies. The nurses helped me into the chair.

Chad gathered up all my personal items without being asked. I packed most of it into my backpack already, but he shoved my charger and phone inside too. Along with a small assortment of cards from well-wishers. I propped the crutches on my lap and Chad wheeled me toward the exit.

"Home, sweet home!" I said when Chad pulled the wheelchair to a stop alongside Vanessa. I hopped toward the passenger door, keeping my weight off the broken leg. Chad took my crutches once I was in the van and placed them behind the seats.

"It is an awesome van," Chad said. "The drive here was smoother than I expected. Although using a camera to back up will take getting used to."

"Thanks, she's my baby." I patted the dash.

"And you're trusting me to drive her?"

"Not much choice at the moment." I gestured toward my broken leg. "Besides, splitting the driving responsibilities is one of your primary roles as my PA, even when the doctor gives me the all clear to drive. You still on board?"

"I'm still here, aren't I?"

"Great, so I guess we can start by heading back to the Miller house and getting a few final exterior shots for this week's video."

"You're the boss, let me just return the wheelchair and we can get going."

I settled into my seat and watched Chad walk back toward the hospital. I couldn't help noticing that my new PA was hot. Totally off limits, but hot.

# EIGHT

## *Chad*

Daniel Collins was even more attractive in person than in his videos. That might be a problem. The camera didn't capture the magnetism of his full wattage smile.

It might just be me, but I could listen to his silky voice describing the history of the rundown building we filmed in front of all day. He was so passionate about what he did. It lit him up.

He gave me a crash course in setting up the camera equipment once we parked on site. Daniel insisted on getting the camera and lenses himself. Once he had what he wanted, I helped him get settled on the creaky old front porch. Then I dragged out the various bags of gear from the back storage compartment under his guidance.

I set up a tripod for the camera. While Daniel walked me through where to place three big lighting stands, I adjusted them. His instructions for attaching shades to them to diffuse the lighting for the shot left something to be desired.

More went into this than I would have expected, considering we were filming outside. Still, I knew how to follow directions. It wasn't too long before I had all the filming paraphernalia arranged to Dan's exacting standards.

Then he made me take a photo of the shot on my phone to show him the camera frame, a few more subtle adjustments and we were ready to roll.

"Hi, I'm Dan Collins with Hauntastic Haunts. At the camera helm today is my brand spanking new PA, Chad Brewer. Say hello, Chad."

"Hello," I squeaked. Daniel winked at me. Good thing the camera sat on the tripod or I'm sure I would have mangled the shot when I jerked in surprise at being included in the video.

"Behind me is the old Miller House. New viewers, this month's previous videos feature the Miller House haunting. Click the links below to view those first." He gestured to where he would add the link after uploading the video.

"We checked out reports of paranormal activity at this site this month for a few reasons. For one, we here at Hauntastic Haunts love a good mystery and the Miller family disappeared under strange circumstances in the 1890s. We covered the mystery of what happened to them in the first video in this series, it's quite a story.

"The current owner of the property reached out to me to request we try to put the disgruntled spirits here to rest. As always, I strive to uncover whatever unfinished business the ghosts might have and try to help them find peace.

"Unfortunately in this case, my presence dismayed the spirits here. In last week's video, you can see a ghost manifested before I fell. I'll be the first to admit I'm not a professional in cleansing a haunting.

"If I can help spirits to pass on, that's great, but I'm not equipped to deal with malevolent spirits. I focus on helping lost or confused spirits. Those looking for closure. Vengeful impulses are outside my scope of experience.

"I hope this video series will highlight the need for a cleansing at this location. In my opinion, a strong medium can help the angry spirits haunting the Miller house. Madame Karen, I know you work in the Northeast. If you're watching, this is one haunting where I defer to your expertise on these matters.

"I intend to reach out to the property owner to put him in touch with a medium. I hope they can take further measures. It seems clear to me that whatever happened to the Miller family, at least one ghost haunts their home to this day.

"Much as I wish for a more decisive outcome, I must move on to another haunting after this webisode. As I've mentioned elsewhere, the city condemned the property after my accident, so it's not safe for me to explore further.

"Remember, don't try this at home folks. Even with years of experience under my belt, accidents happen," he swept his arm toward the bulky cast on his leg with a wry grin.

"If I uncover more of the house's secrets or details of the spirits haunting it, I will post another followup video and share that information with you all. Be sure to like and subscribe if you enjoyed this series and if you're looking for exclusive behind-the-scenes video check out my Patreon. The link is in the video description below.

"As always, thanks so much for watching Hauntastic Haunts Investigates. Tune in next time when Chad, Vanessa and I will be on the road reviewing the hottest new ghost hunting gear courtesy of Paranormal Outfitters Inc. Have a hauntastic day!"

Daniel waited a beat then spoke again.

"Okay, great. Let's do another take. This time, join me for the catchphrase? So after I do the shout out to POI, I'll pause and we'll both wish the viewers a hauntastic day, sound good?"

It took three more takes before I satisfied him with my enthusiasm. After that he had me traipse around the exterior of the house to get more footage in case we needed it to film a followup episode from the road.

I think Daniel would have preferred to get fancier with zooming in on the entrance. My skills weren't up to replicating the little camera tricks I'd noticed in re-watching his newer episodes in my downtime last night and on the train from Connecticut to Exeter this morning.

I was too much a camera novice to capture more than basics. I did my best to get the shots he wanted framed to his exacting standards. No cutting the gables along the roofline out of the frame.

Daniel talked me through angling the camera so the giant tree limb from a nearby oak didn't obscure the architectural details. Shooting with the light behind me to avoid glare. Not getting Vanessa's license plates in the shots, stuff I wouldn't have thought of without Daniel mentioning it.

It was exhausting. And it took hours to get enough footage to fill what amounted to enough clips for a twenty-minute behind-the-scenes webisode. Still, I felt good about the work.

It helped that Daniel was patient with me when I had to reshoot the same angles multiple times. He also proved free with his praise when I got things right.

"Thanks, that's a wrap on the Miller house, for now. Let's pack in the gear and find some grub, I can show you the editing software tomorrow."

I disassembled the gear and stowed it all the way I'd found it. Then I locked up the back storage area.

Daniel had already put away the camera bags when I joined him in the main living area. He had his crutches propped against the wall and was leaning on the countertop as he prepped two steaks.

He grinned at me when I entered.

"Hey. Great work today, Chad. How do you like your meat?"

I choked on air, because my crush was talking about meat. *Mind out of the gutter.* "Medium is fine. Can I help?"

"Not much room." He waved me toward the passenger seat, which he had spun to face the back of the van. I sat and watched, feeling a vague guilt at not helping.

He lit the propane burners. "I've got dinner. So, did you have time to look over the list of potential sites for August that I sent you?"

"I did. The discharge paperwork says you shouldn't be sitting for more than a couple hours at a time, so I'm thinking we want to pick something close."

"Good call." Daniel checked the pan before dropping both steaks into it.

"The lighthouse in New York looks neat, but not super accessible with you on crutches. And I don't know how accessible it is during the winter. Could we pencil it in for the spring?"

"I was thinking the same thing," Daniel agreed. "I like the looks of the site in Maine. It's a lake. The area is popular for camping, hiking, fishing and boating. Lots of little cabins in the woods. So the shore should be walkable. The building at the haunted site burned down years ago, so no stairs,

"I agree, but it might be better to save it for September or October. I did some poking around and the fall foliage is popular with tourists. I bet we could get some stunning eerie shots once the leaves turn and fall," I said.

"You did your homework, I like that." Daniel beamed approvingly at me. "Okay, so we'll shoot for Maine in September or possibly October, depending on how the weather is looking. I have another option that I didn't put on the list because I haven't confirmed if we can get access. An old dairy farm in Vermont, we can poke around to see if it would work and contact the owners tomorrow."

"Sounds good. You want me to secure access to the lake site too?"

"That would be perfect. You've got a knack for this. I'll need you to get written permission from the property owners and then check out the pertinent filming permits we might need. Most places are lenient since we aren't a huge outfit, but better to make sure we're following local ordinances upfront."

"On it, boss." I saluted.

Daniel flipped the steaks. He reached above the counter and pulled out a can of corn and grabbed a can opener from a different drawer. Then dumped it into a pot on the back burner. "I'd love to have sites lined up enough in advance to have a proper schedule, make sure all our ducks are in a row on the paperwork side. Stace agreed to cancel the permits she had lined up for our August shoot in Iowa and explain what happened. So no worries on that front."

"Great." I nodded. "So, are we all right to stay here until we get next month's shooting schedule ironed out?"

"No, we can stay tonight, but we'll head to a campground tomorrow. Need to fill up the water tank and empty the gray water, all that jazz. On that note, you're welcome to use the shower. It has hot and cold water. Try to keep it brief since the tanks are only so big. It takes a good chunk of the solar to heat the water. We can use the showers at the campsite tomorrow."

"Sounds good," I said.

Daniel got out two plates, transferred the steaks to them and then drained and seasoned the pot of corn before adding that to the plates too. He got out utensils, turned off the stove and used the walls and counter to ease himself into a chair at the computer desk.

"You mind bringing over the plates?" Daniel gestured to the plates. I brought both plates to the narrow table and sat beside him to eat.

That he could prepare the entire meal without having to move more than a step drove home how small our shared living space was. But it also highlighted the space's efficiency.

"This tastes good, thanks," I said.

"No prob, I've gotten used to cooking simple stuff. We eat most of our meals out of Vanessa's kitchen. Consider it part of your compensation. You can always make requests, or help yourself to the kitchen, do you cook?"

"Some. Mom taught my sister and I the basics growing up," I replied.

"That's good. Got to be honest, I'm surprised you agreed to take the job on short notice like this."

I shrugged, trying to hide how out of character doing something that impulsive truly was for me. It was high time I chose a path I wanted instead of being content just to get by in life. Live a little. How many times had Kay goaded me with that phrase? Well, now I was doing it—living. "I wasn't about to pass up the perks."

Daniel chuckled, he gestured to the van. "Living in the lap of luxury, right?"

"Yep," I agreed. Luxurious it was not, but the chance to get to know someone I'd admired for ages thrilled me. Between college and working at Chorus I'd been stuck in a rut since Mom died.

When Daniel offered me the job, joining him on the road sounded like fun. Any other day, I would have laughed at his offer, but with my job at Chorus gone, what did I have to lose? I was due for some adventure in my life.

# NINE

## *Dan*

I 'd spent less than a week with my new PA and I was already in trouble. It wasn't just that he was alluring. He was. Or that he had this dogged determination to give every task I set for him his all.

There was just something about him. Some quality that made him the perfect fit for the job. Which meant I had to keep my growing attraction to myself.

By the end of his first full day, Chad had made arrangements with the owners of the haunted dairy. We took our time driving there, overnighting at a scenic campground along the way. Under any other circumstances, the drive from Exeter to Vermont would be an easy distance to cover in one day.

Chad insisted on following my discharge instructions to the letter. I needed to stop every couple hours to get my blood circulating after the surgery to repair my broken bones, so we stopped and I hobbled around on my crutches.

It was nice having someone who cared enough to make a fuss over my health. The leisurely pace was a nice reprieve from my usual scramble to travel between film sites.

Our stay at the campgrounds proved uneventful. Chad was good company and we chatted about inconsequential stuff.

Since we broke up the short drive, it was well before noon Thursday morning when we arrived at the sprawling dairy farm with our haunting location. The reports of spirit activity centered around an old barn that had fallen out of regular use. The dairy's owners had long since replaced it with larger modern facilities.

The current owners were a couple. Lara and Jane Goodman. The pair hadn't seen my videos before Chad approached them on my behalf. But they welcomed any publicity the webisodes might help them garner.

We met Jane in the dusty driveway between a stately white farmhouse and the postcard perfect big red barn. The barn was where they allowed visitors to pay to tour a working dairy farm. Tourists could pet calves, milk a cow, and buy farm fresh dairy products.

A display of local cheeses held pride of place on their website. The interior pictures showed a long counter that held tubs of homemade ice cream available for purchase by the cone or the pint. The Goodmans had created quite the little tourist trap to supplement their agricultural income.

"You must be Chad and Dan?" Jane greeted us as we stepped out of Vanessa.

"Dan," I said, offering my hand to the petite blonde. She shook with a firm callused grip. This was still a working farm, despite the trappings I should have expected her to be stronger than she looked.

"Pleased to meet you, Lara is handling an unexpected vet visit. Injured heifer, scratched her leg on something bad enough to need stitches. I can show you the old facilities, where the ghost rumors started and give you a tour of the grounds."

"That would be great, hope the injured cow gets well soon," I offered.

Jane nodded in acknowledgment. "Great, you can park here for now. We'll ride in the four by four so I can give you the rundown of how things operate here at Goodman Dairy."

"Sounds excellent," I said. Chad nodded along.

"Can we get some footage of the farm to use in our videos?" Chad asked. "And were you able to sign the filming releases I sent over? Ideally, we would sort the paperwork before we head out."

"Let's start with the tour," Jane suggested. "You can film if you'd like. No flash photography with the animals, and try not to get images of our visitors, but otherwise knock yourselves out. We want you to showcase the farm. Lara and I will get your forms back to you as soon as possible. It's been a wild morning here so we haven't looked everything over yet. That a problem?"

"Not at all," I cut in before Chad could reply. I was used to dealing with property owners.

He was accustomed to being the one standing between the public and their insurance claims. I appreciated his efficiency, but I figured there would be a learning curve.

In my business, we couldn't get too pushy with any people generous enough to let us record on their land and research the histories of their properties. More often than not, my research turned up someone's dirty laundry. Shoots always went better when the owner had full buy in, so I tried to charm our hosts.

"Tell me more about the farm, it looks like quite the operation," I said, giving the proud farm owner a chance to brag about her business.

"Goodman Dairy has been a family owned and operated dairy since the 1800s. Lara's many times great-grandfather bought the first few acres, and the family has grown it into the business you see today. We're proud to be a family-run farm. Lara's twin brother, Leon, owns a stake too. He runs our distribution operations.

"Their parents started the tourist attractions about ten years ago, to give the public a peek at farm life. Lara and I added the dairy bar after she and her brother bought out their parents' stake so they could retire.

"We adhere to Good Agricultural Practices and our herd is grass fed. We don't use growth hormones or antibiotics. Goodman Dairy is a labor of love and we're proud to provide wholesome dairy products to the market."

"Sounds great, can't wait to hit the ice cream counter after we check out the old barn," Chad said.

"Right." Jane nodded. "The old barn. I suppose you'll want to know the history of the building?"

"Yes, please," I said.

"Well," Jane said, "the barn where the rumors originated was the first structure built on the original plot of land where the family patriarch, Edgar, established his homestead. The original house burned down decades ago, but the fire spared the barn. We continued to use it for some of our stock until the 1960s."

"What happened?" I asked.

"They built the new larger milking facilities. Kept using the old building to house older calves," Jane replied.

"But that stopped?" Chad asked.

"It was an old building." Jane shrugged. "Too expensive to keep it heated or try to look at retrofitting it with modern electricity and plumbing. Besides, there were rumors of a dark presence. Voices that weren't there. The usual complaints, when people believe the dead haunt a place."

"Have you experienced anything strange?" I pressed.

"Nothing major. The building gives me the creeps," Jane shuddered, "but it's old and falling apart, so it's expected that it's spooky, right?"

"I see," I said.

"Anyway," Jane continued, "Lara can tell you more, she and Leon used to play there as kids. Lara was telling me they slept out in the old loft overnight once, as a dare, but they didn't last the night. She'll tell you about it over dinner. Will you two join us for the evening meal?"

"If we're invited. We wouldn't want to impose," I said.

"Nonsense, it isn't any trouble at all," Jane insisted. "Good old-fashioned farm hospitality. I'm sure you boys could both use a proper home cooked meal, with all the traveling you do for your show."

That was true.

"In that case, we'd love to join you for dinner," I agreed with a grin.

"We eat at five O'clock sharp." Jane smiled at me. "Before we installed the new automated system, we started the evening milking at six. So that's still when we go around to do a final check on the cows and handle whatever urgent work might have slipped through the cracks all day. Dinner gives us time to socialize before we get the cows tended to for the night."

"Sounds great," I enthused. "And we can park the van near the haunted barn, right?"

"Sure can," Jane confirmed. "You mentioned it's a camper van? There's a campground not too far down the road if you need hookups for water and electricity."

"That's okay," I assured her. "We've got solar power and a water tank, no need for the campground while we are filming. Though I might bring the van over there in a couple weeks to refill the freshwater and dump the gray water. I find ghosts are more active at night, so we'd like to stay on the grounds, if it isn't an imposition."

"No imposition at all," Jane said, she gestured expansively toward the farm. "We pride ourselves on our hospitality."

# TEN
*Chad*

Jane Goodman directed us to the alleged haunted barn. My first impression was of a derelict building, falling to the ravages of time. Part of the roof had collapsed, buckling the back wall. The rough wood looked rotted out in places.

I had real concerns about the structural integrity of what remained. Not Daniel, though. My boss charged right inside. He faced the darkness of the abandoned barn armed with nothing but his cellphone to light his path.

It shouldn't have surprised me when he recorded his first impressions of the place. If I'd learned nothing else about him, I now knew that Daniel loved to film for his show. The way he talked about it animated his entire body with excitement.

Before we left the van, he mounted his cell on a selfie stick. When we got out of the four by four, he clutched the stick along with the grip on his crutch. I marveled at his ability to maneuver on crutches while holding his phone. It did not look comfortable, but the guy managed.

Resigned to my fate, I followed on his heels. At least the floor seemed solid enough. Hard packed dirt with a few pale weeds eking out their survival in the weak sunlight that penetrated through the holes in what remained of the roof.

Other than its state of terrible disrepair, it looked about like I expected based on our tour of the more modern facilities. A large open aisle down the center with partially enclosed slips for cows along the exterior walls.

A couple were partitioned off with sliding doors to form the larger box stalls Jane said they used for horses. At the far end, there were more interior walls blocking off two rooms.

"That's the feed room and a tack room for the horses at the end, they were later additions." Jane pointed to the enclosed rooms.

I had no interest in venturing near where the wall had given way under the weight of the fallen roof.

"This barn used to have four box stalls for cart horses. The rest was for the cows. Lara's great-granddad converted one stall into a small farm office later."

Daniel peered into the room Jane described and made some approving sounds.

"When they used this building, a couple farmhands bunked up in the hayloft. A sizable chunk caved in when the roof collapsed. Elmer Goodman kept a cot in the office for someone to stay close when they expected a cow was close to calving."

"Interesting." Daniel gave every appearance of being absorbed in Jane's words.

As though the building's creepy atmosphere didn't put him off in the slightest. Something about the barn made my skin crawl.

The thick coat of dust on all the surfaces and the cobwebs made me imagine spiders skittering over my body. I chalked it up as nothing more than a primal fear of creepy crawlies making my hair stand on end.

"You can see there's not much worth salvaging. Lara's dad was sentimental about the old place. He wanted to fix it up, preserve the history. We've talked about demolishing it, but anytime we look at budgeting for it, we find money needed elsewhere, so it's just been moldering out here."

"But there have been incidents, right?" Daniel asked.

Jane twirled a lock of hair around her finger, considering her answer for a little too long before she said, "A few."

"Would you care to share?"

"Lara swears that when they were kids, she and her brother were playing in the loft when they heard voices that couldn't have been there, screaming."

"Anything else?" he asked.

"Lara's brother fell from the loft and broke his arm," Jane answered. "Leon swears someone pushed him down the ladder, Lara says she was on the other side of the loft swinging on an old rope they had rigged up here."

"A rope?" Dan prompted.

"Sure, they tied it to the beams when the loft was full. They used to climb up into the rafters and swing down into the hay. Their mother swears it's a miracle Leon's arm is the only bone they broke between the pair of them."

"Anything else?" he asked.

"Lara says they always checked the rope before they played, but once she says when she was climbing it snapped and dumped her into the hay. She got a concussion out of it. She says that after both incidents she and Leon heard laughter and footsteps. Otherwise it's just minor stuff."

"Care to elaborate?"

"Bad feelings, doors opening and closing. Weird noises. If you ask me, I think Lara's just spooked about a couple of weird incidents. She gets the heebie-jeebies or forgets whether she left the doors open or locked. Or it could be Leon messing with her. The two of them enjoy their pranks," Jane tacked on the last as an afterthought.

"Well if it's a prank, we might find evidence of that. Are you and Lara prepared for evidence of a real haunting?" Daniel checked.

"Lara is. I'm skeptical, but if you can put her mind at ease, that's all I can ask. We have some stipulations about the videos you're making. We don't want the farm or the family portrayed in a negative light. You must understand, we are trying to run a business here."

"Understandable," I fielded that one, since handling the legal release nitty-gritty of the negotiations was my job. "We can discuss your terms now that we've seen the proposed film site. Dan, are you ready to get back to the office to handle the paperwork?"

Daniel turned in a slow appreciative circle, taking in the broken down stable like a medieval lord surveying his domain. I shook my head at the silly image. He patted the support beam closest to him with a proprietary hand and nodded.

"Let's get to it," he said. He leaned on the beam as he collapsed the selfie stick and shoved his phone in his pocket. He looked more comfortable using the crutches without trying to film at the same time.

Jane led the way out and I couldn't follow fast enough. The whole structure made me feel like I needed a long hot shower to scrub myself clean. An oppressive air of grime and rot lingered and the ethereal brush of cobwebs over my exposed skin made me shudder with revulsion. The less time we spent inside the barn, the happier I would be.

The warm sun on my face as we exited made me glad to be out of the gloomy building. I understood why people called it haunted. It had an odd atmosphere about it, strong negative vibes, if you believed in that nonsense.

Not that I was a true believer. That title went to Daniel, and the barn thrilled him. I understood his enthusiasm. The Goodman barn was picture perfect for the part of a haunted building.

# ELEVEN

## *Dan*

"Right, I've changed the line here, to grant you and Lara the right to review the edited video before we post it online. In exchange, we reserve the right to refuse to make any edits that materially alter our findings. After seven days we may assume the video proofs are to your satisfaction if we don't hear from you. Is that agreeable?" Chad asked.

Jane pursed her lips and nodded. "We just want to be sure there isn't anything in it that will hurt business, you keep full creative control."

"I understand," Chad commiserated, "but we stick to a production schedule. The usual turn around on Dan's videos is only a few days once he gets them edited. I think you'll agree, giving you a week to review is lenient on our part."

"It's fine, Janie," Lara soothed. "We're good with that, and we'll do our best to get back to you ASAP once you send the proofs. Jane is our marketing expert, so she has the final word, but we'll want to loop Leon in on this too. It shouldn't be a problem."

"Great, so if you are in agreement I just need you both to initial here, next to the addendum." Chad handed the pen to Lara.

He pointed to the line he'd already changed and initialed on both copies of the filming contract. Lara signed. Jane read the new verbiage for herself before adding her initials.

"Perfect." Chad sorted the paperwork into two piles. "So, if everything else is agreeable, we just sign here, here, and here on both copies, and that should cover everything."

They signed, then Chad passed me the pen. I added my name to both copies with a flourish.

"We're looking forward to working with you." Lara offered me a handshake.

Her grip proved as calloused and strong as her wife's. I'd observed Lara wrangling an injured cow earlier, so I knew that the woman was strong from hard work. She shook Chad's hand too.

"We're old fashioned here, still like to close a deal with a handshake," she said, sounding sheepish. I liked her already.

Chad's handling of the papers impressed me. His grasp of my business needs in steering the negotiations pleased me. He had secured all hours access to the haunted site. The Goodmans agreed to provide dinners at the farmhouse.

As a bonus, they offered us an electric hookup for Vanessa from the house if we needed it. Not relying on solar power meant we could use my editing suite without worrying over depleting our battery reserves. It was a small extra that made my life easier. I often lost track of time during editing and worked late into the night. If we were low on power, I risked losing hours of work if the battery died.

I'd mentioned that tidbit during our drive from New Hampshire to Vermont. Chad asking about it meant he had paid attention to my rambling. His attention to detail would make him excel at this work.

In addition, he got permission to film on the entire farm grounds. Lara and Jane had each signed a release for on-camera interviews. They had also agreed to arrange for us to interview current staff and Lara's brother.

We still needed individual releases from anyone who appeared in the final cut. After today, I had confidence in Chad's ability to handle that with as much efficiency as he'd handled everything else I'd thrown at him. I never wanted to let him leave.

Lara even offered to supply the names of former farmhands who had worked the farm when the haunted stable was still in regular use. This was going well so far.

With the contract out of the way, Lara invited us to tour the rest of the facilities. Jane had already provided a personalized version of the tour they offered to the public. Lara was eager to show off their automated milking parlor to us, an area off limits to tour groups.

Chad and I sat in the back of the four by four while Lara motored around the grounds, taking us to the employee only areas. Jane explained farm operations and what they used various fields and buildings for. Lara interjected with fun facts about the herd, the history of the place and her family.

We wrapped up the tour with a meal in the stately farmhouse. After some brief banter to establish whose turn it was to cook, Jane prepared a hearty dinner of steak, potatoes and salad.

While Jane cooked, Lara sat with us on the front porch and regaled us with stories about the dairy's history. When we sat at the table, I stuffed myself with thick slabs of home-baked bread slathered in the dairy's butter. It was delicious.

Lara and Jane were gracious hosts, though the meal was a little rushed so they could go take care of evening chores. If today was indicative, I had a fantastic feeling about the next month.

# TWELVE

## *Chad*

Our first full day at the farm started to the sound of the rain drumming down on the van's roof. I must have rolled in my sleep because I woke up lodged against the solid dividing wall between my bunk and Daniel's.

In the hazy moments as I came to awareness, I could almost imagine I felt his body heat through the divider. Pure fancy on my part. A product of my overactive imagination.

Much like the pleasant dreams in which I had vague memories of kissing someone who looked an awful lot like my dashing boss. Not that I planned to snuggle with Daniel. It would be nice to have *someone* to snuggle with, someday. Not Daniel.

He was my boss. Someone I admired—that was all he could ever be. He'd been upfront about his no dating employees policy. Simple as that.

Too bad the van didn't offer much privacy. My vivid dreams left me rather in need of a few moments to take care of things below the belt. I could hear the sheets rustling on the other side of the divider, a telltale creak in the bedframe that heralded Daniel worming his way out of his bunk.

With his injured leg, it took him some time to get out of the raised bed. Thumps, bangs and muffled curses serenaded me as I stole a few more moments of rest. The swoosh of the fabric curtain on his bunk as he drew it back into place followed. I

listened to the asymmetric thuds of his footsteps as he
maneuvered around the kitchen area. My cue to rise and shine.

By the time I'd squirmed out of my bunk, Daniel had coffee
brewing for us over a propane burner. The large hourglass
shaped stovetop espresso maker he used produced a strong cup
of joe. I had zero complaints there. Bonus points for not
dealing with filters.

"Morning," he said, glancing over at me as I got my
bearings.

"Morning," I replied.

"Ready to dig into some editing?"

"Video editing?"

"Yeah," Daniel confirmed, "we've got to finish the video
wrap up for the Miller House series. Releases tomorrow.
Might as well give you your first lesson with the software
while I'm working. Then we can sink our teeth into the history
here."

"You know it. Where do you want to start? With the
Goodman Haunting, I mean."

"The local library should have archives of the town paper,
we can look back around the stories Lara mentioned at supper.
The farmhand who disappeared in the 30s. The injuries in the
old barn. Check for anything newsworthy leading up to the first
incidents."

"Sounds good," I agreed.

"We should set up interviews with the old stable hands Lara
mentioned too. They might offer some insights."

I scratched my jaw, enjoying the feel of bristly stubble under
my fingers. I needed to shave, but I liked the tangible reminder
of my masculinity. Confirmation my appearance reflected the
real me now never got old. Not even after years on T.

"I don't want to be that guy, but do you think it's possible
this might be a publicity thing the twins have cooked up

between them?" I suggested what I'd been thinking since we first arrived at the dairy.

"It's always a possibility," Daniel allowed. "Hauntings can be a draw, especially going into the fall. We'll investigate and let the facts speak for themselves."

"I guess."

"If it's an elaborate hoax, our investigation should uncover that, too."

"Will you go public, if it is?"

"I doubt the Goodmans would sign off on that. You agreed to give them editorial control over what we say." He reminded me.

"Sure, but we won't lie, right?"

"No. We won't. Let's not borrow trouble. If they are trying to use us for publicity, we'll cross that bridge when we come to it. Honestly, I'm flattered that you think I'm popular enough to be worth the effort to fool me into covering their farm."

I flushed at the teasing note in his tone. He *was* that popular. Daniel and his show might not be a household name, but he had a sizable following. His audience only grew the more videos he produced.

"You know what they say about publicity, it's all good, right?"

"Right." Daniel shot me his million watt grin and my heart pounded at being its focus. "So, like I said, we'll devote today to editing. Tomorrow we can dive into background research. Sunday, I want to film a bit for the product review and unboxing video. Just as well that we aren't filming today, the rain will screw with the sound quality on anything we record in the studio this morning."

"That sounds like a plan." I considered a moment. "The only problem will be if the library isn't open on weekends, if we need to go today instead, we could edit tomorrow?"

"That's a possibility," he mused. "I hate to cut it too close to the wire though. Why don't you check the library hours while I make us breakfast? Is French toast okay? Need to use up the bread."

"Sounds delicious. Is your leg up to standing?"

"I'm fine." Daniel waved away my concern. "Yet another advantage to having a tiny home, everything is within arm's reach. I'll just prop myself up at the counter, almost no strain on the leg. If you'll grab the eggs and milk out of the fridge for me?"

I got out the requested ingredients. Daniel rummaged around for everything else he needed to cook. True to his word, he gathered his supplies without moving from where he had his hip leaned against the cabinetry.

"I can call around to the witnesses and try to set up appointments for next week, too," I offered.

"Good thinking," Daniel enthused. "The sooner we get those scheduled the better."

"My thoughts exactly."

The coffee maker grumbled and hissed as the last of the water boiled. Daniel flicked the burner off and poured the brew into our mugs. I took mine, sipping from it even though it was still piping hot. Daniel grimaced as he added heaping spoonfuls of sugar and whitener to his cup.

"Don't burn yourself," he commented.

My only response was a contented sigh. He made good coffee.

# THIRTEEN

## *Dan*

I stole a glance at Chad as he pored over the old archives across from me. I'd sweet-talked the chatty librarian on duty until he helped us pinpoint the most likely sources for the information we sought. Now we sat up to our eyeballs in archives.

Chad had the patience of a saint, poring over the documents like it was his job. Well, it was his job for today. I liked the furrow in his brow when he concentrated. It pleased me to see him so focused on learning the job. It gave me hope he felt invested in doing it right and sticking around for the long haul.

Yesterday, he'd picked up the video editing software faster than Stacy or Zack. His grasp of the business side of matters surpassed theirs too. Comparing him to previous PAs set too low a bar, but he cleared it with ease.

If he left, he'd be all but impossible to replace. I knew that already, and it was still his first week. I needed to ensure he wanted to stay.

Priority one, figure out what made him tick so I could make sure he stayed happy working for me. I could almost convince myself that gave me a good excuse for staring at him like a creeper. It didn't though—nothing could happen between us.

To act on my attraction would be a surefire way to lose him. I should quash the little crush I'd noticed growing toward him with ruthless prejudice. Despite that, I had to admit to myself that I had a crush. The fact watching Chad work held more interest than what I should be doing was proof enough.

To be fair, the records made for dry reading. It wasn't a large town and their paper reflected that. New store openings got full page spreads. Event announcements ranging from town meetings and a temperance society social to a local amateur theater production took pride of place.

Plenty of articles extolled the virtues of agricultural techniques. Ads filled much of the space. For everything from local goods to cough remedies. The layout made the paper hard to follow with too much clutter.

The archive read like a typical small town paper from its day. Gossip printed in the guise of editorials. Political rants. Local tragedies rated mentions too. A fire here, an accident there. I skimmed through the pages of death notices, birth and marriage announcements.

The usual fare. I didn't find any significant occurrences at the Goodman farm. Lara and Jane assured me that the entire enterprise had been in the family for generations. Even before they built the haunted barn.

Yet Goodman Dairy never received mention. It seemed odd since many other dairies appeared in the archives. Higgs Dairy, Gaghan Acres, and Smythe Farms to name a few. But no Goodman Dairy.

Not until after the Great Depression started. Chad was the one who found the profile on Goodman Dairy from the fall of 1933. Buried in a short article about the local state of the industry. It dropped a casual mention that Elmer Goodman had turned the failing Higgs Dairy around after inheriting the property from his deceased brother-in-law. That was it.

We looked through the papers for mention of Higgs' death. We searched back to 1932 to find a short obituary for one Frank Higgs. A single line of text stated his birth and death dates and that his wife, three daughters and a married sister survived him. That was all.

Well, the fact he had no living sons explained his brother-in-law running the farm after his death. It also accounted for the change in name while the family insisted the operation had remained in the family for eight generations.

I resolved to ask Lara about Higgs when I saw her. The possibility remained that she hadn't mentioned him because his death was unrelated to the farm. There were countless ways he might have died, on or off the farm property. His death could have no bearing on the haunting.

I had a gut feeling there was a connection though. Call it intuition or experience researching these matters. But I was certain Frank Higgs was our man—or in this case, our ghost.

# FOURTEEN

## *Chad*

S unday morning I got to experience a major perk to Daniel's set up—no commute. I had parked the van near the haunted barn when we returned from our research excursion yesterday. That left us steps away from our work site.

After we delved into public records, we spent last evening interacting with fans on Daniel's website. The final Miller House video was live, so there was plenty of activity to monitor.

Today brought more dreary weather, but the drizzling rain of the past two days had ceased. As we stepped out of the van, an almost autumnal chill gave the air a bite I didn't expect in early August. I shivered. Daniel glanced over at me.

"Cold?" he asked.

"A bit." I nodded. "Aren't you?"

Daniel made a noncommittal sound. He reached inside the van to grab a hoodie from the overhead storage above the cab. He handed it to me along with the camera bag before he climbed out and circled around the back to get out the rest of the gear we needed for filming from storage.

"You aren't carrying any of that," I scolded when he tried to sling a carrying case with lighting stands over his shoulder. "I'm not watching you screw up your leg more. Tell me what we need and I'll get it."

Daniel wore a sheepish expression. "I can grab the carrying cases so long as my hands are free for the crutches," he protested.

"Nope, not a chance, I've got this. You're here to look decorative, boss."

He shot me a smirk, like my words were an admission that I enjoyed looking at him. I flushed, keeping my mouth shut as I gathered everything we'd used to film at the Miller House.

Daniel stood close enough to observe. He told me to switch out a few of the items I'd grabbed, then nodded his approval when we had everything. It was a lot to carry by myself, but I managed.

Armed with our camera, tripod, and the lighting kit, we ventured back into the rundown structure. The dark confines made me wary. Daniel seemed excited to get started.

"I want to get shots from all angles with the camera mounted in place," he explained. "Then a few shots where we walk through the main floor. Lara said she would check into whether the loft can support enough weight for us to get some footage up there. Since many of the incidents seem to involve that area. Otherwise we will have to improvise."

"You are not climbing up into that loft with a broken leg," I said in a flat tone that brooked no argument.

Daniel laughed. "Are you volunteering?"

I most certainly was not, at least not until we got the all clear on what remained of the loft's structural integrity.

"I'll ask Jane about borrowing a ladder that doesn't look ready to collapse so we can at least get some shots up there," I said to appease him.

Daniel beamed at me and ruffled my hair. "That's my problem solver."

I flushed at the praise, but it was dark enough inside the barn to hide my reaction. I busied myself setting up our camera equipment so we could get the shots Daniel wanted to cross off today.

"So, you're familiar with my format, right?"

"We're filming the unboxing today, right?" I asked, to confirm that I was.

"We are." Daniel smirked as he pulled a small oblong white box out of his pocket. I didn't recognize the logo stamped in black on the front, but then I wasn't as into the gear as some of his fans.

"What's that?"

From the way he was watching me, it was obvious he expected a response to the object.

Daniel chuckled, with a rueful shake of his head he answered, "I was beginning to think I'd run out of things to train you on already. This, my friend, is a new thermal camera from Paranormal Outfitters. Top of the line, expensive as heck, and nothing touches it on results."

"What does it do, exactly?"

Daniel chuckled. "That's what this video will be all about, so, I'll keep you in suspense until you're ready to roll."

"I see how it is," I joked. "You trying to bribe me to hurry it up with the grunt work?"

"Yes. While you're working, let's run through the plan. This is our viewers' first impression of the site for the month. It was Zack's idea to do the unboxing like this, the fans responded well, so it stuck. We give a sneak peek of the site and reveal whatever product I'm reviewing."

"I know, I've seen the show," I reminded him.

"Right. So you understand we need to pick a spot that captures the haunting's character without giving too much away."

"Shouldn't we do that before I get everything set up?"

Daniel waved his hand in dismissal. "If it weren't for the leg, and safety concerns, we'd film in the loft. Frame the old rope swing on the screen edge. Since that's not an option for today, I figured right here, with the old ladder up to the loft in the background is the next best thing."

"Hmm, what do you say to borrowing a bale of hay from Lara as set dressing?" I suggested.

"You mean those giant rolls out in the pastures?"

I shook my head. "I mean, that would look rad. But I think the smaller bales I saw stacked near the stable where they keep the horses would make a better seat for you. That way you can show some Goodman Dairy flavor and rest that leg. Plus, it gives you a place to set the device."

"I like it, I'll finish with the lighting. Why don't you see how fast we can commandeer that hay?" Daniel took over fiddling with the tripods, screwing in the expensive specialty bulbs for the lighting. I pulled out my phone and dialed Lara.

"Lara speaking," she answered in a crisp tone.

"Hey, Lara, it's Chad. I was wondering if we could borrow some farm stuff to use as props."

"Depends what you have in mind."

"I saw some bales of hay in the stables, those would evoke the right mood. Maybe some leather stuff?" I asked.

"The little square bales in the main stable are straw, not hay," Lara explained. "We use it for bedding. But you can take as many as you need if you promise to store them properly. If you let them molder, the heat from fermentation and rot inside the bale can cause it to ignite."

"Good to know."

"I can set aside a few pieces of horse tack for you, too. Leon's daughter, Stephanie, is coming to help muck out the horse stables this morning. She should be here any minute. I can have her pick out some gear and show you how to take care of it. Steph can take the four by four to help you transport whatever you need out to the old barn. Ben is working today too, grab him to help if you need the extra muscle," Lara offered.

"That would be fabulous."

"Great, I'll text you when she gets here. You can meet her in the horse stables."

"Perfect, thanks, Lara."

"Very good." Lara hung up. I tucked my phone away and turned to see Daniel watching me as he finished tightening an adjustment knob on the camera tripod.

"We're good, Lara's niece will help me go prop shopping." I summarized the call.

"Great, do you have time to help me move some stuff before you go meet her?" Daniel gestured toward the old feed room and office. With our lights set up, the aisle seemed marginally less creepy. Still gross though. Now I had a clear visual of all the cobwebs clinging to every surface. Much as I didn't want to poke around too much, I wasn't about to leave my injured boss to drag things into position.

"Sure."

I followed Daniel to the former office and helped him pick through years worth of discarded crap. He found a wooden wagon wheel with a few snapped spokes. Near it sat a huge block of smooth curved wood with thick rusty iron eye loops attached to it.

"A yoke," he declared with clear satisfaction. "This will be perfect, we'll prop the wheel and the yoke up behind me. With this and whatever you and the kid find the shot should scream 'haunted barn', without us having to say a word."

"I suppose so," I agreed, reluctant to touch anything in here. If nothing else, there were spiders making their home in the junk pile. I suspected there would be rodents nesting out here too, though, to my surprise, there was little evidence in the form of skittering claws, chittering voices or stinking droppings.

Daniel grabbed the wheel and pulled. I sighed. No getting out of it unless I let him try to move this stuff alone. No chance of that.

I gritted my teeth against the creepy crawly sensations the cobwebs on the curved wood evoked and carried it out to the area we had already lit for the shot. I left it propped against the wall in the camera frame. Daniel trailed behind me and fussed over the placement while I went back for the yoke.

"Perfect, do you think this hook will hold that?" Daniel pointed to a metal spike set in the wall already.

Staring at it, and considering the integrity of the building, I had doubts. But the yoke was light for its size. Made sense, considering. I figured it was worth a shot.

I hefted the block of wood up to the correct height. Daniel helped me maneuver the metal loop onto the spike. I settled the yoke against the wall with care, letting the spike take the weight, but ready to catch the thing if it fell. It held.

Daniel let out a triumphant whoop, fist pumping the air.

"Yes! Perfect, I'll check the framing and mark out where to place the bale of hay. We'll get the shot just right."

Before I could volunteer to help, my phone buzzed with an incoming text. Lara's niece had arrived. I left Daniel fussing over his cameras with an admonition not to overtax his leg. He was so into arranging everything to his satisfaction, I doubted he heard me.

# FIFTEEN

## *Dan*

I t took the better part of the day to get everything staged just the way I wanted it. That was fine by me, we were more likely to capture paranormal activity later in the day.

The ambient noises I associated with old abandoned buildings were eerily absent from the barn. I considered that a promising sign. As though whatever lived there had taken an interest in our recording.

The late afternoon held an expectant silence. I ignored it and signaled for Chad to hit record. Time to turn on the Dan Collins charm for the camera.

"Greetings from Vermont! I'm Dan and this is Hauntastic Haunts. Any guesses about where I am filming this month?"

I paused and gestured to the open area around me. It should be obvious that it was a barn. I was sitting on a bale of straw with two more bales stacked beside me to form a table.

Not the most comfortable seat in the world, stray stalks poked my butt through the soft material of the sweatpants I was wearing. I was sure it would leave scratches if I shifted around too much.

Jeans would have done a better job protecting my tender bits, but they wouldn't fit over my cast. The stretchy sweats were my only option for a while.

The floor overhead creaked. I paid it no heed in favor of keeping up my Dan persona, though, upbeat and earnest despite personal discomfort. I got ready to geek out over my new IR camera.

"That's right. This month Hauntastic Haunts is down on the farm. I am investigating a haunted barn owned by a working Vermont family-run dairy. We'll go into more detail about the dairy and its history in next week's webisode. If you are in the area, be sure to consider visiting once we reveal the name of the dairy. Two more hints, they are open to the public for tours and their homemade ice cream is to die for.

"And speaking of dying, I've got a great new goody to share with you all this week. The people at Paranormal Outfitters Inc have sent me their latest gadget, the GhostCam version 3, and I cannot wait to take this baby for a spin at a real haunting."

I pulled out the narrow white box with a flourish and held it up with the company logo on prominent display. I was itching to get my hands on the new camera it held, but I could be patient if it meant getting the shot right.

After ensuring Chad captured a clear image of the box, I set it down in front of me. The patterned kerchief we'd borrowed from Lara's niece to cover the makeshift straw table made a sharp contrast with the plain white box.

The teen had been wearing the paisley cloth over her hair—she claimed it kept the stink off when she helped strip the stalls in the horse barn bare. I didn't want to think about what caused the stench she referred to. A farm-boy I was not.

I talked up Paranormal Outfitters with the usual platitudes about the company and the quality of their products as I wiggled the box open to reveal its contents.

The new camera sat nestled in a foam insert to protect against jostling. I described the packaging as I tilted it toward the camera to show off the tech. I gestured for Chad to start rolling on the secondary camera I'd zoomed in on the spot where I'd placed the box to capture the details. He gave me a thumbs up and I continued my review, picking up the device with care bordering on reverence.

I monitored my assistant as I worked. He was doing a good job, keeping his cool although I could tell the barn freaked him out more than he cared to admit. I got the sense our spirit didn't welcome interlopers.

We should see strong activity, especially with us both spending most of the day here for it to draw energy from us. The dead fed on the energy of the living. Not that I'd told Chad we were hanging around the barn all day to feed the ghost.

I doubted he would have believed me if I had. For someone who seemed sensitive to the eerie presence here, Chad remained skeptical that ghosts were real.

Chad shivered, drawing my notice to the sudden chill that had descended on us. Like an icy breeze, except there was no wind in the building.

Footsteps pounded overhead, in the damaged loft. Dust fell from above us. Something moved in the murky darkness at the top of the ladder.

"Chad, we should leave," I said.

Chad gave me an uncertain look. I lurched to my feet, stuffed the new IR camera back into the box, favoring speed over caution. If only I'd already had it ready to roll, and had a free hand to record with while using my crutches.

There was no time to lament the missed opportunity though. We needed to flee, while we still could. The level of activity made me think I had underestimated the ghost's strength.

The doors at the end of the aisle banged shut. Chad shot me a panicked look, then he snapped the camera out of the tripod and swung the lens toward the sounds. Good instincts, but I needed to make sure my newbie assistant took care of himself.

"We're hearing strange sounds, and the door to the old office just slammed open," I narrated.

"Dan?" Chad sounded uncertain, but he kept filming even as the disembodied footsteps charged toward us.

"Switch to night vision mode," I commanded.

Chad fumbled with the settings. At his current angle, I could just make out that the glowing screen had picked up a distortion in the otherwise empty part of the barn. I cursed not having the IR camera operational yet.

It would capture much better images than the crummy night vision function on the older model camera. Still, I didn't regret not entrusting Chad with my best DSLR device for his second day as a camera operator.

My fingers itched to use the GhostCam nestled snugly in its protective box to capture some footage. I knew risking damage to the new tech before I even got the review filmed would be bad form. I shoved the box back into my pants pocket to avoid temptation and free my hands.

"What the heck is that?" Chad sounded on the verge of panic.

"Let's go."

I knew better than to stick around and make myself a target for malevolent spirits. Feeding them energy was one thing, risking injury on the first day on the set was another.

Chad's anxiety and fear at his first paranormal encounter would only feed the ghost more. No question, the apparition was angry. It stopped near the damaged far wall. I hopped toward Chad with my crutches.

Chad met me after the first step, sliding under my arm to assist me. He cradled the camera he was holding against his chest with one arm, using the other to support my weight as we fled from the approaching presence. Pity he didn't aim the camera at the ghost as we retreated. Then again, filming while he half carried me to safety might have been too much to ask.

The doors at the far end slammed, open and shut. Footsteps pounded on our heels as the barn's chill intensified until my teeth chattered with it. Chad and I didn't stop until we reached Vanessa and scrambled inside.

We sat in the van in silence, but for our heavy breathing. I could think of much more pleasant ways to get our heart rates up. I shouldn't, though.

Why was I thinking with my dick when Chad had just seen his first ghost? I was certain he would have questions. It was my responsibility to help him come to grips with ghosts existing. He wouldn't be the first skeptic to change his mind.

I watched for his reaction, but when his ragged breathing calmed he met my eyes and laughed. An eerie echo of the voice that had chased us through the barn moments ago.

I sighed, Chad would come around to seeing what was in front of his nose given enough evidence. I had confidence in that fact. But being chased out of the barn by the spirit's malevolent presence wasn't enough evidence for my skeptic.

"You had me going for a minute. Man, the set dressing almost made it feel real in the heat of the moment," he said with a wry smile. So much for convincing him.

# SIXTEEN

## *Chad*

"How did you slam the doors?" I asked. Staring at Daniel as though that might reveal the secrets of his trickery. He just stared back at me.

"I didn't, the ghost did," Daniel said.

"Fine, keep your secrets. I suppose the cold breeze was from a draft?"

"Why so determined to disbelieve what's right in front of your eyes?" Daniel asked. He waved away any response I might give. "No, that's fine. You'll see the truth when you're ready."

With all the barn's structural damage that seemed reasonable. Was the draft strong enough to slam doors too? That seemed logical if Daniel hadn't used some trick to do it, as he claimed. I'd watched enough of his show not to assume he would stoop to gimmicks. Trickery wasn't his style.

Odd for me to acknowledge, since his entire industry predicated itself on trickery, but Daniel was always so earnest about ghosts. I suspected he got caught up in the intense feelings when he explored spooky spots.

After seeing this one first hand, I could understand the impulse to explain away the forces behind the sense of foreboding such places gave me. Easy to cast movement in the shadows as entities.

The intensity of the experience made everything spookier. As we burst free of the barn, though, the fear that had gripped me along with the strange phenomena had dissipated. I felt silly and suggestible for fleeing from nothing. Nothing chased us out into the weak light of sunset beyond the stable doors.

We hadn't stopped until we reached the safety of the van. Now it seemed childish to hide huddled on the floor. My initial glance at Daniel had revealed him looking as unnerved as I was. There had to be a logical explanation besides ghosts. Because ghosts didn't exist.

I just couldn't explain how the heavy barn door slammed shut behind us. There had been no one else inside. A glance out the window as I stood confirmed I hadn't imagined that. The door was closed.

I shifted my focus to Daniel, helping him back to his feet. His breathing was no longer heavy, his face contorted in a grimace of pain as he put weight on his injured leg. I got him settled in the comfortable passenger seat.

"You all right?"

"Jostled the leg in all the excitement, hurts a bit is all."

"Uh, should I go back for the lighting kit?"

"I don't think you should go back inside alone," Daniel said. "Grab the gear from the back, in the black duffel. I have an EM meter in there, maybe we can get some useful readings. Don't suppose you kept rolling on our escape?"

I'd all but forgotten that I'd grabbed the camera in my haste to get away from the unpleasant sensations inside the barn. The camera was still recording. I hit the stop button and handed it over to Daniel to deal with while I grabbed the requested gear.

"Too bad," he called as I opened the rear doors of the van to access the storage area under the bed platform.

"What?"

"You kept recording, good on you. But all you got after the doors started to move was a few frames of the ground before it goes dark. I assume because you covered the lens trying to keep the camera safe and get my butt to safety."

"Sorry," I grunted as I settled the strap to the large black duffel I found there over my chest.

The bag was heavy, and I was glad not to be carrying it over a binder. Wearing straps over my old binders always made the things ride up uncomfortably. The extra pressure on my ribs hurt by the end of a full day of work and classes.

My days of dealing with that discomfort ended when I got top surgery though. Thanks to Chorus's generous employee health policy I'd paid next to nothing out of pocket to remove the largest source of my dysphoria.

I used my foot to nudge the van doors shut. Daniel made grabby hands for the bag when I returned, the camera sat in the empty driver's seat to his side. I slid the bag to the floor at Daniel's feet, in the space between the sliding door and the shower stall.

Daniel looked like he might haul the whole thing onto his lap, heedless of his cast. I took the initiative and unzipped it, pushing aside the flap to reveal a whole mess of stuff I only recognized from watching the show. I'd have to pay more attention to the gear now that I was helping him with it.

"Grab that, right there. The box with the screen and dials. That's an EM meter." Daniel pointed. I grabbed the item and handed it to him. He fiddled with the knobs, as though tuning an old radio. "Aha! Grab the camera and get rolling, time to film a  haunting segment."

He hopped out of his seat, leaning heavily on the doorframe. The pain served as a better reminder to take it easy than any amount of nagging on my part. I leaned across the open space where he'd removed the console to retrieve the camera. I climbed out of the van and traded him for the EM meter.

"Walk me through how to use this, you stay here and shoot while I operate the equipment."

Daniel heaved a sigh, "Fine, ready?"

I glanced at the device in my hands and nodded, even though I would have to wing this segment in its entirety. Better than Daniel doing more damage to his leg.

"I'm rolling," Daniel said, he had the lens pointed at me and a blinking red LED reinforced his words. I was on camera.

I gave an awkward wave and almost dropped the EM meter thing, *shit, so much for looking smooth on camera.*

"Hey, hi, I'm the new PA. Chad. Um, we just got chased out of an abandoned barn here at Goodman Dairy."

"Was that your first paranormal encounter, Chad?" Dan asked with a smirk. It was Dan talking now, the web personality and not Daniel, the guy I was getting to know.

"Yeah. I'm shaken up."

"Aw, if I'd known you were a virgin, I'd have tried to be more gentle. Eased you into it," Dan teased, he shot me a wink and I smiled at him. Banter worked. I could handle banter.

"It's all good," I said, I would not react to him calling me a virgin. Nope. Not at all. Even if it made my knees wobble and my heart pound. "So what now? Do we venture back inside for readings?"

"Yep, that's the plan, so what my assistant has there, for those who are unfamiliar with the gear, is an EM meter from Ethereal Encounters brand. It's a combination meter that gives readings on EM field fluctuations and changes in pressure and temperature. Chad, turn the meter so I can zoom in on the readout. Great, just like that. Okay, so what you're seeing is a normal baseline amount of EM. Chad, bring the sensor to the barn. We'll see what we pick up."

Daniel held up a hand for me to wait. I paused until he gave me a thumbs up and pointed toward the barn. At his okay, I suited my actions to his words, taking the device closer. I could hear Daniel's labored steps behind me as he attempted to hold the camera steady while limping after me. Stubborn idiot was dead set on not letting himself heal.

I glanced down at the dial and saw it jump as I approached the stable doors. I turned back toward Daniel.

"It's moving." I held up the black box to corroborate.

Daniel nodded, then gestured for me to pause. I tried to keep my focus on holding the device steady for the camera instead of the chill going up my spine at being so close to the haunted barn. This was crazy, I didn't believe in ghosts. There must be a better explanation.

"When we exited the barn, we left the doors open wide. The presence that chased us out must have wanted us to stay out because the doors slammed behind us. Chad, are you okay?"

"Still cold," I said, my teeth chattering from the sudden chill, my breath ghosting the air as though it were the middle of winter instead of late summer.

"That's interesting. Chad, can you toggle to the temperature readout? Grab a reading there, near where we observed the manifestation. Then compare it with a reading closer to Vanessa."

"Sure," I agreed. I shot Daniel a questioning look. He nodded for me to get on with it. I found the switch to change modes, and the screen lit up with weather data. Temperature and barometric pressure. I held it up for the camera to capture and started walking back toward Daniel. I'd seen him do similar on the show, so I maintained a slow, steady pace, the way he would.

The readings were strange. Forty-four degrees by the barn doors. It abruptly rose as I neared the van, rising back to a seasonal seventy-three degrees. That couldn't be right. I went back to the barn to confirm it was a glitch.

I paused as I drew close, sudden anxiety gripping me. Ridiculous, there was nothing to fear here. At worst, the Goodman family had rigged up a few tricks to gain publicity. Whatever was going on, it couldn't be ghosts. I stepped back up to the barn doors. The reading dipped a few degrees, down to sixty-eight.

I breathed a sigh of relief, a few degrees could be the difference between being in the shade or not. No ghosts, only my mind playing tricks. Not real paranormal activity. I flicked the meter back to EM mode.

The flick of the dial on the EM meter jumping caught my eye as a wave of cold air bowled me back a pace.

"Oh shit!" I exclaimed.

"What's going on, Chad?"

"Something pushed me. Shit, Dan, the meter moved, and it got cold and something pushed me!"

"Take a temperature reading, quick."

I did. Fifty-five degrees. It had dropped over ten degrees in less than a minute. What could cause that? I angled the meter readout so that Dan could catch the readings on the camera, I hoped I wasn't shaking too much, making the readings unintelligible.

"Okay. We can take a hint, the spirit wants us out for now. Let's see what our friend has to say. Grab the EVP device from the bag. We use it to record electronic voice phenomena. It's early enough in the investigation I'm inclined to back off for now. But we'll give our ghost a chance to communicate first."

My hands were shaking, so I gripped the meter with both hands as I walked back over to Daniel.

"Relax, Chad, you're doing great. Put the EM meter away and grab the EVP recorder," Daniel coached me. His warm voice thawed the icy fear in my chest at what had happened. Was it real or a hoax? Was Dan in on it, if it was the latter?

And if it was real—it couldn't be real—how dangerous was the situation? What would have happened if we didn't run when we did?

I rummaged through the duffel bag until I found the device he wanted. Glad for a distraction from my racing thoughts.

"Chad."

"Yeah?"

"You're safe. I wouldn't let anything happen to you."

I gave a stiff nod of acknowledgment. "What do I do now?"

"We will offer the spirit an opportunity to chat, bring the recorder close to the door and ask if it has anything to say to us."

I went, with more trepidation than I should have felt at approaching an empty building. I turned on the device and spoke, loud and clear. "If you're here, we're listening, spirit."

Nothing happened.

"Are you Frank Higgs? Do you have a message for us? We're listening," Dan called out, too.

My trepidation had all but evaporated, leaving embarrassment that a part of me had expected a dead man to talk to me. Still, we were recording, best make a good show of it.

"If you have something to say, speak now, Frank." I stumbled over the words because they made me feel like a kid playing pretend. I didn't believe this stuff. I didn't.

There was no response. The abnormal chill in the air had faded again. It shouldn't disappoint me. Of course the ghost didn't talk to me. It wasn't real.

"Nothing?" Dan asked.

"Nothing," I confirmed.

"That's all right. We have plenty of time to get the ghost talking. They sometimes respond better if they have a connection to the person contacting them."

"Should we call Steph or Lara?"

Daniel took a moment to consider before nodding. "It can't hurt. We can see if the spirit is more talkative for the family. I don't think we should risk going back inside today though. No need to feed the ghost more living energy tonight."

I sent Steph a text explaining what we wanted to try. Within moments she confirmed that she and her aunt were on their way. With nothing better to do, we waited.

# SEVENTEEN

## *Dan*

C had paced while we waited for Lara and her niece. I stood, propped on my crutches, gritting my teeth through the pain in my broken leg.

It hadn't bothered me much up to now, other than my reduced mobility. Our panicked flight from the building had wrenched it something awful. I should rest it, maybe pop a pain pill. Instead, I kept as much of my weight off it as possible and observed my assistant.

I'd known going in that he was a skeptic, but so far he'd done a good job humoring my enthusiasm about the paranormal. Now he was struggling to accept what he'd seen.

From his reactions today, I doubted he would remain a disbeliever for much longer. There was only so much a person could rationalize, and this haunting was already proving to be one of the most active I'd investigated.

The familiar four by four rattled along the packed dirt field road. A large black and tan dog from the farmhouse loped along at their side, tongue lolling. When they took the last bend in the road, where the vehicle's destination became clear, the dog lagged.

Hackles raised, the animal dropped to its haunches with a low whine. Lara pulled up beside us. Steph whistled to the dog, trying to coax it closer to no avail.

"None of the animals like this field, it's why we don't graze the cattle here anymore," Lara commented, tipping her head toward the overgrown pasture land around the abandoned structure.

What remained of the fencing out here was in disrepair, boards broken and bowed, posts tilted at odd angles. The whole area was subject to the vagaries of rot and decay.

If nothing else, it created the perfect esthetic for filming Hauntastic Haunts. I made a mental note to capture the disrepair in our exterior shots of the barn before we wrapped filming. Later.

At the moment, I hoped to take advantage of the spirit's activity. See if the apparition would confirm their identity or failing that, help us determine what held them to this place.

Lara and Leon's stories weren't much to go on. I had my suspicions after our preliminary research though. There was only one noteworthy death that fit all the details.

I hoped the interviews Chad had arranged for the rest of the week would shed some light on who Frank Higgs had been in life. And whether he was behind this haunting.

"Hmm, wonder why that is," I said. In my experience, animals were more aware of the paranormal than humans. They had the sense to avoid hauntings.

"It's creepy out here," Steph observed, hugging her arms over her chest in a protective gesture.

"No argument here," Chad said.

"Right, well, if we send the spirit to their rest that should help," I offered.

"Do we know who we're dealing with?" Lara asked.

"Nothing confirmed yet." I shook my head. "I know you said at dinner you didn't know of any deaths happening in or around the barn. No accidents or anything?"

"I don't remember the family mentioned anything serious anyway," Lara replied.

"Well, we had something manifest," I revealed. "I've got a tool that allows us to communicate with the spirits if there are any auditory phenomena. While we were filming, we heard disembodied footsteps, but you mentioned you've heard voices before?"

"*A* voice," Lara confirmed, "talking to the cows, it sounds like. Might be a trick of the acoustics. We spend minimal time there."

"Right, well, it's worth a shot. Chad, do you have the EVP recorder?" I asked.

Chad, ever the helper, strode to the van and rummaged around for the gear I'd requested. He returned to my side and handed over the device. I handed him the camera.

"Roll on this," I directed. "I want a single continuous shot. Try to capture all the audio, I can edit it down to just the pertinent shots after. Focus on reaction shots to whatever happens. A few zooms on the device readout as the results merit. But viewers get more out of seeing a person's facial expressions and honest reactions than numbers and dials on a display readout, got it?"

"Gotcha," Chad agreed, he raised the viewer on the camera to his eye and hit record. I put on a bright smile for the camera. My leg wasn't up to standing without my crutches, so I stayed in place, cognizant that the framing could be better than me propped against Vanessa's open door.

"We're standing outside the haunted barn after a manifestation drove Chad and I away," I narrated. "I've got two members of the family who have lived on this land for generations with me to get the ghost talking. This is Lara Goodman, and her niece Stephanie. Are you two ready to make contact?

"Sure," Lara agreed.

Steph looked less certain about the whole thing. "Is it dangerous?"

"Most spirits cannot interact much with the physical world," I assured her. "It takes too much energy. To be on the safe side, we won't push too hard today, but it should be safe. If you're both ready, we'll give our spirit one last crack at communicating before we finish filming for the day."

"Ready. Tell us what to do," Lara said.

"Take the EVP recorder and approach the barn door," I instructed. "We recorded EM activity and a cold spot in front of the door earlier, so that area is within the ghost's range. Stand there and offer to talk. We'll record whatever happens."

Lara took the recorder. I showed her how to make sure it was on. Then Chad and I watched as Lara and Steph tried to entice the ghost into revealing their identity.

Nothing happened. The earlier display must have zapped all the juice the ghost had gathered from Chad and I. Or, a more disturbing thought, they were biding their time. Either way, we were wasting time here. Nothing more was likely to happen today.

I let them mess around a while longer with nothing but static to show for their efforts. Then I called it a day.

So much for convincing Chad the ghost was real. By the time a disappointed Lara drove away, he'd bounced back to his usual self. His earlier nerves about the barn and our experiences there banished.

# EIGHTEEN

## *Chad*

Falling asleep after what happened in the barn was a challenge. I still had that jittery keyed up feeling that came with being chased from the haunted barn. Allegedly haunted. Creepy without a doubt.

Absent the intense emotions of the moment, I felt unspeakably foolish for believing a ghost was in the barn with us. Mere suggestibility had me thinking I'd experienced things that couldn't be real. That was all it was, getting caught up in Dan's excitement and his ghostly expertise.

It was Daniel and his magnetism, not ghosts. Ghosts weren't real. But Daniel, Daniel was all too real.

With only the thin divider between us, sleep was getting more difficult by the night. My internet crush was easy to ignore. Far harder to dismiss my growing feelings for Daniel when I spent all day with him. And all night with him inches away.

The way he looked at me last night, so full of concern after our mad dash from the barn, well, it went to my head—and my heart. Foolishness. Nothing could happen between us. He was my boss.

A guy could fantasize. But perhaps not when there was only a thin wooden barrier between me and the object of my desires. This whole living and working within eighty square feet of my crush might take more willpower than I'd expected.

I spent far too long tossing and turning before slipping into a restless slumber. It was just as well I didn't remember my dreams, I'm sure they were a jumble of my boss in compromising positions and ghoulish apparitions.

I crawled out of my narrow bunk first the next morning, unable to sleep any longer. My imagination had me almost believing the soughing of the wind outside was a moaning vengeful spirit. It wasn't. Only the wind.

The van was chilly this morning. I pulled on a hoodie before breaking out the coffee grounds. Daniel had shown me how the stovetop coffee maker worked on my first day.

I filled the bottom with water, added a few spoonfuls of grounds to the metal filter. After I screwed the contraption together, it was ready to go. I flipped open the stove's covering to turn on the propane burner and waited for the coffee to flow.

Either the sound of the water boiling off, or the aroma of fresh-brewed coffee woke Daniel. He squirmed out of his bunk with a wide yawn.

I busied myself getting down mugs from the cabinet above the stove to avoid ogling him. Still, the sounds of him wrestling with his bulky cast and thumping closer to me to grab the sugar captivated my full attention.

"Morning," Daniel said as he heaped sugar into the mug I'd gotten out for him.

"Morning," I said, pouring myself a cup of strong black coffee. Daniel took the pot from me and filled his own mug.

He added shelf-stable whitener from the cabinet and sipped his coffee. He set his mug on the desk under the wall-mounted video editing display and pulled out a chair to sit.

"So, who are we interviewing today?" Daniel asked.

I leaned against the counter, sipped my coffee to buy time and recalled the schedule I'd worked out for the interviews.

"Today we've got Mr. Dawes, a retired farmhand and Mr. Smith, who still works part-time. Dawes worked here when Lara was a child. Lara says Leon will join us for dinner tonight, so we can get his take on the childhood incidents over the meal."

"Sounds good." Daniel took another appreciative swig of his coffee. "It occurs to me you aren't familiar with the gear. I figure we can film a short refresher segment to help you learn. We can set up here. Where we filmed the end of the IR camera review. You saw how I rig the backdrop across the bunks. After breakfast, we'll set everything up in here and I can give you the quick and dirty rundown on the most common gear we use. How it works, the meaning of various readings we might find."

I nodded. After the excitement of yesterday, we'd finished filming his new IR camera unboxing and review inside the van. He called the seat in front of the editing monitors his studio. I deemed that a generous description for a chair next to a green sheet draped to cover the bunks, but I didn't call him on it. The truth was, he made it look professional in his finished videos.

We'd gotten into a groove working together inside the van. Wrapping up the GhostCam version 3 segment lasted us until dinner at the farmhouse. After which Daniel spent a few hours editing our footage from the day. We worked well together.

"So, we're making a paranormal investigations training video for the gear?"

"Yeah," Daniel grimaced, "I guess with the number of assistants I go through, you'd imagine I would have filmed something like that already. I have some Paranormal Investigations 101 videos out already, but they're scattered, this will be more focused. It can double as an intro for new subscribers. I hope it will make it easier for you to do your job if you have a basic grasp of our tools, right?"

"Right," I agreed.

"So, let me preface by saying you were fantastic yesterday. The camera loves your energy. And so you know, your job is secure, okay? I've already mentioned you don't have to believe in the paranormal to work for me, just have an open mind. And you know, don't outright contradict or obscure our findings on camera. Not that I'm suggesting you'd sabotage us or anything."

"Sabotage, huh?"

Daniel face-palmed. "You know, I will not keep digging there. My point is, after what we saw yesterday, I wanted to say, you can talk to me about any of this stuff. If you have questions or doubts. You might be a skeptic, but what you saw yesterday got intense. So I just wanted to check in with you, see how you're handling everything. Heck, I started out skeptical myself. I got my start in paranormal investigations taking cheap dares to stay in haunted locations overnight."

"I'm fine," I assured him. "Emotions were running high. It's all good. And I know about the dares. I saw the vids. You really changed your mind, though, huh?"

"Impossible not to, after everything I've seen over the years."

"I guess. Like you said, yesterday got intense. Is it like that all the time?"

"When we investigate a haunted site, yeah. Not all of them are—sometimes an old abandoned building is just an old building." Daniel gestured with his coffee cup.

"You think this one is real, though?"

Daniel nodded. "Seems that way."

"So, what does that mean?" I asked. "Not to say I've changed my mind, but what's the end goal here? Are we trying to put the ghost to rest?"

"Yep, if we can. For now though, finish your coffee, it's almost time for you to start Ghost Hunter 101."

# NINETEEN

## *Dan*

Once we'd eaten a quick breakfast, I set up for filming while Chad fetched the bulky duffel bag full of my most used gear. I pulled the backdrop curtain across the bunks and smoothed out the wrinkles. Then I attached the camera to the wall mount I used for filming inside Vanessa.

That just left adjusting the lighting and clearing the table of our coffee cups. I unlocked the arm to let the desk swivel up and away from the wall. I angled the table between me and the camera mount to best display our gear, then locked it into position.

"Where do you want this?" Chad hefted the duffel.

"There." I gestured to the table.

He set it down, and I rifled through the contents, pulling out the parts I needed for this segment. Once I'd selected what I wanted, I lined everything up in a neat row.

"Set that aside," I said. Chad stowed the duffel in the cab, between the chairs.

"What now, boss?"

"Ready to play the attentive student?" I arched a brow at Chad.

"Sure, what should I do?"

"Stand beside me and look interested in learning about each tool. Ask whatever questions you have. You can touch, but be mindful of camera angles, so our viewers get a clear view of the details."

"I can do that." Chad nodded, sidling around the table to join me behind it. It was a bit of a tight fit, but I didn't mind his proximity. I jostled his shoulder, and he shot me a grin.

"Great, so live in three, two…" I hit record on the remote control in my pocket instead of finishing the countdown. With a big grin, I waved into the camera as the red light blinked to life to let me know we were recording.

"Greetings from my crew to yours," I said. "Today I am breaking in my new assistant, Chad. Say hello, Chad."

"Hello." Chad waved at the camera, taking his cue from me.

"Chad here isn't familiar with the tools of the trade." I slung a companionable arm around his shoulders and pulled him into my side. "And that just won't do. So we are filming a short bonus series I'm calling Ghost Hunter 101 to familiarize him with the gear. It should be a good refresher for everyone watching.

"If you already have a good understanding of the gear we use, rest assured, this is a bonus supplemental video. We're still sticking to the usual release schedule as well. If you're watching this as soon as it drops, the August unboxing came out a few days ago and the haunted history vid will post to the channel as usual on the second Saturday of August. I guarantee it'll be a hauntastic time.

"Speaking of the unboxing video, Chad, you are already familiar with two of these tools now, right?"

Chad nodded and brushed his fingers over the EM meter I'd set up in front of him. "I am."

"So verbose," I teased.

"We used it yesterday, it makes noise and lights up when there are electromagnetic fluctuations. Like if someone is using a microwave," Chad joked.

"Or if a ghost is present," I countered.

"Or that," Chad said, dry as dust.

"We can also use it to monitor cold spots." I rattled off the make and model of the meter and a summary of its tech specs. Then I moved on to the IR camera. The new one from POI. "Anyone who has watched the channel long will know, I love getting gear from companies to review and this camera did not disappoint.

"So, Chad, we use infrared cameras to capture clearer images of ghosts than your typical camera will pick up. You may have seen IR images of people, appearing at the warmer end of the spectrum. Ghosts show up in the cool end. You can capture some stunning spooky images with a good IR camera and a cooperative ghost. I've had an older model for a while, but POI's latest model, the GhostCam version 3, has some exciting new features. For one, it comes equipped with a motion activated surveillance mode. For another I can stream the video feed to a mobile app via bluetooth. Now, that might not give the clearest reception with a ghost around since the EM will interfere with connectivity, but it's still a fun feature to have."

"You know the best part, though?" Chad asked, a mischievous glint in his eye that alerted me I was in for a ribbing.

"What's the best part?"

"Well, considering your accident prone nature, the best feature you mentioned to me yesterday is that it sends automatic backups of whatever it records to cloud storage at regular intervals. So even if the camera gets damaged, we should be able to access the footage."

I laughed. "Way to call me out. Okay, you're right, that is a handy feature."

We filmed for the better part of an hour to go over each of my top five most used tools. I figured that would give us plenty of material to edit down into a twenty minute segment.

Chad was a natural in front of the camera. The more I placed him there, the more comfortable he seemed. That suited me fine.

If I had my way, he'd be standing in the spotlight with me well into the future.

# TWENTY
## *Chad*

We filmed for over an hour to get the raw footage for the Ghost Hunter 101 video. Daniel seemed happy and energized when he called cut. I helped him tidy the gear away afterward, locking the table back into position under the dual monitor display bolted to the wall.

By the time we'd packed all the gear, paranormal and otherwise, we only had enough time for a quick lunch before our first interview. Daniel threw together sandwiches to eat on the road. I drove the van to Mr. Dawes' address in the neighboring town.

It was a pleasant enough drive through scenic pastureland. The smell of cows and manure was strong, but I was getting accustomed to it after a few days out here.

Dawes lived in a well-maintained ranch home with a single-car garage. An old pickup truck, its paint peeling, sat parked in the drive. Someone had propped open the hood.

When we parked behind the truck, an older guy with a wiry build and a beer gut straightened up from where he was working on the truck's engine. He set aside his tools to watch us get out of the van.

"Mr. Dawes?" Dan stepped forward and set his crutches to offer a handshake.

"That's me." Dawes wiped his hands on a rag already stained black with grease. He gave Dan a firm handshake and an appraising look.

"Hi, I'm Dan, this is my assistant Chad. Do you mind if we film this interview?" Dan asked.

"Don't see why not." Dawes shrugged. "Let's sit. My Aggie has lemonade sitting on the porch for us."

We both followed him up the front porch steps. He and Daniel took the pair of rocking chairs on either side of a low table set with a tray of refreshments. Cookies accompanied a pitcher of lemonade dripping condensation in the warm late summer sunshine. Three empty glasses sat beside the tray.

I helped Daniel prop his crutches in easy reach while Dawes poured drinks and set a cookie on a napkin. I declined mine so my hands were free to film. Daniel took an appreciative sip and complimented Aggie's culinary skills.

Dawes beamed at the praise. "Thanks, but you aren't here for the hospitality."

I took that as my cue to hit record on the camera and get the interview on film.

"You boys are the ones investigating Lara's ghost, right?" Dawes broached the subject.

"Lara's ghost?" Dan repeated.

"Sure." Dawes nodded. "That girl's convinced the old barn is haunted. Ever since she almost hung herself with that darn rope swing, playing in the loft."

"Do you think it's haunted?" Dan asked.

"Ain't no such thing as ghosts," Dawes replied. "But I'll warrant it's a creepy old place. With the history, well, I can see why her imagination runs away with her."

"What history?" Dan prompted.

"You know." He sided-eyed us. "Old man Higgs killed himself out there, back in the 30s, 1933 I think. Farm was failing all around him, I suppose he couldn't face it. After his death, Goodman took over, he was Higgs' brother-in-law, married Martha Higgs, the rest is history."

"I see," Dan said.

"I worked for the family since I was a sprout myself, though not in Frank's time," Dawes elaborated. "I was still a babe in arms. My father drove the milk truck back in those days. He was the one who found the body when he arrived to pick up their morning milk. I didn't start working for Goodman until years later, but everyone knew the story. Dad took it hard. They were friends."

"Understandable, how awful for him. I often find cases where someone dies by suicide stick around, looking for closure on whatever drove them to the act. Care to share any other details about Mr. Higgs?" Dan asked.

The old man scratched his chin contemplatively. "Frank Higgs left behind his wife Catherine and their three daughters. Elmer and Martha Goodman moved the widow and her girls into a guest house on the property. Treated them right, gave them work and a decent wage."

"Was that unusual?" Dan asked.

"Times were hard, but they were family," Dawes replied. "They helped find good marriages for the girls when they came of age, even though they had two grown daughters of their own to arrange for. Not everyone would have done that."

"The family was close then?" Dan pressed.

"Sure. Elmer's oldest son, Robert, is Lara and Leon's grandfather. Good family. I worked for Elmer and Robert for years before my bad back forced me to retire. Lara's a good sort too, loves the farm," Dawes said fondly.

"And Frank's girls," Dan prompted, "are any of them still local?"

"No." Dawes shook his head. "They've all passed. Robert's oldest son, Will, retired to Florida with his wife a few years back. I think one of Robert's sisters is still alive, she moved out of state when she married though."

"You said the farm was failing, how did Elmer turn it around?" Dan steered the conversation back to the historical events around the haunting.

"Every dairy farm struggled in those days, it was the Great Depression. Prices kept going lower. Elmer stuck it out, pushed through it with good old-fashioned hard work and determination. Helped that he had a whole passel of brats old enough to help with the milking, he put the Higgs girls to work in the milking shed too. Nothing like free labor," Dawes observed.

"I can imagine." Dan shot me a look I couldn't quite decipher.

Dawes said, "Elmer provided for his family and Frank's girls. Frank would have been none too happy about that, Martha's man showing him up like that. Then in 1938 they worked out price controls to stabilize the industry. The farm turned profitable enough they could afford to hire on hands. A few years after that, they hired me."

"What else can you tell us about the barn, did you experience anything strange there?" Dan asked.

"Nothing strange happened to me beyond the odd noise." Dawes scratched his chin. "You wouldn't know it from its current state, but that used to be quite the enterprise. Could hold almost fifty head of cattle. We did the milking all by hand. Takes longer that way for less yield, you know?"

"Yes, Lara mentioned when she showed me the new facilities. Very impressive," Dan sipped his lemonade.

"The old place is falling apart now, have you seen it? Still gives me the creeps to think about Frank climbing up to the loft and looking out over his land before he did for himself you know?" Dawes shuddered dramatically.

"I can't imagine," Dan commiserated. "So, when did they stop using the old barn?"

"Well," Dawes drummed his fingers on his armrest, "when they passed the rural electric act, Robert convinced his father it was time to build a bigger barn with fancy electric lighting to take advantage. Around that time, one of the younger Goodman boys got trampled by a spooked horse out at the old stables. Damn near lamed the boy, leg broken so bad it was a miracle he didn't take sick and die."

"That sounds serious," Dan observed

"Serious enough that Nate never liked to talk about the barn after that, he was superstitious about it," Dawes agreed. "Couldn't blame him after Frank's ghost tried to kill him."

"He blamed the ghost?" Dan asked.

"That he did," Dawes confirmed. "Anyway, in all the fuss someone knocked over a lantern. It would have set the whole building ablaze if Robert hadn't put it out quick. That more than anything decided Elmer."

"I don't follow," I interrupted.

"Well, the animals acted funny sometimes, spooking for no reason we could tell, or behaving ornery. Anyway, after Nate broke his leg, the hands refused to go up in the loft. There were rumbles before, but afterward their imaginations ran wild. They claimed they heard strange sounds up there."

"I can't imagine that helped morale," Dan said, then he sipped the lemonade.

"Nope." Dawes took a sip too, then cleared his throat. "That settled it, Elmer agreed to build the new barn. Elmer kept the old barn up, added in box stalls for the horses and kept the cows in the new barn. They still used it some until Will's twins got hurt in the loft. Fixing it up to modern standards wasn't worth the cost, easier to build a new stable for the horses, so they just let the old one go to ruin."

"Can you think of anything else?" Dan asked.

"The original farmhouse was out near there too, but that burned in the 40s. They rebuilt closer to the new facility and the cows," Dawes scratched his jaw contemplatively.

"A fire? Was anyone hurt?" Dan leaned in close at the new tidbit.

"No, they all escaped." Dawes shook his head. "The youngest kid, Evie, said she heard footsteps and a man laughing. It scared her, she woke the household when she saw the smoke. I remember Elmer said it was the darndest thing. Something blocked the door, he had to muscle it open to get them all out. It was an odd story."

"And then they rebuilt away from the haunted barn?" Dan asked.

"That's right." Dawes nodded. "More convenient to the milking barn, worked out for the best. I remember Robert saying he slept better at the new house, no strange noises waking him at night. All of them looked less tired after the move. Little Evie smiled more even. She'd been a fussy child, but that stopped after the fire. Like night and day."

"Strange."

"It was," Dawes agreed. "Anyway, in the 90s Lara convinced Will to install a new state-of-the-art automated milking system. They built the new facility around that installation. Don't think they've kept up maintenance on the old place since."

"Do you remember anything else about Frank?" Dan asked. "Were there any incidents in the building prior to his death?"

"Nothing that I can recall. Mind, I was a child when it happened, I didn't hear everything. Frank, though, he was a good man. A good friend to my father, a good husband and father to his family. But Dad said he used to get these black moods. His death was a real shame. It shocked the community, but not Dad, he said Frank used to get maudlin in his cups.

Before he died, he asked my father to watch out for the girls if anything happened to him. Afterward, Dad figured Frank'd already decided when he asked."

"Sounds like it was rough on him," Dan said.

The old man shrugged. "That's life, now, if that's all your questions, boys, I've got to get the old rust bucket running again."

Alex Silver

# TWENTY-ONE

## *Dan*

Our second interview of the day was less useful than
the first. Mr. Smith tried to answer our questions, but
he either remembered nothing useful or it happened
before his time. Still, after chatting with the retired farmhands,
we had new avenues to pursue.

We had confirmation that Frank Higgs died in his barn in
1932, despairing of his farm's prospects. So after the
interviews we hit the town archives for more research.

Chad found old articles online about the dairy industry in
the 1930s. It didn't paint a pretty picture. After oversupply
issues caused dairy prices to drop in the late 20s, they never
made a full recovery until the late 30s, years after Higgs' death.

I could understand Frank's despair at seeing everything he'd
worked for falling to ruin around him. Higgs' obituary hadn't
told us much, too short on details. But the names of his
surviving family gave us more leads.

Looking them up returned more dead ends. All three of his
daughters were deceased. They had children local to the area,
but I wasn't sure they would know anything.

Chad volunteered to look into getting in touch with them
and track down Evie Goodman, the only still living member of
the family old enough to remember Frank. He slipped outside
to make some calls. I immersed myself in records research
until he returned.

What we'd already learned looked grim. Frank Higgs killed himself in the loft of the haunted barn—and then the strange incidents started.

Spooked animals, odd noises, the fire in the original farmhouse. Accidents. This situation had all the hallmarks of a true haunting.

The only question in my mind was whether it would be safe to continue our investigation. Higgs had already proven dangerous and powerful. His ability to move heavy doors was nothing to sneeze at in a spirit. It proved he was strong enough to interact with the physical world.

So far, a few broken bones were the worst of Higgs' bad behavior, if the stories were true, but would it be too risky to make a further attempt at communication with the ghost? My natural inclination was to encourage the lingering spirit to move along as best I could.

What would Higgs want? The farm was thriving. His great-niece and nephew owned the operation. It had remained in the family. Was there more to the story?

Only the dead man could say. Or his relatives. They hadn't connected the spirit haunting the barn to their deceased relative, yet. Odd that. Chad's return pulled me out of my musings.

"What did you find." Based on his grim expression, Chad didn't have happy news.

"Nate's son is a resident of a local nursing home, Alzheimer's. The nurse I spoke to said he isn't lucid most of the time and won't see visitors who aren't family. Evie I can't seem to find. Maybe Lara can shed some light on where her great-aunt ended up. Probably she isn't a Goodman anymore and I doubt Evie is her full given name since I can't find a thing about her. Beyond a birth record for an Evelyn Goodman who would be the right age. Not much else." Chad slumped into his seat.

"And Frank's grandkids?"

"Two of the daughters stayed local. The third, Lettie, married a politician. They moved to Burlington. I got several hits on her when I searched the database. Her children aren't local. I called around to the Goodman descendants I found listed in the phonebook, but none of them seemed to know much about the old barn or Frank. I'll keep digging," he promised.

"Do you recall Lara or Leon mentioning Frank at all?" I asked.

Chad looked up from the archive records he was perusing. "No."

"Don't you find that odd?"

"You would think if they bought into the haunting stories, they would have connected their great-great-uncle's death to the events, yeah," he agreed.

"Right." I nodded. "So, I'm thinking Lara should be our next visit. I don't know how much more useful information we'll find here."

"Sounds good." Chad stretched. "I guess it makes sense that people would associate the death with the bad luck on the farm after and eventually the story snowballed into the idea the place is haunted. Too bad Frank's name got lost in the retelling."

"We'll bring that up with Lara, too. It's getting late, let's wrap up here before they kick us out, and get back to the farm before we miss dinner."

# TWENTY-TWO

## *Chad*

W e returned to Goodman Dairy around six. Lara and Jane had left a note taped to the unlocked farmhouse door. They had saved us plates of leftovers to reheat, wrapped up in their fridge.

They were already out at the barn to do the evening chores. We ate a quick and quiet meal in the empty farmhouse. After we ate, we took care of our plates and returned to the van.

Daniel directed me to park near the old barn for the night. On the drive, he'd mentioned staking out the place with the new infrared camera. So I ended the evening digging through his piles of gear in the fading light of dusk to find a tripod with the correct mount for the new GhostCam.

It would be a challenge to set up everything before we lost the daylight. I didn't mind working into the night with Daniel though. The sky at sunset was a sight to behold so far from light pollution.

The chirping of insects serenading us was peaceful. Soon, dark would leave Daniel and I alone with nothing but the stars and the waning moon above to bear witness to our presence.

I saw how this lifestyle appealed to Daniel. It was like his life was one big exciting camping trip. The cramped quarters weren't bad, other than the lack of privacy. Jerking off with the object of my fantasies inches away was too unnerving to contemplate. But otherwise? I had no regrets.

I found the right attachment to connect the GhostCam to a stand in a jumble of camera accessories Daniel kept in a storage bin in the back. The plan was to set it up in the entrance of the film set. I found it less unnerving to think of it as a set than as a haunting when it was dark and the lengthening evening shadows seemed almost alive.

Despite the foreboding the barn engendered in me up close, I thought this would otherwise be a very nice spot to spend a peaceful evening. With no other agenda than to admire the vast expanse of country sky with a special someone at my side.

Someone, not Daniel, but perhaps very like him, who would be content to enjoy the view and my company. It was utter nonsense. I refused to start something with my boss.

Workplace romances were a bad enough idea when work was a nine-to-five grind in an anonymous office. It would take downright catastrophic levels of stupidity to date my boss when we lived and worked in a six by twelve space.

No way that could end well. Best to banish the thought right now. Better to keep working with my semi-celebrity crush than to risk this shot at a job I was getting into. Even if it was just so much high-tech table-rapping, Daniel made it fun.

"You got the camera ready?" Daniel checked.

"Yeah." I nodded. "Sorry about that, woolgathering."

"Great." Daniel grinned. "Once you set it up by the doorway it will capture the main aisle and the ladder to the loft. That's where we sensed the presence before. I'll log in and stream the video to my phone. I love the new features with version 3 already. It's so cool that we can monitor the footage from Vanessa live."

"Are we using the EM meter too?" I asked.

"Not yet. But we'll have it ready to roll if we detect any spirit activity. Sometimes they're more active at night."

"Okay," I agreed. "Sounds good. I'll get everything set up, you take it easy."

"I'd argue with you, but to tell the truth, I appreciate you doing the legwork," Daniel admitted. "My leg has been sore since our mad dash to safety yesterday."

"Should we get it checked out?" I asked, alarmed at the possibility he'd done real damage.

The last thing Daniel needed was another medical issue. Like an infection in his broken leg. Or to have screwed up his healing.

At least we'd filed the paperwork to get him switched to the higher premium policy for the interim. It would cover him until open enrollment made it possible to change companies.

That Daniel's compensation package offered me coverage too was an unexpected boon. If I stuck around for three months, he would purchase a plan for me. It meant having coverage for my T. Not that testosterone was the most expensive medication to need, all things considered.

At Chorus I'd seen some eye-popping drug prices. Still, insurance meant not paying for the bulk of the cost out of pocket. And I wouldn't have to worry about the bill attached to my monitoring blood work while we were traipsing around the country.

"No," Daniel assured me. "It's nothing like the warning signs on that discharge paperwork you have memorized, just a tad sore from overdoing it. I'll rest it as much as possible for a few days and I'm sure it'll be fine."

"I hope so, hate to see you in pain. You got painkillers from the hospital, right?"

"Yeah, I took some Advil. It helps, no worries." Daniel patted his cast. "If it's still bad in a couple days, we can find a walk-in care place. I doubt it will come to that."

The walk from the van to the barn had me jumping at shadows. We'd only parked about a dozen yards from the door, but it seemed much further with the wind rustling the tall grass and weeds around me.

I imagined they sounded like low whispering voices. The sounds of the barn settling transformed into creaking moans. And I could have sworn I heard something moving within. Likely squirrels, based on what Stephanie and Ben had said about the place when they helped us set up to film the other day.

Still, I wasn't keen on coming face to face with anything living in the creepy husk of a barn.

I was glad Daniel didn't want me to go inside to film. Even standing in the doorway raised goosebumps on my arms. I made fast work of attaching the IR camera to the tripod and setting it to surveillance mode.

It took a few moments to get the shot framed just so, and then I made sure the camera was turned on and ready to transmit to Daniel's phone app.

My task completed, I didn't linger outside. Something about that old barn gave me the creeps. It was probably just the chilly breeze making my skin prickle, but I still walked a little faster than necessary to get back to the safety of the van.

It was silly. Ghosts didn't exist, no matter how sure Daniel seemed. He was playing a role or believed because he needed the comfort of certainty about the afterlife. No judgment from me, I understood the appeal of knowing. But if they were real, surely Mom would have stuck around to check in on us?

At the least, she would have visited with her grandkids. Zoe had been born after her death, wouldn't she want to meet her? Or maybe check in to make sure I was okay once I started college. If any part of my mother still lingered, she would have said something or given me some sign.

So, no—ghosts weren't real. I just couldn't shake the sense that something malevolent was watching me from the shadows.

# TWENTY-THREE

## *Dan*

C had seemed shaken after setting up the IR camera to record the barn. I gave him some time to hide his nerves as I fiddled with the app on my phone that let me stream the video feed from the GhostCam.

We could observe any spirit activity from the comfort of Vanessa's well-lit interior. I loved that feature already.

I sat in the passenger seat, swiveled around to face the back. Chad helped me prop my broken leg up on the toilet and took a seat on a chair he dragged closer to me.

"So, is it working?"

"Sure, want a peek?" I turned the screen to face him.

The interior of the barn appeared cast in shades of greenish gray. Nothing spectral had happened yet, but I didn't expect much so early in the evening.

"So, it picks up heat signatures, right?"

"Thermal energy. It can detect cold spots too, that's what we're looking for tonight. The cooler shades, so greens and blues. If you put your hand in front of the display, it would show in oranges, yellows and red tones. My old one couldn't do streaming so this is fortuitous timing with my leg. But we covered that this morning."

"Yeah, I remember. Just making sure I had the details straight. Next time you should quiz me." Chad winked at me.

"Next time I will." I smiled back. I hoped to have lots of next times with him. He was probably the most competent assistant I'd ever hired. And he was a willing pupil, even if he was a skeptic. "I'll set up an alert for if we catch anything moving around overnight. Care to stay up with me a while longer to monitor the feed? I'd love to grab more readings if the ghost makes an appearance tonight. We can hang out and chill while we wait."

"Yeah? I'm game."

"Nice. So, on that note, let's play a game," I suggested.

"A game?"

"Yeah, getting to know you stuff. Two truths and a lie, ever played?"

Chad nodded. "I have. I can go first. I once got chased by a rabid raccoon, I was valedictorian of my high school class, and I'm a stickler for following the rules."

I laughed. "I'll guess you don't follow the rules, is that a jab at me assuming you were a straitlaced father of two before we met in person?"

"You got me. I bent the rules all the time, it sucks being the person telling someone we won't cover their medical procedure, you know? So I did my best to push claims through, even if I had to stretch the limits of the rules to do it."

"That's why they let you go, huh?"

"Yep, that's the long and short of it. I got caught bending the rules one too many times."

"I was someone you did that for, huh?" It wasn't really a question, I knew he'd put his job on the line for me.

"You were. Don't go apologizing about it, though, I'm a grown man. I made the choice to go to bat for our clients knowing the consequences. I'd do the same again."

"Few people would," I observed.

Chad shrugged. "I understand what it's like to be in desperate medical need only to learn my policy denied me coverage or it isn't an important enough priority."

"Because of your transition?"

"That too." He nodded.

"What else? Or is that prying? You don't have to tell me if it's too personal. You don't owe me answers just because I'm your boss, or anything."

"It's fine, I brought it up." Chad shrugged. "My mom died of breast cancer when I was a teenager. First, they wouldn't cover the screening because she was 'too young'. She fought for it, because she had a family history. Then we had to fight with them to cover treatment."

"That's awful," I said, horrified.

"She was already stage four when they found it. She fought, Mom was always a fighter, but it wasn't enough. From diagnosis to her final hospitalization, she lasted eighteen months. Long enough to attend my high school graduation and meet my oldest niece. My older sister, Kay's, kid. She had a good policy too, so it covered most of her medical expenses. But we spent way too many of her last days battling with the company to get claims approved and arguing about rejections. She had life insurance so Kay and I didn't go into debt giving her a nice funeral."

"Is that why you worked in insurance?"

Chad barked a laugh. "Hell no. I hated those bastards for what they put my family through. But they offered a decent benefits package and they had flexible hours. A few years into community college, my college fund and Mom's life insurance had run dry. I was hitting a brick wall getting my transition care covered through my school's policy beyond them offering me a few sessions a semester with a mental health counselor.

"Chorus Insurance was hiring. The starting pay was enough to afford the rest of my degree courses if I stayed enrolled part-time while I worked. Plus, their policy covered top surgery and getting started on T. The monitoring early on can get pricey with the regular blood tests, so it worked out for me. I'd always planned on it being temporary, but then I saw a chance to help people out. People like my family, and you, just looking to get the services they'd paid for with their premiums, you know?"

"I get that." I nodded.

"Right. Well, that delved deeper than I meant it to. Figured for sure you'd ask about the raccoon," Chad forced a weak laugh.

"Seemed too obvious. I'm sure that's a story though, what happened?" I asked, sensing the story might break the heavy mood of his confessions.

"Kay and I were playing in the woods at our grandparent's house. Kay threw a ball into a blackberry bush. I followed in after it, ran back out with a raccoon chasing me. We ran into the house and slammed the door behind us. Kay thought it was hilarious."

"It sounds funny, were you hurt?" I asked.

"In hindsight, maybe it was funny," he allowed. "I was fine. That animal was freaky though. We assumed it would lose interest and go back to the berries. It didn't, though. It stayed right in the doorway hissing and making a terrible racket. Grandpa ended up shooting it an hour later when it was still there."

"Did the raccoon have a personal vendetta against you? Now I'm picturing a tiny Rambo Raccoon shaking its adorable little fist at you."

Chad shook his head, but he was smiling. *Mission accomplished,* I loved his smile.

"Not a vendetta, rabies. They got it tested and sure enough, it came back positive. I didn't get bit, I don't remember the raccoon touching me at all. I ran like the devil himself was after me when that thing hissed at me. The branches left my arms scratched to ribbons, so I had to get vaccinated just in case. It was miserable."

"How old were you?"

"Nine, Kay was fifteen."

"She's your only sibling?" I asked.

"Yep. What about you, any siblings?"

"Only child. My friends all said it made me spoiled." I laughed it off. "I think it was just that my parents didn't know what to do with a kid so they figured throwing money at me constituted parenting. But enough about that, my turn. Hmm, let's see, how do I top rabid wildlife and an altruistic streak a mile wide?"

Chad pinked at the praise. So cute. And why had I mentioned topping? Not where my mind needed to be with my employee. Time to think unsexy thoughts.

"My grandmother, who died before I was born, used to visit me when my parents were working late. The first time I tried to stay overnight in a haunted house I chickened out after the first hour and lost a five hundred dollar bet. My first kiss was with a girl named Trixie behind the bleachers at our high school."

Chad laughed. "Well, since you know that I know you're gay, I'll guess Trixie is true, too obvious to be the lie. And I can picture you swearing never to lose another bet after failing the first one. You're stubborn like that. So, I'll guess your grandmother didn't appear to you as a kid."

I laughed. "Nope, it wasn't Trixie, it was her twin brother Trent. They were my best friends, but Trixie didn't speak to me for three months after she found out."

"Did she have a thing for you?"

"No, she was just pissed that I screwed up the dynamics of our friendship. It was weird dating my best friend's brother and when we inevitably broke up, things were weird between Trixie and I for a while. Can't say she was wrong to be upset, in retrospect."

"Do you keep in touch?" he asked.

"Some, Trix doesn't believe in the paranormal. So, she thinks I'm being ridiculous traveling around the country with Vanessa to film make-believe. What can you do, right?" I shrugged it off.

"So, you believe your grandma's ghost was looking out for you?" Chad asked.

"I saw her. My parents told me that ghosts aren't real. They assumed it was an imaginary friend thing. We moved when I was ten, and I stopped seeing her. Convinced myself that it was a product of my overactive imagination, and ghosts aren't real."

"But you believe in them now." It wasn't a question.

"Yeah, at first I didn't. I figured haunted sites were just creepy abandoned old buildings, and it was our collective consciousness that made them seem ominous or whatever. People read patterns into situations that aren't there. There are logical explanations for hauntings, right? So, I was initially planning to go around sleeping in haunted places to debunk local urban legends about hauntings."

"What changed?" Chad asked.

"I saw that the spirits are real," I said, a simple statement of fact.

Chad wasn't someone talking would convince. He'd have to conclude the paranormal was real for himself. Like I had.

I could only pray that when he did, he didn't run the other way. Because I already suspected he was irreplaceable.

# TWENTY-FOUR

## *Chad*

Van life was growing on me. Tuesday had marked a week with Daniel, and it was already Thursday. Time flew when you kept busy. I hadn't realized how lonely and boring my life was when I was working at Chorus until everything changed.

My studio apartment was in a building full of young professionals. We all lived in similar solitary units. Most of them worked the day shift and had established groups of friends.

My flex schedule at the customer service center often had me working evenings. I never saw my neighbors unless one of us was arriving home while the other was leaving for a work shift.

Work was always busy. Clients on the phones, managers breathing down our necks. The evening shift was a little more lax on that score, but still, the general mood in the office was that we were co-workers, not friends.

I couldn't remember the last time I'd shared a cup of coffee in the mornings. Probably my last year of high school.

We found out Mom's diagnosis was terminal at the end of my junior year. My heavily pregnant sister and her husband, Brad, had moved Mom and I into their suburban cookie cutter home. Mom took an upstairs guest room, and I got the pullout couch in their finished basement.

Kay took care of Mom during her illness. My sister made sure I made it to graduation. When I turned eighteen, she had insisted on getting us both tested for the BRCA mutation that made Mom's cancer so aggressive. She only waited that long because that was the minimum age for our insurance to cover testing.

We all breathed a sigh of relief when that came back negative. Still, the worry that it might claim me too had been another tick mark in the pro column for getting my chest surgery ASAP when it became an option for me. There was still a risk, but it was much lower with most of my breast tissue removed—good riddance.

Kay had held our family together through everything. She was the reason I made it through that last year. The reason Mom hung on as long as she did. Kay had been our rock, all while adjusting to becoming a mom herself.

Those last few months with Mom had been bittersweet—awful and wonderful. Awful to know we were losing her, to see her get sicker with each passing day. And full of the wonder of hoarding a treasure trove of family moments. Moments of being together stolen back from the illness that ravaged her body.

Watching her play with my niece, and getting to see Sadie every day for the first few months of her life. Feeling like a burden on my sister when her focus should be on her baby and instead she had to deal with my emotional crap.

The simple ritual of gathering around Kay's table to share a hot cup of coffee and a meal in the morning encapsulated all that emotional upheaval. Intense highs and lows. We'd embraced those shared moments of being a family in Mom's last months.

It had all fallen apart after the funeral. I couldn't face the painful memories, so I stopped joining my remaining family for breakfast.

When the fall semester started, I moved into a cheap apartment near campus. I worked my ass off to afford it without having to take out student loans. I'd been on my own ever since. Kay gave grudging acceptance to the excuse I had a penchant for solitude and wanted the quiet to focus on my studies.

This morning, as I sat cradling a warm mug of coffee in my hands, I recognized it for what it was—I'd been lonely in my old life. Daniel sat across from me, reciting an animated account of one of his earlier ghost hunting exploits. I'd spent years lonely and alone, and now, because of him, I wasn't either of those things anymore.

Daniel had given me so much more than a job when he made the offer to hire me. Not that I could tell him that without it coming off creepy and clingy. He was my boss. Even if I was technically one of the show's financial backers, so in a way I was, in part, paying myself.

My phone pinged with a notification, interrupting Daniel's story. This one was about a former PA. A ghost's sudden presence in the room spooked her into dropping an expensive camera. The fall broke an even more expensive lens.

I doubted there was a spirit, just a drafty old house. The broken equipment made me cringe though. Daniel babied his cameras almost as much as his van. He touched them with the same tenderness Kay reserved for her kids.

"Need to get that?" He broke off in his telling and gestured to my phone.

I waved away his concern, "It's just a calendar reminder to do my shots today, every two weeks."

"Sho—Oh, right, T? Do you need help with that at all?"

"No, I'm fine, thanks. You don't mind me doing it here in the van though, right?"

Daniel snorted. "No way, man, as long as you're here I want you to consider Vanessa your home. Do whatever you need to do. Should I give you privacy?"

"It's fine." I waved away his concern. "I'm doing the shot in my gut this week, so nothing you wouldn't see at the beach."

"If you're sure," he hedged.

"I am," I said firmly. "I'll wait until after we eat, though," I said, nodding to the swiveling table we were eating on. The ritual of a shared breakfast in the mornings, sitting across from each other, had fast become a highlight of my day.

With the table perpendicular to the wall, it would be a pain to climb up to my bunk. Much easier to retrieve my injection supplies, let alone use them, once we restored the table to its usual position, and put away the breakfast dishes.

"Oh, right," I said, "speaking of the beach, I tracked down Evie Goodman. Well, her daughter, Annette."

"How is that related to beaches?" Daniel asked, puzzled.

"They live near Myrtle Beach," I explained the non sequitur. "I guess Evie is in a nursing home with dementia, but Annette told me her mother kept a diary. I guess she reads entries to Evie when she visits her."

"Any chance of us getting our hands on the diary?" Daniel demanded.

"It's possible." I shrugged. "Annette offered to dig through the ones from the 30s and send screenshots of anything that sounded relevant. From talking to her, I think she'd like the chance to do a televised interview. Although she seemed fuzzy on the difference between broadcast television, streaming services, and a vlog webisode."

"Think she'd be willing to return to the family home to get her shot at social media stardom?" Daniel asked. The twinkle in his eye made it seem like I was in on some private joke with him.

"I don't know about that, but I bet she would do a video interview with us if she finds anything of note in the journal. I think she'll be telling everyone she knows about the show when we get it online too."

"I never say no to word-of-mouth advertising. Well, it would be nice to read the journals, but I can understand the sentimental attachment. Digital versions will have to suffice."

"In the meantime," I reminded him, "I've got Lara's brother coming to film an on camera interview with us this afternoon."

"Perfect." Daniel beamed. "I want shots of the loft too. We can play them with a voice-over of him giving us a firsthand account of the time the ghost pushed him and he broke his arm."

"Oh, I had some thoughts on that. Lara said they had a structural engineer check out the building to see if it was worth refurbishing after the roof caved in. Looks like the loft is still sound. Let's do one better. What if I cast local kids to do a dramatic reenactment?"

"Filming kids can get dicey, we need all kinds of releases…" Daniel trailed off.

"I'll handle it," I assured him. "I looked up the regulations. We just need to follow some common sense guidelines as far as work hours and safety regulations. And have all the releases signed by the kids and their guardians and we should be golden."

"Well, so long as you've got the legal side covered, I like it. If we can get the raw footage, it's a piece of cake to slap a filter on it. Like they do in the big budget productions. Then we add a voice-over of Leon telling the story over top of the video, splice in some modern day shots of the interview and the loft.

A healthy dash of sound effects, and bada bing, bada boom, we've got an awesome segment."

"*Spooky* sound effects?" I asked, amused at how enthusiastic he was about my suggestion.

"Yeah, I've got a whole library of them to use when we get to the editing portion. I'll show you when we get around to that part. For this one, I'm thinking we can go simple—children laughing, creaking boards, maybe a bit of a crash as we have the actor fall out of frame. And some ominous mood music."

"I'll get right on casting then," I said.

I hadn't seen him do dramatizations in past episodes, but I had seen them on other paranormal investigation shows. I figured it would give our webisodes the feel of a higher production value, without too much of an outlay.

A warm glow of happiness filled me at his approval for my idea. It made me feel like a bigger part of the show.

"It'll be a good exercise to show you the basics for compositing video."

"I'm always up for learning new tricks."

"I've noticed, I'll teach you on the fly. The editing is one of my favorite parts so it isn't like I need you to take over that role. It would be ideal for you to know the basics if I ever need to delegate it to you for any reason."

"Reasons like you being in the hospital with a broken leg?" I deadpanned.

"Exactly like that. It's almost like you've known me a while," he teased.

I chuckled. "Well, at least long enough to realize you are the uncrowned king of accidents."

"Spoken like a true insurance salesman."

"I didn't sell the stuff." I wrinkled my nose in distaste. "I just tried to help people access the coverage they already paid for."

"True. Well, you did a better job of it than anyone else I spoke to at Chorus. There's a reason I had you on my speed dial."

I didn't have an adequate response to the praise, my cheeks heated, and I ducked my head trying to hide my embarrassment behind a sip of lukewarm coffee.

"Well, anyway, their loss is my gain. In case I haven't told you, you're doing a splendid job of managing things for the show. I don't know how I'd have gotten on without you."

More praise, my face was in danger of catching fire. "I just made a few calls, arranged paperwork and did the heavy lifting, nothing major."

"You pulled everything together to get a film site on short notice and you're picking up the technical details fast. I'll make a proper paranormal investigator out of you yet, mark my words."

I laughed at that ridiculous statement. Still, the job suited me well enough, and I enjoyed working with Daniel. There were worse things in life than a job I didn't wake up dreading every morning and a boss who appreciated my talents.

# TWENTY-FIVE

## *Dan*

I cleaned our breakfast dishes while Chad climbed into his bunk. He muttered to himself as he got his prescription out of the overhead cabinet where he stored his personal effects.

I smiled to myself. Cramped as Vanessa could get, I enjoyed sharing my space with another person. It didn't hurt that Chad was adorable and devoted to making Hauntastic Haunts the best show it could be.

He seemed to grasp my vision for what the program could become. I meant what I said, that I was lucky to have snapped him up when I did.

Chad slid from his bunk with his supplies. The coffee pot needed a quick wash, so I took care of that, then set about returning our dishes to their secure spots in the cabinet over the sink.

My chores complete, I turned to face Chad. My offer to get out of his way so he had room for whatever the shot thing entailed died on my lips. I stood frozen in place when I saw that he was shirtless and held a vial and syringe in one hand.

The grip required to hold both in place looked uncomfortable, and the syringe seemed to fill in slow motion. It distracted me for a moment.

I'm not sure what I'd expected. The syringe wasn't big. And Chad had laid out his other supplies on the table at his side, all familiar from my many hospital stays. Another needle, still capped, an alcohol wipe, and a small sharps container.

My eyes caught and held on him. He wasn't a gym bunny. He had some pudge around the middle. But he'd inked his chest with a pair of gorgeous tattoos.

The bright scales of a dragon in vibrant blue and green curved around one pectoral and the other bore a roaring lion in shades of gray.

Chad caught me staring and gave a self-conscious chuckle.

"I'd do it in my bunk, but there isn't enough room." He nodded toward the narrow partition.

I swallowed. "No problem, just admiring your ink."

It sounded like a flimsy excuse for staring at him, even to my own ears. The truth was, I liked him. And the part of my brain that processed that attraction didn't give a rip for higher morals and not hitting on my employee.

The guy half naked in my home had my dick taking notice. Even though nothing could happen between us.

It was a strange realization. To go from professional admiration of the man to acknowledging that the warm feeling in my chest when I saw him was genuine attraction. I hadn't had a real life crush in years. It threw me off balance.

"Hello?"

"Sorry, what?" I'd missed what he said.

"I was saying I got them to cover up the top surgery scars. Plus, it draws the eye away from my pudge, so win-win. What about you, have any tattoos?"

"Um, no," I said, swallowing hard. "I do not, don't much care for needles. I can see you know your way around them, though." I gestured.

Chad laughed. "Necessity, you should have seen me fumbling around with the vials the first few months. It was a travesty."

I watched as he expertly finished preparing the injection. He set aside the vial, and pushed on the plunger to expel any air, before capping and replacing the used needle with the safety needle from the table. He set the prepared med aside while he swabbed a patch of skin near his hip.

I should have looked away when he pinched the spot he'd cleaned and pushed the needle into his flesh. I winced, but couldn't seem to tear my eyes away as he slowly injected the testosterone.

"Why is it taking so long?" I demanded, squirming at seeing the needle still lodged in his skin.

Chad glanced up at me, looking far more amused than anyone with a needle in their flesh should. "It's an oil suspension. That makes it a time release depot, so I only have to inject once every two weeks. I'm lucky that I don't notice too much of a taper effect between doses so I can get away with biweekly injections. The tradeoff is that the suspension is too viscous to push in fast like a flu shot or something."

"Oh." I somehow closed my mouth on any unhelpful commentary about that. Even the thought of giving myself an injection made me squeamish. The prolonged injection time had my skin crawling.

"You get used to it," Chad said, reading me like a book. He removed the needle, activated the safety cap, then put it in the sharps container.

A drop of blood welled to the surface of his skin. Chad pressed a square of gauze over it, massaging the area for a while before applying a band-aid.

I realized I was still staring when he reached for his shirt.

"Sorry, I can give you privacy for that."

"It's fine. I mean, I don't mind doing it in front of you. It's not like there's much place for you to go, especially with your leg. Unless you think you might faint at the sight of it?" Chad added the last with a teasing lilt.

"No. That's fine. I only want you to feel comfortable."

"Okay. Well, we have work to do, right? Did the IR camera pick up anything interesting after we went to bed?"

My mind tripped over the phrase 'we went to bed'. Going to bed with him would be wonderful. And wrong. So wrong. Head out of the gutter.

I cleared my throat. "Um, good question, let's check."

Chad tidied away his injection supplies while I logged onto the computer beside him at the editing station. I pulled up the files the camera had sent to my email inbox.

I focused on the screen instead of watching him wriggle back into his bunk. No checking out my employee's ass, that would cross a line. There would be no line crossing here.

Work was a welcome distraction from the fact that I had it bad for my assistant.

# TWENTY-SIX

## *Chad*

I'd made Dan Collins tongue tied. The gorgeous guy I'd spent the past couple of years pining over had noticed me. *Me* of all people. The guy who was so shy he could barely speak up during roll call as a kid.

And I couldn't act on it. Not when a workplace romance had the potential to ruin everything between us. Better to make a close friend in Daniel than risk my new job over a fling.

Daniel was becoming a good friend too. A friend I could talk to about Mom and Kay. Someone who worried about me when I shared the raccoon incident instead of laughing at me.

A friend who cared beyond the surface stuff. Something I'd lacked for too long. So it wasn't worth risking that connection to get laid.

Even if Daniel looking all sleep tousled first thing in the morning was my idea of a walking wet dream. Okay, objectively, he was kind of average looking—I got that. Brown hair, brown eyes, slightly above average height, medium build. But that didn't capture the way his eyes sparkled when he got passionate about a topic.

It didn't account for how safe I felt with his arm wrapped around me when we fled the barn the other day.

The sheer power of his belief almost had me convinced the incident was more than a mere flight of fancy. That there was an enraged spirit on our heels.

It was nonsense, of course, but that was the power Daniel had over me. He made me want to believe in the fantastic.

Or maybe that was the part of me that wished I'd gotten the chance to be honest about myself with my mother. To know, without a doubt, she still loved me.

That was pure fantasy on my part. I never told her I was trans, so I never got to hear her call me her son. Never heard my name on her lips.

No ghost would fix that empty ache in my chest at not knowing for sure how she would have taken the news. Kay had hugged me and offered me whatever help I needed figuring stuff out when I told her.

I'd only had the guts to come out after I'd moved into my crappy student apartment. Proven to myself I could put a roof over my head if she reacted badly.

Kay claimed Mom wouldn't have cared. She loved us too much to care about that. In my head, I knew my sister was right.

Mom had never been a bigot. She'd asked me near the end if the reason I hadn't dated through high school was that I liked girls. Assured me that who I loved didn't matter to her. I figured who I *was* wouldn't either. But in my heart, I still wished I'd taken the chance while she was alive.

That might be the real root of my fascination with Daniel and his paranormal investigations. He could offer me the hope of getting that absolution from my mother. Of confirmation she loved me as much as her son as she had as her daughter.

And I was being maudlin while Daniel worked. I stashed my stuff and rejoined him at the editing desk. The overnight footage revealed little more than a boring still shot, no signs of a ghost.

The only movement was a squirrel scampering down the ladder around dawn. It looked kind of cool in the infrared. A blurry blob of red and yellow color gradients.

Dan seemed unperturbed by the lack of results.

"We'll try again tonight," he declared. "What's on the agenda today?"

"Interviews with dairy staff this morning. If you want to handle those without me, I can look into casting for the flashback scene. I got the impression talking to Ben and Steph the other day that no one working here has much to add to what we already know, but it never hurts to be thorough. I'll meet you for lunch and to prepare for the Leon interview."

"Great. Depending on how long the interview with Leon takes, I'd like to take another look at the library archives today. The librarian the other day said that the woman who works today is a local history buff. She might point us toward more useful information."

"If nothing else, having a segment with a local historian will make for a more interesting means to present the background information to our viewers," I said.

Daniel would know that already, but I wanted to show him I took his show and my job seriously. It must have worked because Daniel grinned at me in response.

"My thoughts exactly. We can get her on film talking about the plight of the dairy industry in the late twenties through to the thirties. Have some film releases ready to sign, all right?"

"You got it, boss." I saluted.

Daniel took his time gathering what he needed for the interviews, then I drove the van over to the dairy offices. He left to do the staff interviews. I got on my phone to double check the regulations for child labor in Vermont and sent the film release forms to Daniel's blue tooth printer.

My immediate jump to prepare the paperwork was optimistic. Nothing said I would find someone to sign those forms today, but I liked to feel prepared. I shrugged off my doubts.

Once they were ready, I slid the printed pages onto a clipboard and went to find Lara. She was my best bet to point me toward local candidates to play her and her brother as kids. I was excited to make it happen. If we could pull it off, the flashback scene would be epic.

# TWENTY-SEVEN

## *Dan*

The morning spent conducting employee interviews dragged. I didn't mind this step most months. Loads of people repeating the same urban legends was par for the course with these shoots.

When so many people agreed about spirit activity, it often meant there was some kernel of truth to the claims of a haunting. Experience informed me this was a good sign. But it made for a dull morning.

Or maybe it was just dull because Chad wasn't there with his shy smiles and his way of anticipating my every request. He excelled at making sure I had what I needed in arm's reach this past week. He shouldn't be indispensable already, but there it was.

Probably just the injury making it seem that way. Normally, it was no effort to get my own drink. With my crutches and the lingering ache in my broken leg, simple tasks became a pain.

I was glad to finish with the last employee. I made a triumphant return to Vanessa for lunch. It didn't even surprise me when the side door slid open as I approached. Chad must have seen me leaving the farm office.

Once again anticipating my needs. I climbed into the van with some difficulty, stiff from my morning sitting in Lara's office.

"Interviews ran long?" Chad asked, sympathy in his voice.

"A little. Nothing we haven't heard already, but they all put their own twist on it. I'll edit down the footage so we can use the best-worded quotes for the video. Ben films well, he's very animated."

"Perfect, here, sit. I made grilled cheese, nothing fancy, but it's a quick meal. And it uses the fresh bread Lara and Jane sent home with us the other night. Saves us time to get set up for Leon, since I figured this segment will be a big part of the video, right?"

"Yeah, that's the plan," I agreed, pleased with his enthusiasm for the show. "How about you? Any luck?"

I bit into the sandwich he slid in front of me and suppressed an appreciative moan—it was good. He'd put more than just cheese inside. I thought I tasted bacon and something sweet and crunchy, closer inspection revealed apple slices. Weird, but delicious.

"As luck would have it, yes. Lara told me Steph babysits a brother and sister who might fit the bill. They're the right age and general appearance. She gave me their mom's number. When I called, the mom sounded delighted. She offered to bring them out to the dairy this weekend. I sent her a summary of what we want to film. So, as long as she still approves after reading through everything, I'll get her to sign the release forms first thing before we film with the kids."

"That was fast, I'm impressed," I said.

"It helped that Lara let me offer them a free tour package and some ice cream vouchers to sweeten the deal. With the budget you gave me for this episode, we can cover enough to pay the kids at least minimum wage for a few hours of filming."

"Great! Also, you are the official grilled cheese maker now."

"You like it?" Chad shuffled around nervously.

"Yeah, it's good." I assured him.

"Mom used to put the apples inside because I wouldn't eat my fruits and veggies as a kid. She tricked me into eating all kinds of stuff by covering it with cheese." He chuckled. "Hidden broccoli and cauliflower lurking in my mac and cheese. Or shredded carrot and zucchini. She put those in cupcakes too. Made me think I was getting dessert when, in actuality, I was getting the next thing to a salad. The beetroot ones were a pretty shade of pink though."

"Beetroot cupcakes?" I wrinkled my nose. No amount of sugar and chocolate could make beets palatable. They were hands down my least favorite vegetable.

"Yeah, you'd think the flavor would have given up the game, but she made this fantastic frosting so it hid the flavor of the veggies in the actual cake. Mostly."

"Why not lick off the frosting?" I asked. That's what I would have done as a kid.

Chad guffawed. "That question proves you never met my mom. The only time I tried that, she took away my dessert privileges for a week. She informed me that if I didn't like carrot cake, she and Kay could eat the entire batch of cupcakes without my help."

"You poor thing," I commiserated.

"I thought so, taught me to eat the hidden veggies if I wanted sweets though. Anyway, the grilled cheese with surprise fruit was one of my favorites."

We finished the rest of the meal without saying much else, beyond my making more comments about how good it was and Chad looking flustered at my effusive praise.

Then we got set up to film Leon's interview. I figured it would be neat to capture the mood of a working dairy, so we were filming outdoors. The weather was cooperative. A nice shade of overcast without too much wind to screw with the sound.

I had Chad stand where I intended to be for the segment. Then I framed the shot, so we captured the big iconic looking red barn that housed the ice cream bar and where Jane sold tickets for the dairy tours. I also wanted to capture the bucolic feel of rolling green pastures with the lazy black and white cows dotting the landscape.

My exacting instructions had always left my previous assistants fed up well before I got the shot perfect. Chad got me, though. He tolerated my meticulous attention to detail over the show with good grace.

Once I had the shot framed, I had Chad mark out the positions for Leon and I to stand. That should make sure Chad's inexperience with filming wouldn't mess up my perfect background. He was a good sport about it.

"Move a step left, no my left, okay, now stop." I checked the shot, frowned and gestured for him to move again. "No, sorry. Take a few steps back. Wait… um, come forward." I spared a glance at him over the top of the camera, still not right. "A hint more to the left. Now up on your toes, you're a little shorter than me, I want to ensure my head will fit in the frame."

Chad took it in stride, waiting until I had everything perfect. I had him mark his spot with a chalk line then repeated the process with him playing the role of Leon. He marked Leon's spot without complaint too.

I clipped a mic to my shirt collar and showed Chad how to get Leon mic'd up, when he arrived. With outdoor filming the sound quality would be better with microphones.

Filming the interview with Mr. Dawes on his front porch was one thing. The open fields of a working dairy would create more background noise to cut out in post. I'd worry about that later, it would be a learning exercise for Chad at any rate.

We'd accomplished a ton in just over a week. I still needed to make time to reshoot a bit of the barn scene to finish editing this weekend's gear review episode. We hadn't gone back inside since the spirit drove us away on the first afternoon, other than a quick trip to retrieve the lighting kit.

Chad seemed leery of the barn so I hadn't pushed him about going back inside yet. I needed to shoot the footage today or tomorrow though. We needed to leave time for editing before the Saturday evening release. A thought occurred to me.

"Chad, you negotiated pre-approval for the shows about the dairy specifically, right?"

"Yeah, they get to review whatever we film on the farm."

I winced. "Including the unboxing video for Saturday?"

"Oh, shit, I'm not sure if they'll want to see that first. Um, I'll call Jane. She's the one who handles publicity and paperwork stuff. We never got around to reshooting the actual unboxing take that I screwed up the zoom on, huh?"

"We need to get it today or tomorrow at the latest for me to get it edited in time to upload Saturday. If they want to do a quick screening Saturday afternoon, I can make that work. Otherwise we can cut the segment in the barn and just use the GhostCam review you and I filmed inside Vanessa." I said.

"The benefits of taking your studio on wheels, huh?" Chad quipped. "I should have stayed on top of this situation. I'm sorry. I'll explain where we're at and see what Jane says about waiving the review clause for the unboxing video. If she won't budge, we can roll the unboxing footage into the site history episode we're working on for next week, right? I've seen you do that before."

"No worries, we can make either option work. But, yeah. If you could call now, that would ease my mind."

"On it." Chad pulled out his phone and dialed just as Leon pulled up to park his pickup truck next to Vanessa. I went over to greet Leon, confident that Chad could fix the problem. He had a way of doing that.

# TWENTY-EIGHT
## *Chad*

Returning to the barn to film retakes for the unboxing video should have been easy. I'd marked the spot where Daniel positioned the camera in case we needed to do retakes, so that part was simple enough.

I got the tripod set up and framed the shot so it matched what we filmed on our first day. Then I tidied the bale of straw where we laid out the gear Daniel was reviewing and placed the box for him to open.

I had to help Daniel get comfortable seated on the other straw bale. He was trying to play the tough guy, but I could tell his leg bothered him after over an hour standing on it to film the interview with Leon. He'd popped an Advil and declared himself good to go.

At least Jane had been understanding about the timeline and agreed to carve out an hour for a quick review screening with us late Saturday afternoon. My oversight with not getting the review process arranged sooner and letting the filming for this week fall through the cracks felt like a huge failure.

I'd been so paranoid about making sure we stuck to our filming schedule, I'd almost made a botch of the whole job right out of the gate. My scheduling let us pack the key witness interviews into the first week, but left little wiggle room to correct my screwup.

Daniel didn't seem upset, at least. He trusted me to fix my mistake. And I had.

I rolled the camera and this time we got the unboxing video retakes done without a hitch. The biggest problem we hit was when Daniel got tongue tied listing out some tech specs. We did several takes of him opening the box while he thanked the company and plugged their other products.

I held the backup camera so I could get some zooms on his face and the product as we went through his lightly scripted spiel. Daniel needed to hit a few points from the company's ad copy as part of their arrangement. I'd prepared a checklist to make sure we got multiple takes for each of them.

It took the better part of two hours to get through everything to Dan's satisfaction. We didn't pick up any ghost activity. That was more of a relief than I expected, considering I didn't believe in ghosts. The barn still gave me the creeps, though, I felt like the spiders from all the cobwebs in the rafters might drop onto me at any moment.

A hot shower to scrub away the grime and sense of impending doom would have been nice. Instead, we had to rush as soon as we wrapped. We had to drive into town to meet the amateur historian at the library.

I called ahead to confirm we were still on to meet her around closing. She agreed to wait for us to arrive, even though we were running late.

We filmed our last scheduled interview for the day to a backdrop of bookshelves in the library. Dan enthused over the authenticity of the head librarian's office and how official it would look in the final cut of the film. We got some stills of relevant articles.

The old headlines with the faded pictures of era farmers would add some ghostly touches. I'd seen what a whiz Daniel was at video editing and I was sure he'd turn out something cohesive from everything we were gathering.

Leon brought an old family photo to his interview. In it, Martha and Elmer Goodman stood in front of the original home and barn with their children. The image would add interest.

That and the newspaper picture of the burned out farm house after fire destroyed the original building leant the weight of reality to the story we were spinning here. I enjoyed working with Daniel to bring all the pieces together. I couldn't wait to see what our collaboration looked like when it was complete.

# TWENTY-NINE

## *Dan*

"Hey, gang." I waved into the camera. "I'm doing another live feed to let you all, my most loyal fans, get the first official introduction to my new PA. So, here's the man himself, Chad," I panned the camera over to him. "Say hey to the fans."

"Hey, fans," Chad said, ever dutiful.

I knew he was nervous about the spotlight, but the crew would love him. He raised a hand in an awkward little wave and his cheeks flushed at being the center of attention as comments rolled in. I chuckled at Drew's heart reaction to Chad.

BriBri: Aw, he's adorable. Camera shy, Chad?

I nudged Chad and pointed to the comment off screen.

"How could you tell BriBri?" Chad's chuckle had a nervous edge.

RadRaf: Don't be nervous, I'm sure our Dan won't bite.

Drew: Unless you ask real nice.

A string of laugh reacts followed.

RadRaf: Come on kids, keep it PG.

"Yeah, what Raf said. Come on people, keep it classy. I like this one, don't scare him away!" I protested, zooming out the shot, so we were both in the frame.

BriBri: Oooh, like, as in like-like?

Drew: Dan has a crush.

I only just managed not to roll my eyes at their obsession with my nonexistent personal life. "Like as an employee. Let's steer this conversation away from skirting the line with workplace harassment on the guy's first live appearance, people. Sorry, Chad, you can see they're a little enthusiastic. As soon as we're done here this month's unboxing vid will drop."

A handful of excited exclamations scrolled through the chat.

"I know, I can't wait to share this month's haunting with you all either. The suspense is killing us, right, Chad?"

"Right." He nodded.

"So, I'll get right into the big announcement I teased earlier. In honor of this being Chad's first paranormal investigation, we started a series of short gear tutorials. I plan on making it a mini-series titled Ghost Hunter 101. Those videos will supplement each of our films on location this month. Sort of like training videos for Chad here to pop his filming cherry."

"Hey! I've been on camera before," Chad protested.

"Home videos don't count," I teased.

"Fine. Doesn't this count though?"

"Oh, my darling sweet summer child—no. This is a select audience of our most devoted fans. When our next video hits the net, it throws us to the wolves of public opinion. Considering the viral video of me falling, we're likely to face unprecedented trolling. Brace yourself, it will be a bumpy ride."

I slung an arm around his shoulders, giving him a quick side hug to soften the prediction. The fans met my words with a spate of support in the comments.

"Aw, I love you all too," I replied. "Chad, since this is your intro, care to tell everyone a little about yourself?"

"Um, sure, like what?" he asked.

"Anything at all. Fun facts, hobbies, hopes and dreams, deep dark secrets… it's all fair game, right crew?"

A few affirmatives and a bunch of likes floated past.

"Well," he considered, "I don't have deep dark secrets. Sorry to disappoint. I have tattoos, I guess that's a fun fact?"

Drew: What are they of?

BriBri: Where? Pics or it didn't happen.

Chad flushed, "On my chest. Can we do partial nudity?"

I suppressed a smirk at his wide-eyed innocence.

"You can take off your shirt, dude," I assured him with a smile. "That hardly counts as nudity. No pressure, though."

Drew: Do it!

BriBri: Show us your ink.

A few more comments egged him on.

"You really want to see?" Chad gave a nervous laugh.

A cloud of likes followed.

"Guess they want to see your ink," I said when he glanced at me for confirmation.

"Better give the people what they want. Now I'm afraid I won't live up to the hype."

Laughter responses appeared.

Chad hesitated with his fingers on the hem of his shirt.

"You don't have to." I patted his wrist to forestall him. "Or if you'd feel less shy about it, we can take a pic after the live stream and post it on the private site."

"Let's do that. I feel weird stripping on camera."

"Good thing we aren't making those kinds of videos then," I teased. There were a few wheedling comments complaining about it, but no way was I letting anyone make my assistant uncomfortable. "Come on, people, you'll get to see his badass ink later. Don't harass the guy while he's working."

"Sorry, folks, no under the shirt action on our first date," Chad teased. More laugh reacts.

I was glad to see him loosening up and interacting well with my fans. That was important. The fans needed to embrace him for me to keep him on the show.

BriBri: Oooh does that mean you've seen his mystery ink, Dan? Are you getting personal with your PA?

"Bri, how many times do I have to explain workplace harassment to you?"

BriBri: Come on, he's adorable.

"He's my employee. Moving on. Let's get back to Chad. So we know you have some sweet tats, your dream job is chasing ghosts around the country with me, obviously. So that only leaves two questions, what do you do for fun and what's your biggest fear?"

"I have a bit of a weakness for watching vloggers," he replied.

"Oh, do tell, who's your favorite?"

"You, obviously," Chad joked.

"Other than me," I pressed.

"Hmm, should I admit to watching the competition?"

"I prefer to think of them as our colleagues."

"Cool." Chad nodded. "Well, I enjoy watching them, too. But Hauntastic Haunts is my number one fave."

"Of course it is." I wondered if he watched the show for real, if he'd been a fan before I hired him. Was it possible Chad wasn't playing up his fandom for the camera?

It didn't matter either way. As I'd told BriBri, I was still his boss. Even if he liked me as much as I was coming to like him.

"For greatest fear, can I say I used to fear needles?"

"You did?" I asked, surprised considering how expertly he'd handled his injection the other day.

"Sure. I mean, I had to get over it when I started on T. As a kid I once locked myself in my pediatrician's bathroom to get out of shots."

"You didn't!" I laughed.

"I did." He nodded. "My mom didn't know whether to be furious or laugh at my determination."

"So, did it work?"

"No, I still got the shots. I only bought myself fifteen minutes to get worked up about it while they figured out I wasn't coming back and tracked down the spare key."

We both laughed and then Chad glanced at the comments, eyes going a little wide.

"Oh, yeah no worries asking, Raf, I'm trans, he/him pronouns. That's the reason behind the testosterone injections."

Questions scrolled in. We had discussed whether Chad wanted to come out to the patrons tonight before filming. He said he'd play it by ear, but he was comfortable with people knowing as long as we didn't make a huge deal out of it.

He'd agreed to field some questions for the fans so I made no effort to redirect them away from the topic. This part was Chad's show to run as he saw fit. I would step in if they pushed his boundaries, but otherwise he was in control of the stream for now.

"Um, so, I will not tell you my deadname, BriBri. My real name is Chad. I'm sure you didn't mean to be rude, but that's a question that a lot of trans people hate hearing. It's personal and I prefer to focus on who I am, not my past. I *am* Chad. I don't want to be the guy who used to be a girl, or used to be my deadname. I can't speak for everyone, but that's my experience. And before anybody asks, I will not discuss my sex life here, or anywhere else in public. That includes questions about my genitals and surgery. If you have general questions about surgical procedures I can point you to resources. You'll see when I post the tattoo pics, I've had top surgery, that I don't mind talking about."

"Are you cool with fielding questions about being trans that don't relate to surgery?" I clarified.

"Yeah." He nodded. "I get that a lot of our viewers might have questions. I might be the first openly trans person they've met, so I'm fine answering some questions, within reason."

"Awesome, I'm sure everyone appreciates that. Here's what I'm thinking, I will open up a new 'ask me anything' thread behind the privacy filter for Chad to respond to your burning questions about what it's like to work with yours truly. Behind the scenes exclusives on Hauntastic Haunts, getting to meet the famous Vanessa in person, and any transition related questions."

"Sounds good." Chad shot me a grateful look for cutting off the barrage of questions. We had discussed the AMA before filming, it wasn't a surprise. But I knew he'd been nervous about the response to his coming out.

"Chad reserves the right not to answer anything he deems too personal. He'll try to get back to you this week. We've got a busy week of filming coming up, so be patient waiting for a reply if you take part."

"I'll be looking forward to your questions. And we'll get the tat pics posted later tonight, promise. I will also include my artist's deets, I think she did an incredible job."

"It's almost time for the new episode to drop, my upload bar looks like it's about to go live." I cut in smoothly. That was an exaggeration. I'd preloaded the video as soon as the Goodman's gave their approval, but I was about to change the privacy settings to release it to the world.

"So we will wrap up here. Be sure to drop a like and a comment on the video. Tell all your friends, and post your thoughts in this week's spoiler thread in our Hauntastic Haunts forum. See you next time, people."

"Bye!" Chad waved for the camera, I grinned and nudged his foot with my toe, hoping he remembered my instructions about our catchphrase.

"And as always," I said, Chad bumped my ankle back and joined me for the last line. "Have a hauntastic day!"

I ended the livestream with us both smiling and waving at the camera.

"That went well," I said.

"Yeah? You don't think they hated me?" Chad bit his lip.

I snorted. "They responded well to you. Trust me, if they didn't like you they wouldn't be trying to set us up."

He flushed. "That was awkward."

"BriBri and some others get a tad overenthusiastic, but they mean well. Are you still okay with doing the ask me anything? I know we talked about the possibility before going live, but you can back out."

"No, it's fine. We promised the fans, and I'd rather they ask. How are they supposed to learn otherwise?"

"If you're sure. It's not your responsibility to be the ambassador of trans-ness. Just like it's not my job to explain being gay to them. A good number of my patrons are LGBT+ anyway. So, most of them probably won't ask anything too terrible or invasive. You did a good job handling Bri, so I'm sure I don't have to tell you, but only answer questions you feel comfortable answering."

"Yeah, I've gotten decent at that over the years. As coming outs go, that one wasn't too bad."

I chuckled. "Yeah, they're a good group. I come out to new subs every few months it seems. We lose some over it now and then, but the core group is solid. I'm surprised Red wasn't online, they almost never miss the release day livestreams."

"Red?" Chad asked.

"RedHerring99," I elaborated. "They're one of my most devoted patrons. They and RadRaf are our top supporters."

"Oh, um, cool." Chad sounded flustered for some reason. "Must have been working or something."

"Yeah." I frowned. "I haven't seen them on the forums much lately either. I hope everything is okay in their IRL life."

"I'm sure it is," Chad assured me.

"If they aren't around in the next little while I'll send them a DM."

"Yeah, sounds like a plan," Chad said. He still sounded a bit off, but the guy had just done his first live segment, so he was probably still nerved up about it. I brushed it off and reached for the good camera.

"Ready for your closeup?"

Chad chuckled as he shucked off his shirt without hesitation now that it was just us with no live audience.

"Hit me with your best shot." He spread his arms wide to expose the pair of tattoos. I gestured for him to step back, toward the front of the van. He took two steps away and arched a brow.

"Perfect," I said as I took the shot. "Should I stick to closeups of the ink or are you cool with baring your entire torso to the adoring public?"

Chad brushed his fingers over his abs self-consciously.

"Maybe just stick with the tats?"

"No problem." I zoomed in to capture some closeups while Chad flexed for me. I was glad to be hiding behind the camera so he wouldn't notice how much I enjoyed looking at him. I should feel more guilty about that than I did.

"Perfect," I said. "I'll get these uploaded."

I turned to fiddle with the dongle to connect the camera to my computer. I could have done it through wireless, but that wouldn't require as much focus and attention. The wires gave me an excuse to turn away before I embarrassed myself or made Chad feel uncomfortable with my staring.

I selected two images, a single shot of each ink animal on Chad's chest and cropped them to show minimal bare skin. It was easy to manufacture tasks to occupy myself while Chad pulled his shirt back on a few feet away. I messed with the color balance, screwed around with some filters and then removed them.

I flinched as Chad plopped into the chair at my side, his knee bumping against mine.

"Good to go?" he asked.

"Yeah, you approve of these?" I pulled up the two images I'd selected.

Chad whistled through his teeth. "Still can't get over how good they came out. Janice is the best. Here, let me pull up her website so the patrons can check out her other work if they like what they see."

I bit back an inappropriate comment that I liked what I saw. We got the pics uploaded along with the link to Janice's shop and the AMA post. Chad sat back and smiled at me.

Notifications had already started to roll in on the 'Goodman Dairy Unboxing' video we'd uploaded, making my phone buzz.

"Your phone is blowing up," Chad commented.

"Yeah, new vids do that."

"You don't turn off the notifications?"

"No, I kind of like the confirmation that it's live."

"Are you going to check out the comments and stuff?"

"Oh, hell no. Here's the most important rule for doing this stuff, Chad, never read the comments on the internet."

"Never?"

"Well, almost never. If we need to pull quotes for promo, I might have you go through recent comments. The comment section is for the viewers, not for us. I have the Hauntastic Haunts website and other social media set up to interact with the viewers, but the comments are their domain."

"Did you need me to do anything else tonight?" he asked.

"No, you've put in a full day already between shooting the flashback sequence, wrangling diva child actors, and everything else."

"Cool, well, I guess I'll hit the hay." He favored me with a shy smile.

"Good night," I said.

I resisted the urge to watch him crawl into his bunk. And I stayed up editing footage until I was in danger of dozing off over my keyboard. Because the thought of sleeping next to him, with only the partition between us, threatened my resolve not to think about him like that.

I was too exhausted to think about the proximity of his soft breathing or his soft lips by the time I crawled into bed.

# THIRTY

## *Chad*

"What's this about you being in Vermont?" Kay asked on our weekly phone call. I was still riding high on the buzz of endorphins from the live chat the morning after my first livestream with Daniel. Not even my sister's third degree could bring me down. I might have neglected to mention changing jobs on a whim and fleeing the state in our brief chat the previous week. To say she wanted answers was an understatement.

Chorus had me scheduled to work through last weekend so I'd cut short last week's call without arousing Kay's suspicions too much. My luck at keeping her in the dark ran out when I didn't drop by to see her and the kids this weekend. I should have been free, and she knew it. I always spent my weekends off with her family.

"Didn't I say in my email last night? I got a new job that requires travel." I spoke softly so I wouldn't wake Daniel. It wasn't early, but he'd been up for ages last night. Not that I'd lain awake in my bunk for hours listening to him mumbling to himself as he edited our raw footage. Okay, so I had done that. Did that make me a creeper?

"I read your message. I'm just shocked that my baby brother —the prototypical stable boring career man—took a job working for a freelance vlogger. With no notice. And left the state to follow him."

"It was a good offer, and I needed a new job," I defended myself.

"Uh huh, and the fact that the vlogger in question is the guy you've been crushing on for years had nothing to do with your decision?" Kay asked.

She sounded amused rather than accusatory but I still felt defensive. I glanced toward the bunk where Daniel was still asleep. Then I ducked inside the shower stall for what little privacy it offered.

"I like his videos," I hissed into the phone.

"Uh huh, and I read playgirl for the articles, Chad. I'm not judging you, bro. For serious, I'm glad you are doing someone —oops Freudian Slip—some*thing* that makes you happy for once in your life."

I rolled my eyes at my sister, I needed to end the call before I gave myself eyestrain. There was no reasoning with Kay when she got her teeth into an idea. "So how are the rugrats?"

"Sadie's grumpy that summer is almost over. Zoe is beside herself because she gets to go for a full day of school this year and ride the bus with Sadie. They both missed your cartoon date yesterday."

"Tell the squirts I missed them, too. I can't believe I won't be there to send them back to school this year. Next week we can video chat for our cartoon brunch," I offered.

"I'll tell them," Kay agreed. "And I'll send you pics of their first day outfits. Now, stop trying to change the subject."

"Who, me?" I feigned innocence.

"Yes, you," Kay said in her most authoritative mom voice. "You can't send me an email saying you're uprooting your life for a hot guy and then leave me hanging. How am I supposed to relive my youth vicariously through you with no details?"

I snorted at that. Kay and her husband were sickeningly in love and I knew it. "Ha, if either of us needs a vicarious love life we both know it's not you, Kay."

"Fine. Still, dish. Is he as hot in person? Is he a good boss? Are you still crushing on him or did familiarity breed contempt?"

I considered hanging up on her. But there was no sign of Daniel being awake yet so I figured there wasn't any harm in talking to my sister. Besides, she would just keep calling back until I satisfied her curiosity. And it might help me process how I felt to put it in words.

"I'll admit he's cute, alright? And I suppose he might not hate the way I look," I admitted.

"Oh? Elaborate!" Kay demanded.

"I showed him my tats and he couldn't seem to keep his eyes off me. But I mean, he was probably looking for my scars or something."

"You can tell the difference between appreciating a view and that kind of staring, Chad. So he's into you too then. What's the problem?"

"He's my boss," I whined.

"Sure," Kay agreed, "but it's not like you need the job."

"Um, I kind of do. Living isn't free, sis," I joked.

"Ugh, you know what I mean. You can get a different job. You're more than qualified to be doing much more than you have been with your fancy degree."

"It's an MBA, hardly fancy," I scoffed.

"Fancier than anyone else in our family."

"Kay, I love you, but seriously, drop it. So what if I've got a hopeless crush? I enjoy working with him, that's worth more to me than risking a relationship. Nothing can happen between me and my boss."

"It worked out for Brad and I," she said.

She would bring that up. Brad was a manager at the restaurant where Kay worked when they met. She'd earned her way up from a part-time hostess position at sixteen to a bartender after she graduated high school at eighteen.

At first she'd hated Brad because her boss overlooked her for the management position to bring him in from another franchise location. Then he'd set out to woo her and won not only her workplace cooperation, but her heart too.

That was how they told the story whenever prompted. I assumed Kay was glossing over hate sex with that story. I was disinclined to think about my sister fucking so I accepted her sanitized version of events.

Anyway, they still worked together, though it was at Brad's family's restaurant these days. I guess his family wanted him to bring his own *bona fides* back to the restaurant before hiring him. Either way, working together didn't seem to pose a problem for them.

"You and Brad are one in a million, Kay," I said.

"We are pretty awesome. But you can have awesome too, you're related to me."

"There's more to life than sexual relationships, Kay. I'm enjoying this job, okay?"

"Okay, I'll drop it for now. I saw your video, though, you two are cute together."

"We aren't together," I grumbled.

"But you could be. Take chances, Chadrick," she said. I rolled my eyes at the ridiculous nickname. Two could play at that game.

"Whatever, Kaybar," I teased back. "Kiss the kiddos for me, I need to get my caffeine fix."

"Oh, is that why you're being such a grump? No coffee yet? Did something catastrophic happen? Is your coffee maker broken? Do I need to send help?"

"Daniel's still asleep," I mumbled, and then over her peals of laughter I added, "I didn't want to wake him up."

"Aw, that's my sweet, thoughtful brother. It's after ten—wake that fucker up."

"He was up late last night."

"No excuses. Wake him up, share a cup of coffee and give him that irresistible smile of yours, you'll have him curled around your finger in no time."

"I don't want him curled around my finger." The protest sounded weak, even to my own ears.

"Keep telling yourself that and go caffeinate. And call to dish when you kiss him."

"I will not kiss him."

"Uh huh, were you there for that segment you filmed? You two couldn't keep your eyes off each other."

"He was talking to me about his gear. And I was just handing him crap."

"Not just a river in Egypt. You've got it bad, little brother."

"I'm not in denial."

"Go make your man coffee, Chadrick," she said with an air of finality.

"I'll text you about video chatting with the kids later this week, Kaybar."

I hung up before she could say anything else. Daniel was still in his bunk so I tried to keep the noise down while I made coffee and rummaged around for breakfast stuff. Daniel had a box of pancake mix so I figured that would work for a late breakfast when he woke up.

He eased out of his bunk as I was flipping the last pancake with slices of banana in it.

"Smells awesome in here," Daniel said with a sleepy smile for me. Kay was right, I had it bad for the guy.

"Uh, yeah," I said, tongue-tied.

"You didn't have to cook." Daniel reached for a coffee cup.

"I wanted to. It's no trouble. Help yourself."

Daniel swung the table into its dining position, poured us both coffee, and set the table without asking. I added the last pancake to the stack.

We filled our plates in silence. Though Daniel raised an eyebrow at me when he noticed the fruit I'd added to the batter.

"More hidden fruit, huh?"

"It was looking overripe."

He took a few bites before talking again. "This is good. So I heard you on the phone this morning, is everything good back home?"

"Oh, yeah. Just my sister giving me a hard time."

"Oh?" He raised an eyebrow.

"Yeah, I'm not what she'd consider impulsive." I stabbed a bite of pancake.

"You dropped everything to come work for me on short notice. That was way out of character, huh?"

"That about sums it up. In hindsight, I'm surprised it took her this long to call."

"Glad to hear your family is well."

"Yeah. They're good. Great. She watched our Ghost Hunter 101 video. Er, I mean your video."

"You were in it too." Daniel grinned at me, his eyes sparkling with good humor. "You can call it our video."

"Right, well she watched it. I sent her the link to the Hauntastic Haunts channel."

"Did she like it?"

"She said we made a cute couple," I grumbled. Then I covered my mouth wishing I could take the words back when his eyes snapped to me and time seemed to slow. We stared at each other for a long time before he averted his gaze.

"I would never do anything to make you uncomfortable, Chad," Dan said, studiously not looking at me.

"I know. You've mentioned a few times that you aren't interested in anything with me," I said. And boy, could I sound more like a petulant child denied a treat? I'd been spending too much time with my nieces if I was whining like that.

Daniel sighed. "It's not about you, Chad. You're great."

"You don't have to explain anything."

"It sounds like I do. I've been enjoying getting to know you, I love working with you. Heck, you are hands down the best PA I've ever had. You take our work as seriously as I do. But that's just it. I'm your boss, I sign your paycheck and provide your housing and meals as part of our arrangement. How can we even consider starting a relationship on equal footing under the circumstances?"

That he'd jumped to relationship talk instead of just a hookup told me what I needed to know. He was as into me as I was into him. Maybe Kay was right that we both deserved a chance to see where the mutual attraction might lead.

"My sister married her supervisor. People make it work," I blurted.

Daniel sighed. "I don't want to put you in a position where you feel like you have to say yes to me."

I rolled my eyes. "I'm capable of telling you no. You're my boss, not my guardian. I can make my own choices."

Daniel shook his head. "I don't want to cross any lines."

"Okay, fine. How about this? During work hours we keep it professional."

"That's exactly what I'm proposing," Daniel said. I held up a finger to silence him

"I'm not done, during the workday we are only employer and employee. But once the cameras stop rolling and the editing is in the can, we put aside the work stuff and try dating.

Not as a big shot vlogging superstar and his lowly PA. But just Daniel and Chad. Two guys who're into each other?"

"You really want to date me?" Daniel narrowed his eyes. "You aren't just saying what you think I want to hear?"

"Do you believe I'd do that?" I challenged him.

"No, I guess not," Daniel allowed. "You've always been upfront with me. Are you sure this won't screw everything up though?"

"I don't have a crystal ball to tell you how things will turn out. But I can promise to be professional with you if things don't work out between us."

Daniel scrubbed a hand through his hair, considering. From the way his intense gaze locked on mine, I knew I'd convinced him, though. We were trying this.

"Deal. I don't know if this is the best idea you've had yet or the worst, but right now I want to kiss you," Daniel said.

"Same. Do you understand how hard it's been sleeping less than a foot away from you all week? Dude, at the risk of you thinking I'm an internet stalker, I've had a crush on you since I looked up your videos."

"When I offered you the job?" His confused blinking was adorable.

"No, I got curious after I got a call from a guy's PA. That was a first for me. I wanted to see what sort of fancy deal you had going, so I looked you up and found Hauntastic Haunts."

"And you've been a fan ever since? Wait, are you a creepy internet stalker? Is this the part where you send me dead flowers and creepy love notes with letters cut out of magazines and decorated with dismembered body parts? Should I be afraid?" Daniel quipped.

"Too far." I waved my fork at him. "Don't even joke about that. I'm not a stalker. No creepy dead things of any kind, I promise."

"Well, maybe some ghosts," Daniel said.

"That is our business," I agreed with a wry grin.

"Our business. Yeah. I like that there is an 'us'. I guess since you admitted to being smitten with me for ages I can admit that I had a bit of a thing for you too."

"Really?" I asked, skeptical. "But you thought I was some boring suburbanite dad."

"Well, if you were a dad, you'd be a total DILF. Besides, you have a nice voice. It was comforting when I was freaking out about my medical bills. I think that might be why I assumed you were older, because you sounded like you had your shit together."

"You think so?"

"Sure." He nodded. "I mean you've done a great job keeping filming on a schedule. We've already got tons of raw footage to edit for next week's site history video and the haunting videos for the rest of the month. At this rate we'll wrap with time to spare for doing retakes instead of scrambling to cut together whatever we can get at the last minute. Seriously, you're a godsend."

"The Goodmans are accommodating."

Daniel snorted. "They want days to review the footage for the other three videos. I normally don't even get around to editing stuff together until the Thursday evening before a film drops."

"Well, it's a good thing I'm such a hard-ass about the schedule then."

"Yeah. You have a great ass," Daniel said. We both flushed as the words sunk in.

"You think so?" I asked.

"Yeah, I mean, not that I've been ogling you or anything, I just... noticed. Sorry, god, I feel like such a creeper."

"Don't, you aren't. We've established we both like each other. We're both adults, no reason we shouldn't explore our attraction."

"Okay. Sure. But we agreed to keep the relationship stuff after hours. If we plan to make the Goodman's deadline I need to stay on top of editing."

"Fair enough. What's on the agenda for today, boss?" I asked.

"I'm thinking we have some fun working on the big flashback scene. That will take the most manipulation. Best to start early."

"Sounds good."

"Great, once we're done eating, I'll get set up while you handle the dishes. Then you can observe me working my flashback magic on the scenes we shot yesterday with the kids."

# THIRTY-ONE

## *Dan*

Keeping my focus on work all day with Chad sitting close enough that our thighs brushed was one of the hardest things I'd done in a while. He was just as antsy as I was, but he tried to stay engaged with the work.

In addition to observing my edits, he checked in on the AMA thread we'd promised the fans. He answered questions as they popped up throughout the day.

On the editing front, we got about as far as cleaning up the footage we'd taken. We made a few splicing decisions about which camera angles to use for which shots. But my heart wasn't in it and I called it a day around four. "That's a wrap, for now."

"Already? It's not even five," Chad protested.

I made a show of stretching. "My ass is going numb from sitting in this chair. We made a solid start on the scene. Tomorrow we can add in the filters and sound effects. If you insist on putting in more time, I can put you to work trawling my FX catalog. You can pick out just the right creepy kids laughing, barn boards creaking, and mood music."

"Sure, I can do that."

"And I thought I was a workaholic." I laughed. "Okay, I'll pull up my top contenders from what I remember having in the files. You can take a listen while I get cleaned up for dinner, I'm still in my sleep pants here."

"Nothing wrong with taking the occasional lazy Sunday," Chad replied.

"Sure, but tonight calls for something special," I insisted.

"Oh?"

"Yeah, I've got a hot date tonight, hoping to get lucky."

"I have it on good authority your date likes you in lounge wear," Chad deadpanned.

I ignored that in favor of pulling up the sound files I wanted him to listen to. Once I set him up with a pair of headphones, I reached for a change of clothes in my overhead cabinets.

It took a bit of contorting to reach, but better that than climbing with my leg being what it was. I sent Lara a quick text asking about friendly local establishments to take a date. Then I wrapped my cast in a garbage bag and ducked into the shower while I waited for her response. Years of habit with a limited hot water supply had me washed up in less than five minutes and ready to roll.

It took longer to shimmy a nicer pair of sweatpants over my bulky cast. I couldn't be rid of the dratted thing soon enough. My leg had been hurting less, but now it seemed like it was always itchy.

Once dressed, I checked my phone and found that Lara had already gotten back to me.

Lara: The Bistro is good. Jane loves their desserts, check out the chocolate mud pie. The owners also run a B&B and they get lots of LGBT+ clientele, if that's what you're worried about.

Dan: Sounds perfect, thanks, do I need a reservation?

Lara: Not on a Sunday night off peak tourist season.

Dan: Thanks, you're the best. Can't wait to show you the finished video about the history of the haunted barn, I think it will be one of our best ones yet!

Lara: Looking forward to it.

Chad still sat facing the monitor listening intently. I touched his shoulder to get his attention. He spun to face me, pulling off the bulky noise canceling headset I used for edits.

"Come on, I'm taking you out to eat."

"Aren't we eating with the Goodmans?" Chad asked with a confused expression.

"I mean, we could, but that hardly seems like an ideal first date."

"Oh! Right, I wasn't sure if we planned on doing that tonight."

"We are. Unless you've changed your mind?" I checked.

"No, not at all," he replied.

"Well, I know it isn't five yet, but what do you say to knocking off early since it's a Sunday? What kind of tyrant are you working for, anyway?"

"Oh, he's a real taskmaster, just intolerable," Chad teased.

"Hm, well, I won't tell him that you're shirking if you don't."

"Deal. So I'm officially off the clock?"

"Yep," I confirmed.

Chad slid from the chair and turned, putting him right in my personal space. I backpedaled, but my cast got in the way, so I almost tipped over when Chad leaned up to kiss me. A quick brush of our lips, there and gone before I could react.

"I've been wanting to do that for ages."

"Yeah? Worth the wait?" I couldn't keep a goofy grin off my face.

"Hm, I think I need to try it a few more times to be sure. Wouldn't want to jump to any hasty conclusions."

"I can get on board with that plan." I leaned in to kiss him, and he met me halfway. This time our lips parted, and I tasted him.

His fingers tangled in my hair, and I reached for him too, wanting more contact. Unfortunately, that meant letting go of the chair back I was holding and I wasn't ready for the shift in weight. I stumbled, breaking the kiss.

Chad laughed. "Wow, did I just bowl you over?"

"Swept me right off my feet," I teased as I recovered my footing. "Though, I'd like to take you on a date before we let ourselves get carried away."

"Hmm. Not implying anything, but hypothetically—how removable is the bunk partition?"

"Removable. It latches into place at the top and bottom and I kept the foam cutout where it fits into the mattress, just in case. I don't always have a PA."

"Good to know." He licked his lips lasciviously.

"Yeah. Good," I agreed, my mind consumed with thoughts of what we might do once I took down the partition between our bunks.

"I like that I can get you all monosyllabic, it's a good confidence booster." Chad laughed. He lifted onto his toes to kiss my cheek. "Come on, if we're getting dinner before we remove the partition, we should go now."

"Yeah. Dinner, now."

He was still chuckling as he steered me toward the passenger seat.

"Sit, I'll get ready and you tell me where we're going."

I sat, and for once I didn't have to tear my eyes away when he used a chair to lean into his bunk for clean clothes. I had permission to watch him openly. I glanced away when he stripped down to his boxers to change, not sure if he wanted privacy.

"It's fine, you can watch," Chad said. I looked up, taking in the sight of him in nothing but his silky black boxers. It was a killer view, and I learned he had more ink. The upper curve of black text peeked over his waistband where it wrapped around his hip. I wondered what it said. Wanted to trace whatever words were so important to him he had them etched into his skin with my fingers, or my tongue.

"I'm not the most modest guy," he said as he wriggled into a pair of worn jeans that hugged his ass. "I think it comes from growing up with Mom and Kay. We only had one bathroom, so they were always doing their makeup and hair and stuff while I was showering.

"We also changed together, no big deal. So that's what was normal for me." He shrugged into a polo shirt I hadn't seen him wearing before. He said he didn't mind changing in front of me, but the constant patter as he did so seemed to hide nerves.

He made a quick check of the living area to ensure we'd latched everything into place for driving. I only reviewed the checklist with him once before he got the knack for checking. Unlike some of my previous assistants, I went through countless dishes by forgetting to secure everything in my early days with Vanessa. Now my dishes were plastic, and I was in the habit of stowing them between uses.

"You're cute when you're nervous," I observed.

"Who said I'm nervous?"

"Oh, my bad, I didn't realize you were a babbler outside of work hours."

"Only when I'm nervous," he relented. "Fine, you got me."

Chad squeezed past me to get into the driver's seat. He made much less of an effort to avoid rubbing up against me than he had on previous occasions. I copped a feel, and he shot me a shy smile as he got buckled into his seat.

I flicked the privacy curtain shut across the back of the cab, then swiveled my seat to face the windshield.

"Where to, boss?" Chad asked.

Much as I'd resisted a workplace romance, the teasing way he called me boss had my dick hardening even more than our brief kisses.

Me and my big mouth inviting him out to dinner instead of skipping right to the good stuff. I wanted more than sex though, we could enjoy a nice meal first. I gave him the directions toward the restaurant.

# THIRTY-TWO

## *Chad*

B y the time we found a parking spot for the van, I felt like I'd been babbling for hours. No mean feat since it was only about a twenty-minute drive.

Every time I spared a glance at Daniel he looked at me with an indulgent smile. He prompted me to keep talking the few times I'd curbed my tongue.

"Okay, your turn to talk, who was your favorite teacher?" I asked, putting the van in park.

"Does college count?"

"Sure."

It didn't—I was just over being the focus of conversation.

"Then Dr. Landry, hands down. That man was smoking hot."

"You would be hot for teacher," I observed.

"I have a habit of being attracted to people I shouldn't, I guess." He eyed me meaningfully. Not dignifying that with a response, I circled around the van to retrieve his crutches from the back.

"I think it was his glasses," Daniel mused as he made his ginger way out of the passenger seat. He took the crutches to hobble along at my side. "And his accent. He had the cutest southern twang. The way he got so worked up about history was almost enough to make me consider declaring a history major."

"Yeah?" I glanced over at him.

"Yeah, he had this way of making the dry facts from the books seem real and relevant. Like 'today I will tell you how Prussia's biting horses bear responsibility for the shape of the western world as you know it.' Or something like that. I dunno, he made it seem cool. Then I looked up careers for history majors, most of them required advanced degrees. I noped out when I saw how much even an undergrad degree would set me back."

"You dropped out of college?" I asked.

"Yep, dropped out, cashed out the rest of my college fund to buy film gear and make a go of vlogging."

I grabbed the door for him. Daniel smiled at the young hostess who greeted us. He asked for a table for two. She seated us near the front window. The restaurant decor was rustic chic. Lots of wood finishes, polished until it gleamed and lit with eclectic bare bulb fixtures hanging from the ceiling.

"Looks nice," Daniel observed as he watched me taking in our surroundings.

"Yeah." I pulled the menu up to cover my nerves at the intensity of his gaze. Like he meant I looked nice and not the bistro. Time to deflect the focus back onto him. "So you started the vlog right out of school then?"

"I did. My first few videos weren't great, just messing around on campus in my first year. When I decided not to go back, I started an amateur gig where I would take dares to stay overnight in creepy locations. I called it 'Daring Dan'. From there it grew into 'Hauntastic Haunts'."

"Did you consider doing anything else?" I asked.

"Sort of? My uncle Kurt does custom carpentry, cabinets and stuff. He hired me to help around his woodshop. He sold me Vanessa on the cheap when he upgraded his work van. So she had some wear and tear, but she's a gem."

"That worked out for you," I observed.

"Yeah." He nodded. "I worked my ass off doing Uncle Kurt's grunt work to pay him back and afford the renovations. He gave me a sweet deal on custom woodwork and got me in touch with an electrician to wire her."

A server dressed all in black approached to fill our water glasses and take our drink orders. We thanked her, and she left us to peruse the menu.

"The vlog is your passion then?" I resumed our conversation.

"Yeah. I've always enjoyed filming stuff. What drew me to vlogging was the connection to my audience, though. I guess I can thank Dr. Landry for showing me how big an impact you can make when you take the time to connect with people. So, that's why I started with the dares. I hoped to interact with people all over the place, forge meaningful connections."

"Your passion shines through, in your videos," I said.

"You think so? Thanks." Daniel gave me a sheepish look. "It's weird to me you're a fan of the show, to be honest. Most of my assistants hadn't heard of my channel before taking the job. Well, except for Zack, but he's been my friend since we were kids."

"Maybe that's part of why you've gone through so many assistants," I reasoned.

"Huh, could be a factor. I figured it was a combination of the glamorous accommodations, scenic work sites and frequent access to all the best medical facilities."

I chuckled. "Well, when you put it like that, I'm surprised you had any turnover at all. Let's try to keep you out of the hospital."

"No argument here. So, what looks good on the menu?" He gestured.

I glanced down and saw a selection of local cheeses as the featured appetizer. There was a bit of a theme. The menu was a veritable showcase of local agriculture. Grass fed beef. Farm fresh produce.

"Um, they have chicken stuffed with aged Goodman Dairy Gouda and wild mushroom sauce. That sounds good."

"Hm, that sounds interesting, except the mushrooms. Pork tenderloin with fried risotto balls sounds good to me. I like to order things that it would be a pain to make in Vanessa's kitchen."

"I mean, most things fall under that category," I teased. "The van is cozier than I expected, but a gourmet kitchen it is not."

"It's lucky I have you around to negotiate with the Goodmans. I'm counting on you to get us fed a nice dinner on location from now on," Daniel joked.

"I like Lara and Jane. They've shown us such kind hospitality. I guess it isn't always like that?"

"It depends. Some sites I visit have sat abandoned for years. Or they aren't residential so the owner or property manager isn't always available, or invested in the show."

Our server returned to take our orders and drop off Daniel's blueberry lemonade. She refilled my water. Then left us again.

"Oh, speaking of locations, have we settled on where we're filming next?" I asked. "Last week I reached out to some property owners with lakeshore camps for the site we discussed in Maine. I'm still tracking down more than an address for the old schoolhouse in Ohio. Not sure if I'll get a reply, but I sent an inquiry letter about filming. I used Kay's house as the return address, so if they get back to us via snail mail she'll forward it."

"Good thinking." Daniel nudged his toes against mine under the table. "The lake would be nice. Mid-September into October is peak season for foliage. I bet we'll get some killer shots of the leaves turning before moving on to the October site."

"Hauntoween. What's the big plan for that this year?" I asked, leaning closer.

"See, when you say stuff like that it makes me realize you are a true Hauntastic Haunts fan. It's weird in a good way. Most people IRL don't understand how important my work is to me."

"I get it. I like what you're doing with the show. So. Hauntoween?" I wheedled.

"You think you get insider information just because you're dating a star now?" Daniel teased.

"That's exactly what I think, yeah. Or do I only get the NDA worthy deets in the pillow talk after I sleep with you?" I flirted.

Daniel did a spit take. "I wouldn't expect—"

"Relax, Daniel." I sighed. "It was a joke. I want to sleep with you because you're sexy as fuck, not to manipulate you into telling me stuff about work."

"Yeah. Gah, don't joke like that, please? I'm still not convinced this isn't a terrible idea. You're my employee."

"Only when I'm on the clock." I reminded him. "After hours we're just two guys who work together. Equals."

"Yeah. Okay. New rule, let's not talk about work on dates."

"Deal," I agreed.

"Tell me what you do for fun." Daniel changed the subject.

"I like to do those adult coloring books, it's cathartic. And I could work on them while I was taking calls sometimes since I was on the late shift."

"Nice. Did you bring any with you?" he asked.

"Yeah." I nodded. "And a set of pencils."

"Do you draw anything original, or just color?"

"Just color, I'm not an artist or anything. But I enjoy filling in the patterns. It added a touch of brightness to my cubicle. And to my bunk now."

"Show me later?" he asked.

"Sure, I mean, like I said, it's nothing fancy. I can take them down if we're removing the partition." I shifted in my seat at the thought of removing the divider between our bunks.

"You don't have to." Daniel waved away the offer. "Keep them up if it makes you happy, it's your space too."

"Yeah?" I grinned at him. Past hookups had mostly dismissed my coloring as a childish pastime. It was nice that Daniel accepted it so readily, not that I expected anything less of him.

"For sure." He reached over to pat my hand.

Our food arrived and our conversation focused on the meal in front of us for a time. When we finished eating, I was more than ready to move somewhere more private.

The server tried to urge us to end our date with dessert and coffee but we locked eyes and came to the same conclusion. The only dessert we needed was back in the van.

Daniel settled up, and I made a mental note to get the check next time.

I might not be certain how to handle the disparity in our positions, but I was certain I wanted another date with him. He made me feel comfortable. Seen and heard in a way I hadn't been before with anyone outside my family.

"You know what's cool about Vanessa?" I asked as we returned to the parking lot behind the bistro.

"What?"

"We're already home, and I really want to kiss you." I slid the door to the back open. I climbed inside first, then turned back to take his crutches so he could join me.

"Is that so?" Daniel smirked. He was right in my personal space, the two of us pressed together in the confines of the van.

"Yeah." My voice came out as a breathy rasp when Daniel reached around me to slide the door shut behind us. I was grateful he'd had the foresight to draw the blackout curtain across the front of the van earlier. It granted us privacy.

I kissed him. He tasted sweet and tart, like the lemonade he'd been drinking. I got swept away in the intoxicating feel of his lips on mine, the pulsing ache in my groin an answering hardness to the bulge pressing against my hip.

Daniel held my shoulders, using me to help him balance while my hands sought his ass, pulling him snug against my body. It was a very nice ass. Firm and round, with just enough padding for comfort.

Yeah, that was enough kissing. I wanted more. I pulled back, Daniel showed his displeasure with a needy moan.

"I want to suck you off," I said, nudging him backward.

"Yeah?"

"Yeah, lose the pants and get comfortable."

# THIRTY-THREE

## *Dan*

I was more than happy to accommodate Chad's request. It was just unfortunate that his orders were easier spoken than accomplished. I ended up braced against the shower door frame with my pants tangled around my cast.

Hot as it was to have Chad on his knees in front of me, I'd have preferred for him to be doing something other than wrestling with my pants.

He took care not to hurt me, and by the time he'd freed me we were both laughing at the absurdity of it all. I half expected him to call the whole thing off. Levity had taken the edge off my arousal.

The mood between us no longer supercharged with sexual tension. So it took me a little by surprise when Chad finished freeing me and got right back down to business. Or pleasure, as the case may be.

"Take that, pants! You have been defeated." Chad lobbed the offending garments into the shower stall to deal with later. "Now, I've got plans for you," he said, addressing my cock as he took me in hand and licked a wide stripe over the head.

"Do you now?" I asked. His firm grip and playful interest had my erection making a quick recovery. I shivered when he blew over the wet streak he'd left, the sensation intense and leaving me unsure of whether I liked it.

"Hold on," Chad warned. I gripped the door frame harder. My knees almost buckled when Chad took the entire length of my dick into his mouth and swallowed around me.

"Oh, hell." I moved one hand to the back of his head, needing to touch him as he worked my dick. The sight of his head bobbing on my shaft had me seconds away from shooting far too soon. I tugged on his hair and he locked eyes with me without pausing in his ministrations.

He looked debauched with my dick in his mouth, lust and desire clear in his gaze. He pulled back, using a fist to keep pumping my dick so he could talk.

"What's wrong?"

"Nothing. Don't want it to end yet."

A wicked smirk curved his lips. "Who said anything about it being over? This is the amuse-bouche."

"That so?"

"Yeah. Now, quit stalling and fuck my face." Chad's mouth sliding onto my dick drove any coherent response right out of my head. He made eye contact as he went back to sucking my brains out through my dick. It didn't take long before I was coming down his throat and clinging to the kitchen counter to stay upright.

Chad worked me through my orgasm. He gave me time to catch my breath before planting one last—almost chaste—kiss on my dick.

"Good?" he asked, it wasn't quite a tease, as if he genuinely expected critique when I was still floating on orgasmic bliss.

"Huh? Yeah. Very good." I reached for his face, my fingers just brushing his cheek. He turned into the touch. "Come here, let me kiss you."

He stood, biting his lip. His nerves were back in full force.

"What's wrong?" I put a finger to his lips, tracing the soft skin. His tongue darted out, tasting me. On impulse, I pushed my finger past his lips and he sucked for a second, sending tingles of pleasure right to my spent balls. I groaned. He let up on the stimulation, releasing my fingers.

"Ready to head back?" he asked.

I grabbed his hand to stop him when he made a move toward the cab. "What's the rush? Don't I get to reciprocate first?"

"Do you want to?"

"Why wouldn't I?"

Chad fidgeted, at a loss for words, he crossed his arms over his chest and shook his head, mouth open, nothing coming out.

"Do you not enjoy getting head?" I resisted the urge to scoop him into a comforting hug. I suspected I might need a clear head and space for this conversation.

"Dunno." He shrugged self-consciously.

"You don't know?" I raised a skeptical eyebrow.

"Never had much chance to try it," he mumbled.

"But…" I trailed off.

No way had he learned to deepthroat without giving more than his share of head. I might have a biased opinion, considering that having an enthusiastic mouth on my dick felt fantastic regardless of skill level, but still, Chad had experience. He must.

"But what?" Chad challenged, arms crossed over his chest.

"I'm not the first guy you've blown," I stated.

"No," he agreed.

"And none of them offered to return the favor? What kind of assholes have you been dating?" I demanded.

Chad blew out a frustrated breath. "Some of them offered. Dysphoria is bullshit, okay?"

"Okay. Care to talk about it?" I offered, softening my voice.

"Not really," he grumbled.

178

"Do you want a hug?" I leaned my hip against the counter and opened my arms wide. It was a good thing I'd braced myself because Chad took me up on the offer. He buried his face in my neck and clung to me. I squeezed him tight, letting him take a moment to gather his thoughts. Long moments passed with him in my arms.

"I enjoy sucking cock," he mumbled into my neck, so quiet I almost couldn't make out the words.

Then he pushed away. I let him take a step back, though I longed to keep touching him.

"I'd noticed. For what it's worth, you're good at it."

"Practice makes perfect." Chad shot me a teasing grin, then sobered, not quite meeting my gaze. "I guess if we're doing this, we should discuss the dysphoria elephant in the van?"

"Sure, I've told you I don't want to do anything that makes you uncomfortable, Chad."

Chad took a deep breath before he spoke. "I don't like it when the guys I'm with comment on how different my junk looks. I get that it's small, but I can't afford surgery to make it look more cis, even if I wanted it. Also, I don't pack. Not unless I need to, like for sex or if I go to a club where I expect guys to get handsy. Having something in my pants is just a constant reminder of what isn't actually there."

"Okay. What does that mean in bed?" I asked.

"I'd prefer not to have you focused on it during sex. Like with getting blown, maybe it feels great, but the one time I tried it left me so freaking dysphoric I swore I wasn't going there again. I'd rather fuck, or get fucked. Or rimming is okay, I think. I'm not cool with using my front hole. At all—ever. I've had a hysterectomy, so no chance of you knocking me up, I just don't like going there. Anyway, it's uncomfortable to even try these days, since it's atrophied after years of being on T."

"Got it." I nodded, none of that was a problem. "So, you're all about the butt stuff? Do you have a prosthetic to fuck me with?"

"Darling," Chad offered me a tentative smile, "I have an entire collection of dicks for you to choose from if you want to get fucked."

"What's your preference?"

"Vers, for sure."

"Same, so, would sucking you off while you wear one of your dicks be something you'd want to try?"

"Not sure how I feel about that. Might be hot to watch you swallow my cock. Most guys aren't super into the taste of silicone, though."

"Eh, that's what flavored lube is for, right? Anyway, it's not like I suck cock for the flavor."

Chad chuckled at that. "I dunno, you taste fantastic."

"You think so?" I leaned in close.

"Yeah. Better double check though. Just to be sure." Chad closed the distance, kissing me again, long and lazy. When we broke apart, he gave me a soft smile. "You don't even know how much I've been wanting to fuck you."

"Let's get back to the dairy so I can take out the partition and you can show me your vaunted cock collection then," I said.

"Can't decide which one I want to get inside you first," Chad mused.

"Hm, well, I guess we'll just have to try them all," I suggested, that earned me a wicked smirk. Tonight was going to be fun.

# THIRTY-FOUR
## *Chad*

The drive back seemed to take twice as long with my dick rock hard in my pants. I stroked myself off while I was sucking Daniel's dick earlier, but it wasn't enough. I needed more.

My last serious relationship had ended after my college graduation. I'd only had sporadic hookups since. There had been a brief period where I'd fallen into a cycle of letting chasers pick me up on apps.

For them, sex with me was a novelty. I hadn't cared so long as I got off. But that got old after a while and since most of the novelty revolved around using parts I wasn't cool with, I'd stopped.

Now that I'd found someone who saw me as an actual person with my own wants and needs, I wanted to try everything. Like a kid at a dessert buffet, I was ready to glut myself on everything Daniel had to offer.

I parked Vanessa in our usual spot near the haunted barn. Daniel wasted no time going to work undoing the row of latches that held the partition in place to separate the bed into two bunks. It was down in minutes.

I took the partition around to the back to stow it and get out the extra foam Dan told me he kept behind all the paranormal gear. In my haste, I dropped the EM meter on the ground. It bounced closer to the barn with a loud clatter. I winced, hoping I hadn't broken it.

Destroying Daniel's stuff would put a damper on the mood. He was so into his gear. I retrieved the foam first, passing it up to Daniel where he sat perched on the bed, his casted leg at an awkward angle.

"Here, want to get that in place?"

"On it." He took the narrow strip of foam to wedge back into place.

I turned to pick up the meter. It blinked to life as my fumbling fingers hit the power switch. For a moment, relief surged through me at finding it still worked. Then the screen lit up and the little meter spiked a reading, beeping an alert.

Daniel looked up at the sound.

"What's up?"

I lifted the meter. "Sorry, the fall must have messed up the settings or something. It seems to be on the fritz." I shivered in the evening chill. Weird, it had been a pleasant evening when we left the restaurant, but now it was cold enough that my breath fogged in the air.

"Cold spot," Daniel said. I noticed his breath was not fogging, even though he was only yards away in the back of the van. Still, Vanessa had heating and insulation. It made sense that it was warmer inside, even with the rear doors standing wide open.

"The meter says it's forty degrees out here." That must be wrong. The thermometer on the van's dash had read as sixty-seven degrees earlier. Not hot, but the temperature couldn't have dropped so far so fast. I toggled it to EM mode, hoping that it would stop the buzzing alert sound.

I shivered more violently. The cold seeped into my bones. I thought I heard someone moving toward me from behind and a primal fear gripped me. I spun, pointing the meter toward the open door to the stable. The meter squealed with another loud alert.

"EM fluctuations. Grab the IR camera." Dan already had his cell phone camera trained on me. I assumed he was recording the EM meter's beeps and the visual evidence of the temperature.

I wanted nothing more than to get back inside with him, but I reached dutifully for the camera in its protective case. Good thing I'd been setting it up every night all week, I was familiar with its operation by now. It only took moments to have the camera on and aimed into the empty stable.

Dark and empty and not hiding any horrors. I hit record and almost dropped the damn thing as a colorful image in the shape of a man loomed in the center of the shot. If I could believe the camera, he was standing a few paces from the barn door.

It wouldn't take more than a handful of running stride for him to get close enough to stab me with the pitchfork he held in his left hand. Something gave me the sense that was exactly what he intended to do. I took a step back.

"Oh. Damn. Hell. Shit. What the—fuck. Daniel? Fuck. What—"

The figure's face distorted. On camera, the colors flashed into a different hue and then the thing moved toward me. The creak of boards echoed as though bearing a man's weight.

Now that I knew where to look I could just discern the faint outline of a person when I tore my eyes from the display screen. The weapon the figure held glowed with an eerie light all its own.

I wasn't waiting around to confirm the threat was real. I did my best to keep the IR camera aimed behind me as I turned tail and fled toward Vanessa.

Dan pulled the rear doors closed, and I dashed for the side door, slamming it shut behind me.

Something heavy slammed into the van behind me, rocking it. Then a wave of intense cold burned against my back. I was still holding the EM meter, pinging for all it was worth to alert us to supposed spirit activity.

Dan had two cameras out, one trained on my face, the other angled toward the meter.

"You okay, man?"

"Yeah," I said, my voice more shaky than I would have liked. Then the cold faded, the meter dropped from max activity to nothing. And the sense of dread released its hold on my guts, leaving only relief. My heart was pounding like I'd just run a marathon.

"Oh, my god. I just saw a ghost. An actual, real life ghost."

"Seems that way." Daniel stopped recording and put the camera on the bed. He slid down to approach me. I couldn't seem to make myself move from where I crouched against the door.

"Fuck. Damn. I… fuck, Daniel, they're real? A bitter old man who hated his brother-in-law enough to attempt killing his whole family haunts this place for real? A murderous ghost just tried to kill me. Shit."

"Breathe." Daniel reached for me and I flung myself into his arms, clinging to his warmth like my life depended on it. He rubbed my back, soothing touches that dispelled the lingering chill, "Relax, let me hold you, you're freezing cold."

When I felt a little more steady, I pulled back and attempted to crack a joke, "That was scarier than being chased by a rabid raccoon."

"Ghosts can't give you rabies, so there's that." Daniel pulled me toward the bed. "Let's get you tucked in and warmed up."

I let him guide me to the bed. Without the partition, it seemed huge, almost king sized at a guess.

"Raccoons don't wield rusty spectral pitchforks covered in god knows what. I seem to recall you calling me less than a year ago to get an early tetanus booster covered for a puncture wound from a haunting."

"I stepped on a nail," Daniel pointed out. "Spirits don't often stab people, scary as some of them can be. He probably couldn't have hurt you with it."

"Probably?" I repeated.

"Well, nothing is ever certain," Daniel acknowledged. "Most of them can't interact with physical reality—not much, anyway."

"He was interacting with the floorboards enough to make them squeak."

"Right, I said much. I'm sure the boards squeaked when he was alive, just a projection of his memories of how things were back then."

"And when he was alive, the man wouldn't have allowed trespassers on his property. Oh god, I almost got stabbed by a ghost."

"You're safe now," Daniel assured me. "I grounded Vanessa. And I might have laid down salt along with the insulation, you know, better safe than sorry and all that. Haven't had a spirit inside the van since."

"Did you before?" I asked.

"Once, but I'll tell you about it another time. I think we've had enough excitement for one night. Get to sleep."

He pushed me toward the bed again and I climbed up, expecting him to follow. He didn't. Instead, he waited until I'd covered myself in the blankets I'd been using in my cozy bunk, squeezed my foot and said, "Rest now. I'll join you later."

I didn't think I could rest after the night we'd had. I was still horny from fooling around in the restaurant parking lot. But the crash of the adrenaline draining from my system had me out like a light within moments of my head hitting the pillows. I just wished I had Daniel's warmth snuggled up against me.

# THIRTY-FIVE

## *Dan*

Once Chad fell asleep, I retrieved the gear he'd left in a careless heap on the floor. With any other assistant, his disregard would have pissed me off. The gear we needed for the show was not cheap.

Under the circumstances, I cut him some slack. Not just because he was my boyfriend, or might become my boyfriend soon. His first undeniable encounter with a vengeful spirit had him freaked out.

Not lecturing him on the proper care of our gear had nothing to do with exchanging special treatment for sex. It was just basic decency. I had nothing to feel guilty about. No reason to avoid crawling into the big bed we'd planned to fuck in and curl around him as he slept off the fear of the encounter.

I glanced at him, his features softened in sleep. There would be time to cuddle later. For now, I wanted to see the footage he'd captured.

Before I knew it, hours had gone by and I'd completed a first pass on the footage from both cameras.

Chad had captured just under a minute of usable footage. He'd gotten an amazing clear shot of the ghost focusing on him. Then a few seconds where it leveled the pitchfork at him and started to charge.

From there the image was a jolting upside down blur of motion as he ran. Still, I gave him credit for holding onto the camera and trying to keep rolling even as he fled in terror. I'd make a proper cameraman of him yet.

My footage wasn't as exciting. I got a good steady view of the EM meter going mad, and a brief zoomed in image of the readout display on my phone's camera. The quality wasn't perfect, but I would make it work with the other footage.

Chad's breath fogging the air mere meters from where I sat comfortably in a tee-shirt added a nice touch of detail to the cold spot reading. My crappy cell camera didn't pick up much more than a lens flare where the ghost had stood.

I'd seen more detail with my naked eyes, still, Chad's encounter with Higgs would be perfect for the final video in our series. I figured it would work well after the scenes with Leon and the re-enactment of his childhood run-in with the ghost.

I considered pulling up the master file I'd been working on to add in the new spliced footage. A glance at the clock deterred me. It was almost two in the morning.

I shut down the computer. Chad laid cocooned in the blankets on the bed. I dug out a light spare from the shelf above the cab to avoid waking him. I needn't have bothered. As soon as I crawled into bed beside him, Chad snuggled up against me, seeking my body heat and clinging to me like a limpet.

Despite my exhaustion, I stayed up staring at the ceiling for far too long. It was only a matter of time before Chad bailed.

He hadn't taken the existence of ghosts well. Any relationship between us was doomed to failure if he couldn't handle the paranormal.

For that matter, hadn't the ghost proven that we didn't have set hours? Thinking it was possible to separate our work from our personal lives was a delusion. In the dark, with him snuggled into my arms, I couldn't bring myself to say our relationship was wrong.

I tried not to think about it, fretting wouldn't change what we'd already done. We'd crossed a line tonight. It was impossible to return to just being his boss. My only real option was to enjoy this while it lasted.

I'd have time to miss Chad later. After he left. I wished things could be different with him, though.

# THIRTY-SIX

## *Chad*

D aniel was up before me, sitting at his editing console with a mug of coffee at his elbow. I was pretty sure he'd joined me in the bed at some point last night. I had a hazy, half-dreamt recollection of snuggling into him and feeling warm again for the first time all night.

Part of me wanted to coax him into rejoining me to indulge the morning wood I had going. I wanted to finish what last night's paranormal encounter had interrupted. But he was working, and we'd agreed to keep things professional in the light of day.

That didn't stop me from being grumpy about it. I tumbled out of the bed onto my feet and shuffled the few steps to the coffee pot.

"Morning." Daniel sounded too cheerful for the early hour and lack of sleep.

I grunted in response and poured a cup of coffee. I sidled closer to observe what he was doing while I took my first sip. Perfect.

Then I saw the image on the screen and just prevented myself from spraying him with coffee.

"Holy fuck, I actually saw a ghost last night." I pointed at the monitor.

Daniel startled at my outburst, he looked between me and his work.

"You did. Caught some amazing footage too. Pity about the last bit being out of focus, but at least you kept your head enough to hold on to the IR camera."

"I just didn't want to break the damn thing. I know how excited you are to have it."

"I am. If it's ever a choice between your safety and the tech, ditch the gear, please. We could afford to replace it. Our equipment costs are low since we bankroll most of the gear we use through companies that want me to post reviews. But I still appreciate not having to repair or replace it."

"How much danger was I in there?" I asked.

"Honestly?" Daniel ran a hand through his tousled hair. "I can't say for certain, but the spirit has caused accidents over the years. It is possible, however unlikely, that it might have injured you."

"Is it safe to go inside the barn?"

"Ghosts are stronger at night. Sunlight weakens their ability to remain corporeal."

"Seems like a flimsy defense," I observed.

"You wouldn't think it could bleach out stains either, or power our home, but it does."

"Fair point. So, you're saying the power of the sun will protect us?"

"Yes. It should." Daniel nodded.

I sighed, that was not a ringing endorsement. By daylight, I was less inclined to believe what had seemed so real in last night's terror. But the image was right there in the same vibrant shades of green and blue and violet I'd seen last night. I suppose it was possible that Dan had arranged some elaborate trick to get the footage. But I'd seen the apparition, faint, but real as it ran toward me.

The timing seemed off if Dan was pulling a trick. Why would he spring the ghost on me when he could get laid instead? I had a hard time accepting he would perpetrate a hoax without letting me in on it. If not for the ghost, our night would have ended with us together in the expanded bunk.

For now, logic dictated that it wasn't a trick. I'd experienced the paranormal for real. And my first brush with spirits meant I had to examine why my mother hadn't stuck around for Kay and me.

"Daniel?" I asked.

"Yes?" he replied.

"Why do some ghosts stay and others move on? I mean, obviously every dead person doesn't linger, or we'd all be eyeballs deep in ghosts, right?" I shivered at the notion.

Daniel gave me a soft understanding smile. "You're wondering why your mother didn't appear to you?"

"Yeah." I rubbed at my arm with my free hand, conscious of how exposed the question left me.

"Like you said, not everyone sticks around. I don't think anyone knows for sure why, though there are plenty of theories. I think when a person is at peace with death, they are less likely to linger as a spirit."

"So, what, she didn't have unfinished business?" I demanded.

"Yeah," he said, his voice gentle, he squeezed my shoulder. "Or she believed you and Kay would be okay without her there to watch over you."

"It wasn't okay," I snapped. "I needed her."

"I'm sorry, Chad, I don't have all the answers."

Too messed up to trust my voice not to shake, I gave a tight nod.

"If it helps, the fact you didn't see her, or sense her presence doesn't have to mean she wasn't there looking out for you. And even if she wasn't, that doesn't mean she loved you any less."

"I never got to tell her," I admitted. "About me. I didn't come out because I was too afraid. Now I'll never get to tell her."

"That's a hard burden to bear."

"Yeah."

"Would she have taken the news poorly?" Daniel asked softly.

"No. Not really. Kay says she wouldn't."

"Do you believe Kay?"

I sighed. "It's not the same as hearing my mom say that it's okay. I'll never hear her call me by my name. Nothing will ever fix that. If ghosts are real..."

"Then she should have stayed long enough to hear it from you?" Daniel filled in for me.

"Yes. That's it exactly." I hesitated to ask, I didn't want to push his boundaries. I knew he was uncertain about the whole power imbalance between us. But I'd just found out ghosts were real, surely we could bend the rules a little for that. "I know we said we'd be professional during work, but it's only seven and I could use a hug from my boyfriend right now."

"Boyfriend?"Daniel repeated, he blinked at me. For a horrible minute I worried I'd upset him and overstepped.

"Yeah?"

Daniel reached for my hand to pull me into an awkward kiss. "Well, as your boyfriend, I can understand why you might not have wanted ghosts to be real. I can't take away your hurt about your mom, but maybe we can take your mind off it?"

"What did you have in mind?" I asked, hoping he meant what I thought. He kissed me again until the need to get closer had me considering scrambling into his lap. There wasn't room to straddle him. And, despite the rising tide of lust, I had enough presence of mind not to want to hurt his broken leg.

"Bed?" His lips were only inches away from mine. It would have been easy to get lost in his drugging kiss. I tore myself away and climbed onto the bed. Daniel wasn't far behind me. We kissed and touched for a long time, making out like horny teenagers.

Soon ghosts were the last thing on my mind as I rutted against my boyfriend, our light sleep pants the only thing separating us. His dick was as hard as my own where they rubbed together, trapped between our bodies. His rigid length felt so good against my erection.

I got off embarrassingly fast. Daniel didn't seem put off by it, he peppered my face and neck in soft kisses.

"Keep going, or too sensitive?" he asked when I'd recovered enough to do more than cling to him and keep rutting. I reached between us to give his dick an idle stroke. He was still hard. I kept stroking him while I considered.

I didn't need much time to recover compared to most of the cis guys I'd screwed around with in the past. Took me longer to recover than it had before T, but that was an acceptable tradeoff. I figured I'd be ready to go again in no time with Daniel naked in bed with me.

"Can I fuck you?"

Daniel kissed me, his lips a gentle caress on mine. "I would love that, but we've got appointments today and I want to take our time, tonight?"

"All right. Can I suck you off then?"

"Sixty-nine?" He countered.

I shook my head, ready to remind him of my preferences.

"I know, leave your dick and front hole out of it, but I could rim you while you suck me?"

"You are overestimating how flexible I am."

"We could try?" Daniel pouted.

I sighed, we might get his tongue in my hole while I mouthed his cock. But I doubted it would be near as much fun as getting my face fucked or having his full attention on my ass. Especially with his cast complicating any contortions we attempted.

"Nah. I want to enjoy blowing you. Lay back."

Daniel didn't protest, he propped himself up on an elbow to watch me. I positioned myself so I was straddling his abs. That way I didn't have to worry about knocking his leg.

Sometime soon I would take my time tasting every inch of his body. Teasing him when we had no other obligations. But he was right, we had deadlines looming and work to accomplish.

So instead of giving in to my desire to play with him, I pulled out every trick I knew to get him off fast and hard. All the while I worked my sensitive dick with one hand. His hands pawed my ass, squeezing and kneading the flesh, his spit slick finger rubbing over my hole, made me wish we had more time to indulge.

The sound of him moaning my name when he came was almost enough to push me over the edge too. I lasted for a few more furious tugs on my junk. The tip of his finger pushing against my rim—a blatant promise of things to come—had me collapsing on top of him, both of us spent and sated.

# THIRTY-SEVEN

## *Dan*

I t was distracting to sit next to Chad after the orgasms we'd shared not an hour ago. I would have liked nothing more than returning to bed to fuck him. Or let him fuck me.

Both. I wanted both. Instead, we were inside the haunted barn filming again. I wanted to get a few different angles of various shots on film so we had options when we cut together next week's video.

The intro to the monthly haunted history video was always me talking about the haunting on site. We would do a few takes inside. Then a few more outside, getting all our shots from various angles.

The last item on the agenda for the day was filming a stable hand, Ben, who had volunteered to play the role of Frank Higgs. We planned to film a dramatization of Higgs' last moments and his spectral greatest hits.

I would splice in a teaser of what Chad captured last night. The bulk of that gem was going in the final webisode where we explored the actual haunting though. This week's webisode covered the background and set up.

I planned to cut today's footage together with the interviews we'd done last week. Mr. Dawes and the local librarian and history buff, Ms. Clark, would make up the bulk of the webisode. Clark gave the historical context and Dawes had a personal connection to the story.

The segments we'd done with Leon and Lara would fill out the next two webisodes detailing the haunting and our investigation. Most of the camera work was complete. We still needed to film the transitions to segue into the interviews.

I had some ideas about how to portray the fire story. I wanted to print a copy of the old photo of the family in front of the original farmhouse. After I aged the paper I could create a unique effect by burning it on tape to a voice-over of the story.

With the right filter treatment and sound effects it should set the mood well enough. I wanted to do a voice-over track of Dawes telling the story of the house fire. Crackling fire, a child's wail, a slow build with mood music and then fade in on Evie Goodman's daughter reading from the old woman's journal.

It would be perfect. After today's filming, the last major segment I had planned only required footage of the journal entries from Evie's daughter.

"Hey, Chad?"

"Yeah?"

"Can you get Evie's daughter to film herself reading that journal entry she messaged us about finding? It would be awesome if she included a shot of her sitting in a rocking chair reading the story to her aged mother. Think she'd go for that?" I asked.

"Yeah. From talking to her, I imagine she would eat up a chance to be the next big star. At a minimum, I can ask her to photograph the relevant passages and email them to us. Want me to call her?"

"After we wrap this up," I said.

I found it obvious he didn't want to spend a second more in the haunted barn than he had to. I couldn't blame him. Even for a haunting, there was a malevolence here I seldom encountered. Best to get what we needed on tape and then leave the spirit in peace.

I planned to put Lara in touch with a medium to help exorcise the angry spirit of her dead ancestor once we finished filming. This one was well beyond my amateur ghost banishing abilities.

I could track and record the paranormal no problem. When it was a simple matter of putting a restless wanderer to rest, I could manage that sometimes too.

Something like this required a real medium. I relied on technology to interact with the spirit world. I wasn't about to dabble in the powerful arcane rites that would stand a chance against a spirit of this power.

Better to leave that to the professionals. I was here to bear witness to the past and record the effects it had on the present.

The rest of the day passed without incident. I expected that it would, since it was a bright cheery late summer day and Higgs must have expended a great deal of energy in his appearance last night. He shouldn't have enough juice for a repeat so soon.

We got through the takes we needed. Then filmed the scenes with our volunteer stand in ghost. We finished up in the barn well before the shadows started to lengthen in the evening.

"I want to call Annette before we head to the main house for supper." Chad packed away the camera gear with care. I was already itching to upload today's recording and get to work on edits. If I started now, I would work straight through supper, so I refrained. Instead I focused on putting away the stage makeup and costume pieces.

Ben had been a good sport about me dressing him in period appropriate clothing. He'd balked at the pale makeup to make it easier to add a ghostly pallor in post-production until I explained why I was using it.

Ben had gone back into the barn to retrieve his ball cap once I got him out of makeup. I didn't think too much of it when I didn't see him leave. Figured he'd slipped past us on his return to the main facility unnoticed. Until a scream rent the air.

Chad came tearing out of Vanessa. His eyes, wide with terror, met mine.

"Is that Ben?"

We turned to the barn in unison. The scream rose in volume, then abruptly cut off with a strangled gasp. The silence after was even worse than the terrified screaming. I snatched up the camera, shoving it into Chad's hands.

"Whatever it is, we should record it," I said, then grabbed my crutches to propel myself across the yard and into the barn. Chad followed, hot on my heels. He didn't have to say a word for me to realize how much it cost him to go back inside.

Light illuminated the interior through the holes in the ceiling. The setting sun sent a golden shaft through a large window in the west-facing wall. It illuminated the section of the loft nearest the ladder and visible from the aisle.

Ben lay caught in the beam of light inches from the opening in the loft floor, curled in a ball and clutching at his gut.

"Is that—fuck." Chad shoved the camera into my hands and ran for the rickety ladder we'd propped up to access the loft above. We'd filmed a few scenes up there over the past week. Or at least, Chad had.

My leg kept me from climbing up there. The metallic tang of blood scenting the air tipped me off that Ben had sustained injuries. I pulled out my cell and dialed emergency services. From the amount of blood pooling around him, if he'd survived his injuries, I suspected we would need help to save the guy's life.

I explained the situation to an operator as I watched Chad ball up his shirt and press it to the man's injuries. I hoped like hell Ben was still alive. We'd only been outside without him for moments. He had to be alive.

"Call 911, if you haven't," Chad called down to me from the top of the ladder.

"Is he alive?"

After a moment, Chad replied, "His pulse is there, but thready. I'm putting pressure on the wound, but there's a lot of blood."

"Keep pressure on it. Help is on the way," I parroted the calm lady on the phone. If it weren't for her voice in my ear telling me that help was coming I'd have been freaking out. Instead, I relayed her orders to Chad. I needed to stay calm for him and Ben.

"If it's safe to stay up there, it's best not to move him."

"Safe enough, how long?" he asked.

"They dispatched an ambulance."

We waited in tense silence until the distant wail of an ambulance approached. The sound cut out before the vehicle reached us. I'd given instructions about the old dirt road to the abandoned barn, unsure if it had an address in their system or what. Did barns have their own addresses?

The doors burst open and people in uniform took over the scene. They sent Chad and I outside, taking over with Ben's wound. Someone yelled at me to stop recording. It was only then that I realized I'd gotten the whole grim proceedings on video.

No way in hell was I using footage of an actual death, or even near death experience on my show though. I'd have to delete it. Later. There would be time for that later. I stowed the camera in the van, thankful no one had thought to confiscate it.

Lara and Jane arrived to learn what the commotion was about. The first responders loaded Ben into their ambulance and drove away with the lights and sirens wailing. They said something about him being in critical condition, but at least he was still alive.

They wouldn't be rushing him to the emergency room if he was dead, right? I clung to that hope. It had been my fault the man was inside the haunted barn. I didn't want his death on my hands, even if I never could have predicted what happened.

I didn't even know what happened. Had he somehow tripped over some long-abandoned farm implement? That made no sense. He only went back inside to grab his ball cap, not climb rusty old plowshares.

Jane left to follow the ambulance to the hospital. Lara called Ben's family to notify them of the accident. Then the police showed up to ask us questions.

It was hours before they seemed satisfied with our statements. They left with my camera in an evidence bag. I was too shaken to even bring myself to work up any outrage over it. I just wanted to know how Higgs had gained enough strength to inflict the amount of damage Ben had sustained.

# THIRTY-EIGHT

## *Chad*

Once the ambulance left, I took stock of the situation. Ben had survived, at least for now. I'd done everything in my power to help him. Except make sure his attacker never harmed anyone else.

That meant I needed to ensure we stopped the dangerous ghost. Got our video in front of someone who could banish Higgs. This was my first experience with a crime scene. But if TV taught me anything, it was that the police would want to take our camera as evidence.

So while Daniel did his best to answer Lara's bewildered questions, I backed up all the files from the camera. I uploaded everything to Daniel's computer, then backed that up to his cloud storage.

We'd make time to deal with it later. For now, I'd ensured we had what we needed to get the word out about this supernatural menace.

I felt antsy so close to the barn as night descended. The flashing lights of the police car that arrived next lit up the barn in strobing colors. I hoped Dan was right that light would disrupt the malevolent spirit if it tried anything else.

The ghost must have worn himself out trying to kill Ben; he stayed away while we answered questions. After endless hours, they took the camera and left us with an admonition to stay in town. No surprise there, though Daniel seemed taken aback at the implication they suspected us of foul play.

I'd been on the phone with Annette to finish arranging her interview when the attack occurred and time stamped video to narrow down the possible window for the attack would bear out the fact I was not involved.

I had an alibi. Daniel did not. I knew he'd been inside the van, but I hadn't actually seen him there so my word wasn't enough to clear him.

"Would a serious accident on your set improve your ratings?" the officer asked toward the end of the interview.

Daniel frowned like the thought never occurred to him. It should have. His own injuries had proven to boost his views and likes repeatedly.

I knew Daniel well enough to be certain he would never even consider hurting a person as a publicity stunt. The police did not know that.

I hoped like hell Ben survived and could tell us what happened to him. It must be the ghost. I shuddered to think what might have happened to me last night if I'd been any slower to escape. Frank Higgs had struck again, and this time it was far worse than Leon's broken arm.

# THIRTY-NINE

## *Dan*

I operated in a haze after what happened in the loft. One thing was clear now, Higgs' ghost must not remain unchecked.

It would not be enough to document the haunting, this one required professional intervention. If only the police hadn't taken my camera, I might at least review the footage. Check for any evidence of what happened to Ben.

Some sign of the ghost's malign interest in him. Or perhaps some incriminating detail that would prove the ghost responsible for the injuries inflicted on the man.

On that note. How lucky were we to have avoided a serious accident before now? It could have been Chad the ghost harmed. Last night I hadn't credited the true extent of the danger he had been in.

I couldn't fault him for his nerves, considering the attack or for his desire to put space between us and the ghost. I didn't argue when Chad suggested parking Vanessa near the farmhouse. Lara and Jane were too busy to deal with us that night. That left us to our own devices.

"What now?" Chad didn't turn to look at me. Did he blame me for the attack? I was the expert on these matters. I should have taken more precautions.

"We call in a medium to put Higgs to rest," I declared. "End this, once and for all."

"But, isn't that what we do?" Chad asked.

"I'm just an investigator." I shook my head. "I collect all the latest tech, but I'm not a medium. I can communicate and coax the willing. I can't force an angry spirit to his rest—but I know someone who can."

"Who?"

"Karen White," I said with a grimace. She wasn't precisely my nemesis, but we were not on the friendliest terms.

"Karen White?" Chad repeated, incredulous. "The Karen White who posts ragey social media rants about you being a clueless dilettante? You know her?"

"Sure," I feigned nonchalance. "Why else would she bother mentioning me?"

"But isn't she your professional rival?"

"She is," I acknowledged, "but I can respect her expertise enough to know when something is beyond my abilities. Higgs almost killed you last night. May well have killed a man today. I won't risk anyone else."

"Shit," Chad cursed. "I was trying not to dwell on how close... will Ben make it?"

"I'm not sure." There had been a lot of blood staining the ground. On Chad's hands and clothing from trying to stem the flow from the even set of puncture wounds in the man's gut.

"Give me her number, I'll make the call." Chad pulled out his phone. I sighed.

"I appreciate you trying to make this easier for me, but it'll be best if I call her myself. She'll take it as an insult otherwise."

"Okay."

I took a deep breath and dialed Karen's work number.

"Other Side Encounters, this is Tabitha, how can I help you?" Karen's receptionist answered in a warm tone that oozed distant politesse.

"Hi, Tabitha, this is Daniel Collins, from the web series Dan's—"

"I know who you are." Tabitha cut me off, turning brisk and chilly. "Is this about her latest blog post?"

I suppressed a groan, I made a mental note to check out Karen's blog later to see if she'd posted something about me again.

"No, I find myself with a professional matter that she is better suited to handle."

Tabitha snorted, it wasn't a stretch to assume that the staff of Other Side Encounters thought Karen was better qualified than me to resolve any and all paranormal situations. "Karen is in a consultation, what is the problem?"

I gritted my teeth. Cleansing the haunting was more important than my professional pride. Lives were at stake. "I've got a haunting in Vermont where the ghost has been escalating for decades and today he stabbed a man."

There was some commotion down the line, then after a beat of silence, Tabitha's tone changed to concerned. "Did he survive?"

"They took him to the local hospital by ambulance. Word is that he is in surgery to repair the damage. I need to deal with this haunting before something worse happens. I'm more than willing to swallow my pride to make that happen. Can Karen help or do I need to call someone else?"

"Hold on, I'll appraise her of the situation."

New Agey hold music filled my ear before I could respond. I half expected Karen to let me stew on hold for ages. She didn't, though. It was maybe five minutes before I was on the phone with the woman herself.

"I'll help." Karen's melodic voice didn't hold her usual scorn for me. "You did the right thing, calling me."

"Great, when can you get here?" I asked.

"Oh, no, You mistake me, dear boy, I'm amid several sensitive consultations. I cannot get away to visit in person."

"Then what do you have in mind?" I clenched my fingers around my phone in frustration.

"I will provide remote help for you to lay the spirit to rest. If you insist on inserting yourself into my profession, it's high time you learn to do more than excite the spirits before moving on to your next exploit."

"I thought you only taught other mediums," I retorted.

"Yes, well. I could do worse than an apprentice with your persistence and passion for the spirit world. And for once you've shown you can exercise discernment. Are you refusing my offer?"

"No, not at all. I'm grateful."

"Good. Then your first job as my long distance apprentice will be to tell me about the spirit you encountered. With none of your usual showmanship, I am a busy woman," she admonished.

I laid out the details, Karen only interrupted a handful of times to tell me to get to the point. She clucked over my reaction to Chad's encounter last night, chiding me for not taking the threat seriously enough. Only what I deserved. I should have known better. Done better.

When I finished, she made a contemplative sound. "The spirit seems to seek revenge. Who would your Frank Higgs blame for his death?"

"Blame? No one, he killed himself."

"Well, I'm sure he had a reason for that, don't you think?" Karen snarked.

"I told you, his farm was failing."

"Ah, who did he blame for that?" she asked.

That drew me up short. Who would Frank have blamed for his hardships?

"His sister?" I suggested, uncertain.

"That's a strong possibility," Karen acknowledged. "From what you've told me, he's attempted to harm his young nieces and nephews when the stable was still in use. He may have played a role in burning the original house with his sister's family inside."

"But how does that knowledge help us?" I demanded.

"We can give the spirit the closure it needs. Find out the root of his desire and you will learn the key to convincing him to let go. You will only be able to send him to his rest once his hold on the living world is loosened."

"So, we figure out why he wanted to wipe out his sister's family? That's assuming he wasn't just a sociopath?" I clarified.

"Short answer? Yes. Though, it may be enough to convince the spirit we have redressed the wrongs done to him without discovering the finer details."

"How?" I asked.

"That's for you to figure out. If that's all, I am busy. Call me when you are ready to attempt further communication with the spirit."

"Thank you, Karen."

"Uh uh, that's Madame White to you," she chided me. "An apprentice medium must show the proper deference."

I bit back a snarky reply—I needed her help here. "Thank you for your help, Madame White."

"You are welcome. And try not to get yourself killed, if I am to mentor you, I'd prefer to do it with you still on this side of the veil."

She clicked off the call and left me with a sinking sense that I was in way over my head. I was no medium, apprentice or otherwise. I relied on my gadgets and gear to interact with the paranormal. Karen was the real deal. I'd never felt more like the fraudster she'd always accused me of being than I did after that phone call.

# FORTY

## *Chad*

Daniel dropped his phone in his lap and rubbed at his temples. "Any idea why Higgs has it in for his sister's family?"

"Jealousy?" I suggested. "Elmer turned the failing business around. If he'd bothered to pitch in sooner, Frank might not have taken such drastic measures?"

"Resentment." Daniel nodded. "That's a thought. Although, if the negative feelings developed after his death, then that begs the question of why his spirit lingered. A violent death alone is enough to make a ghost. But he's proven powerful, something is holding him here."

"We don't have anything new to draw on," I said. "Speculation is all we have absent more information. I suspect Evie's journals are our best lead. The good news is that I have arranged a video interview with Annette. We hammered out the details just before, well, the incident. We'll have to wait until tomorrow to talk to her and Evie."

"Tomorrow, huh? You're so efficient." Daniel forced a tight smile.

"I try."

Daniel sighed, fiddling with his phone. He looked so dejected. I wanted to make everything better. But the situation was grim. We'd put Ben in danger and the consequences of his injury remained ambiguous.

The officers who had questioned us seemed suspicious of our story. They had separated us while we answered endless inquiries about what we were doing and how Ben fit into things.

It had been a long terrible day. My natural inclination was to go straight to sleep and hope tomorrow was better. Daniel needed a distraction, though. It was obvious from his distant expression. His defeated slouch.

"Come on," I stood and patted his thigh, "we've got footage to edit if we want to have the videos ready in time."

He gave me a startled glance. "We do? But the camera…"

"We do. I uploaded everything while you explained the situation to Lara. Just in case they took the camera."

Daniel yanked me into a hug. I only just kept from overbalancing into the gap between the seats at the force of it. If not for his leg, I would have let him pull me into his lap. As it was, I patted his back then kissed his cheek.

"Come on, time's wasting."

I slipped out of the van's cab and past the curtain into the living area. Daniel followed on my heels, using the kitchen counter to keep most of his weight off his broken leg with practiced ease.

We spent the next several hours poring over the footage for any sign we could have prevented today's attack. Daniel pointed out a lens flare and strange distortions in the sound and light that I couldn't easily explain.

He claimed they showed paranormal interference with the equipment. That it meant our activities agitated Higgs' spirit. We'd been in the barn all day, feeding Higgs our living energy, according to Daniel.

Yesterday, I might have doubted him, but considering my experiences in the past twenty-four hours, I felt a prickle of dread instead.

"We upset him?"

Daniel nodded. "It seems clear he hates trespassers. Access to so much living energy to feed on must have strengthened him. It's up to us to stop him now."

"We will. I can't say how, yet, but we will. We just have to figure out what he wants. You know, other than bloody, violent vengeance on the living."

Daniel's hand on my shoulder was a welcome comfort.

"I won't let him harm you. We will figure this out."

"But not tonight." I yawned. A glance at the clock revealed it was well past midnight. "We should call it a night if we plan to keep our appointment with Annette and Evie."

We got into bed together and I took comfort in Daniel's warmth at my back and his strong arms around me. Neither of us suggested doing anything more than sleeping after the day we'd had, I was in no state of mind for sex.

We overslept in the morning. Daniel rushed to prepare for filming Annette's interview.

She sent me a text moments before our scheduled video chat. For a moment I worried she intended to back out on us. She was our best lead to uncover the reason behind Frank Higgs' lingering presence.

The message was just checking if we were ready for her, lucky for us. I replied that we were.

Moments later Daniel had the call pulled up on his monitor. He made it full screen and unlocked a swiveling mount to angle the screen of one editing monitor toward the camera. He hit the record button on a screen capturing program he'd explained he liked to use for remote interviews.

My job was filming our side of the interview. I had his spare camera set up on a tripod to capture him against the privacy screen he used to cover the sleeping area when filming inside Vanessa.

"Hello, can you see me all right?" Annette sat beside an elderly woman in a wheelchair. Natural light flooded the room and washed out the colors a little. Daniel would want to correct the color balance and lighting for the final cut.

Look at me picking up on filmography. If that was even a thing. I thought it might be.

"Hello," Daniel greeted Annette warmly. "I'm so glad you and your mother could take the time to talk with us today."

"We're happy to help your investigation in any way we can." Annette preened. "Mother was a young girl when her Uncle Frank died. It was a real tragedy."

"It was." Daniel nodded and gave her a sympathetic smile. "You told me your mother kept her journals from that time, correct?"

"That's right. Her mother taught the girls their letters so they could help keep records for the farm. The journal was for Mom to practice. I thought they might interest you. A few entries from the months leading up to and following Frank's death in particular.

"I've scanned the relevant entries and attached them to an email. You can refer to them later, but if you'd like I can read some to you today? Mom loves it when I read to her about her childhood. She gets confused these days, so the reminders sometimes help her."

"I'd love to listen with her, then. And Evie, if you remember any details not written in the journal, please share them with us," Daniel addressed the frail woman at Annette's side.

"Oh, she doesn't remember much these days, Dan, she's ninety-five and suffers from dementia."

"I see."

"Yes, well. Let's begin, shall we? I read through the year of my great-uncle's death and found a few entries, that in hindsight, may shed some light on what happened. Keep in mind, this account is a young child's perspective. Mother was only eight years old, here's what she wrote." Annette opened an aged journal with several paper markers sticking out between the pages. She flipped to the first marked entry and read.

*January 24, 1932,*

*I heard Uncle F arguing with mother again after church. Not sure why they yell so much. Mother says uncle worries about the farm.*

*Father says F is a sanctimonious "B" word. Mother says those words aren't for children. I hope they stop fighting.*

*Uncle F forbid Aunt C and the girls from visiting so I can't ask Lettie what's going on. Lettie knows everything.*

*Last time I saw her, she told me her father is angry because my father was trying to get the milk without buying the cow. Whatever that means. We have so many cows, I'm not sure why Uncle F wants to buy more.*

*When I asked him about buying cows, father laughed. He told me that milk prices are so dreadful he had half a mind to sell his share of the farm and move west. I hope we don't. I would miss Lettie and everything here.*

*April 6, 1932,*

*Uncle F went out of town to trade some bulls. Aunt C brought the girls to visit. Lettie says we need to change bulls sometimes so that the calves will be healthier.*

*I guess that's a good thing. I like playing with the calves.*

*Lettie says our bull is as mean as Satan's teeth, so I hope Uncle F will get a nicer one. That would be good. The cows would be happier. Lettie says happy cows make more milk. If the cows are happy, maybe we won't have to move west.*

*Lettie says Uncle F is still angry at my father. She thinks it's because he's too nice to her mother. I don't care how nice he is. I miss my cousins.*

*Everyone in town says we play so well together we could be sisters. Sometimes I think we even look like sisters. I miss them.*

*August 7, 1932,*

*Lettie told me in Sunday school that Uncle F hit her mother. It scared her. He was screaming something about cuckoos in his nest.*

*I don't know why he was so angry about a bird. Aunt C didn't come to church this week. I hope she is okay and she can bring Lettie to visit again soon. Mother says not to worry, it will all work out for the best. Pastor T says all things work together for good.*

*August 10, 1932*

*Uncle F died. Father says we are moving into the big farmhouse soon. Aunt C will stay there too. I know I should feel sad, but I'm also glad he can't hurt Aunt C anymore.*

*Now I get to live with Lettie, just like sisters. Pastor T won't read Uncle F's final rites. Lettie says he can't rest in peace because he killed himself. Does that mean he'll be a ghost? I don't want him to haunt us. I hope he goes to rest.*

"That's the ones I wanted to share." Annette shut the time-worn journal, set it aside, then folded her hands primly in her lap. "So you see? It sounds like my great-uncle suspected his wife and my grandfather of having an affair. I can't confirm whether there was substance to those accusations, but the man had a mean streak and an issue with grandfather."

"Sounds like it." Daniel looked grim.

As well he might. My stomach roiled at learning Frank had been a violent man in life too. Somehow, that made everything seem more ominous. And it was up to Daniel and I to stop him from hurting anyone else.

# FORTY-ONE

## *Dan*

After talking to Annette I was ready to confront Frank. He'd had a clear problem with his wife and brother-in-law. The journal bore out what we already suspected about Frank's motives.

We had run into dead ends with Frank and Elmer's other descendants. They were either dead or knew nothing more about the events surrounding Frank's death. The only person left to ask about the details was Frank himself.

Around noon, Jane texted that Ben had come through surgery and was stable in the hospital, now. It looked like he would make it. I felt profound relief at the prognosis. If I'd caused an innocent's death because I'd drawn a ghost's ire I wasn't sure how I would cope with it.

I left a message with Tabitha to have Karen get back to me about how to use the information we'd gathered. Then Chad and I spent the rest of the day editing footage.

By the time Karen called me back the next day, we'd submitted the video for this week for the Goodman family's approval and made a solid dent in a first pass on next week's video too. I still needed to add in some FX and clean up the audio, but that could wait.

I answered Karen's call on the first ring, not even caring that it made me look over-eager.

"So, what have you found for me, Daniel?" Karen asked.

"I can't confirm the veracity, but according to a contemporaneous journal, Higgs suspected his wife of having an affair with his brother-in-law. The two of them both worked the family farm, but Higgs seemed to think Goodman was overstepping boundaries there too."

"Good start, what else?" she demanded.

"He took out his frustration with the situation on his wife."

"I see. So it is probable then, that this spirit is seeking vengeance for perceived wrongs done to him."

"I suppose," I agreed with her assessment. "What does that mean, as far as putting him to rest?"

"It means you need to give him justice, redress of his grievances."

"Um, he seems to have moved way beyond forgiving and moving on when he started attacking people who work for his sister's descendants," I pointed out.

"Did I say anything about forgiveness? No, convince the spirit his vengeance is complete. Let him believe that he killed the man he attacked, did he?"

"No, looks like he will survive," I relayed the news.

"Well, you're an actor—act," Karen suggested acerbically. "Time passes differently for the spirits. Tell your apparition he succeeded in his act of vengeance. Get him to believe what he wants to believe. Once he fulfills his purpose, his hold on this world may dissipate."

"Don't we have to, like, find his remains and sanctify them or something?" I asked.

"Oh, are you turning priest on me now? That would be a shame," Karen snarked. "No. We aren't exorcists. We are about giving the dead peace, not forcing them to cross over against their will."

"So you want me to give a murderous old man peace?" I asked.

"Yes," she confirmed.

"I'll see what I can do." I sighed.

"Call me with your results. Oh, and Daniel?"

"Yeah?" I asked warily.

"If you insist on filming at least take precautions not to get anyone else killed."

"I'll keep that in mind," I muttered.

Karen sighed, then she hung up on me.

"So, what now?" Chad watched my conversation with Karen with intense interest.

"Now we try to contact Frank."

By the time we parked beside the barn and got our gear organized, it was mid-afternoon. I directed Chad to get the gear we needed, and we ventured inside to set up.

The bales of straw from our first day of filming still sat near the now bloodstained ladder. In Monday's commotion, someone had shoved them aside, but they remained untainted by Ben's blood.

While Chad got my backup cameras set up on their tripods to film multiple angles of our attempt at communication, I pulled out the supplies I needed. My spare digital camera, my cell phone, and the IR camera were all training on the spot, then Chad adjusted the lighting kit.

I adjusted my EM meter. Then set up a mic to pick up and amplify any EVP. Chad had seen those before, so he didn't comment as I arranged them.

When he saw me pull out an Ouija board, though, he laughed. "Are you serious?"

"Sometimes they work. If Frank has something he needs to get off his chest, why not give him an easy way to tell us?"

"You are serious." Chad shook his head. "He tried to kill a man yesterday, Daniel. What about this situation makes you think he wants to sit down and give us a civil interview?"

I shrugged. It was more a hope than any real conviction on my part. And events around his death might have pissed off Frank, but the goal was to figure out what he wanted. This might be the best way to give him the chance to vent without violence. He'd already proven capable of interacting with the physical world.

"Can't hurt to ask." I favored Chad with a lopsided grin. He looked unappeased, but neither did he tell me what a terrible idea it was, so seize the day and all that.

"Are you ready?" I asked when Chad stopped fussing over the last light stand and returned to the cameras.

"We're rolling," he said, when he had gone to each one, I presumed to hit record.

"Frank, buddy, if you're listening, we're here to talk to you. We're here to tell the world your story. About how those closest to you betrayed you. They tried to take everything from you, didn't they?"

The temperature in the barn dropped.

"Did it just drop about a million degrees in here?" Chad demanded, he continued to man the camera, though, so points for dedication. "Dan?"

"The meter says it dropped about eight degrees, yeah." I read off the display as I held it up for the camera's benefit. "Frank?"

The digital display on my EVP recorder jumped and bounced as a barely discernible scratchy voice spoke.

"What was that?" Chad demanded.

"He's here!" I watched Chad's reaction, but he didn't show signs of bolting yet. I rewound and played back the EVP. Even listening close, I didn't catch what Frank had said. Just a burst of sound. I rewound again, played it back at half speed

219

"Betrayed." The tinny voice played through the speakers, hard to discern. I replayed it again—louder, and a touch slower. The single word sounded clearer this time. "Betrayed."

"Your brother-in-law betrayed you, right, Frank? With your wife? They went behind your back. Isn't that what happened?"

Another burst of EVP. I backed up to replay it. EVP was a pain to decipher.

"Murder."

"Dan?" Chad asked, he shuffled his feet anxiously.

"Whose murder, Frank? Can you tell us what happened? Move the pointer for us?" I gestured at the board I'd set up on the straw bale.

For a long moment nothing happened. I was considering putting my hand on the pointer. Channeling spirits fell outside my wheelhouse, but it should make it easier for Frank to interact with the object if he had a living intermediary.

Before I could touch the pointer, it flew between letters. I read them off to Chad as Frank paused on each one for a fraction of a second.

"S-T-O-L-E-T-H-E-F-A-R-M."

"What?" We took a moment to puzzle out what he'd spelled.

"Stole the farm?" Chad sounded perplexed by the words.

"That's it! That's what we've been missing, Frank, did you kill yourself?"

The pointer flew to the words printed at the bottom. "No."

"Were you killed? By your brother-in-law?"

The plastic moved to the 'yes'.

"They plotted against you to steal the farm that had been in your family for generations. That's the wrong you have been working so hard to correct all these years? The farm belongs to the Higgs family, not the Goodmans. That's what you've been trying to fix?"

The plastic pointer practically vibrated in place over the printed word 'yes'. The ghost's rage was palpable around us.

"How can we help you find peace, Frank?" I watched, knowing we were close to the answer, as the pointer moved again.

"Y-O-U-C-A-N-D-I-E," I read dutifully.

Chad mouthed the letters as I spoke them aloud, trying to sound out the message. Then, as the pointer landed on the final letter, several things occurred at once.

"You candies?" Chad said, sounding confused for a moment. "No, not candy… you can die!"

Chad's eyes widened in fear. My expensive lighting rig surged impossibly bright and then shattered with the pop of bulbs bursting in unison. The yoke we'd hung on the wall crashed to the ground with an echoing thud.

In the darkness, Frank sucked all the remaining warmth from the room. My breath frosted the air in front of me. The interior of the barn was almost dark in the fading light of evening and as frigid as a midwinter midnight.

"Dan, we have to get out of here." Chad dove for me, throwing my arm over his shoulder to support my weight as we ran for the exit. I just had time to snatch up the cell phone I'd propped up to get a closeup of the board before he dragged me away.

Frank Higgs manifested, a faded transparent version of who he'd been in life. He stood between us and the exit wielding a bloody pitchfork and laughing maniacally. We were about to die.

I pushed Chad behind me—it was my fault he was even in this mess, maybe I could buy him time to escape from the menacing apparition.

"Frank, we're here to help you, buddy." I raised a hand in appeasement.

The one with the cell in it, hoping to catch his image on video, despite the lack of lighting. My phone was still recording, it was possible the camera could pick out the soft glow of ghostlight on his form where it floated in midair. Was it morbid to think if I was facing death anyway, I might as well memorialize the event on my channel? Probably.

That would guarantee me loads of hits. Until the community guidelines got the video removed. I seemed to recall they frowned on explicit violence, even if a ghost was the indisputable perpetrator. What a way to go.

While I contemplated the PR of being stabbed by a murderous ghost, Frank lowered his weapon and charged. A shriek of EVP came through my speakers, and I was glad my voice recorder was still recording from where I'd abandoned it. At a guess, I figured Frank was screaming something to the effect of, "Die, scum."

I braced myself to face my death like a man and buy Chad time to escape.

"Wait!" Chad yelled, stepping around me to face the ghost, hands raised in a placating gesture. "Don't kill us, we can help you. We can prove that Goodman stole everything from you. He ruined you, but we can ruin him right back. Wipe him out of local legend. Raise your name back up over the farm. That's the justice you seek, right?"

The spirit flickered, wavering in the air a few feet from where I stood.

"It's simple. All we have to do is expose him for the thief and murderer he was. We have the proof right here. That's what Dan, and I have been recording these past weeks, the evidence of Elmer's wrongdoing. He ruined you. And once we tell the world, we'll ruin him. You'll have your revenge. You just have to let us live to publish the story."

The ghost wavered, not seeming to believe us.

"He's right, let us go and we'll tell the world what Elmer did to you. To Higgs Dairy. He won't get away with it anymore, Frank. We won't let him. We can prove he wronged you."

Some part of the ghost must have believed us. Or he might just need someone to know his version of events, because he faded away. The barn's ambient temperature warmed back to usual. Chad and I stood there alone, side by side in the dim interior of the barn. We exchanged looks as a final crackling burst of EVP came through the speakers.

I scrambled for the recorder to see what he'd said. Frank's parting words were, "prove it."

# FORTY-TWO

## *Chad*

"Oh, my god! You just almost got us both killed, you psychopath," I accused. I was still a touch freaked out.

"How was I to know he'd try to kill us?"

"Hmm, I don't know, perhaps the fact he tried to kill someone yesterday might have clued you in!"

"Granted. But we got through to him. Isn't that what truly matters?"

"What truly matters is not taking stupid risks and getting ourselves killed, Dan."

Daniel waved away my concern and hopped over to where he'd propped his crutches against the wall prior to filming. From there he moved around collecting the recording equipment we'd set up before Frank almost murdered us.

"Daniel?"

"What?" His calm infuriated me.

Did he not realize his obsession with getting the scoop on the ghost had almost gotten us both killed? I'd always thought the persona in front of the camera was separate from the real him. The Daniel I was falling for wouldn't be so cavalier about putting our lives at risk.

Dan the social media personality would, though. Maybe the two weren't as separate as I'd begun to think.

"Shouldn't we get out of here?"My voice pitched higher, with an edge of hysteria, and I hated it.

"I doubt he has the energy to appear again so soon. I just want to grab our gear so we can edit the footage. Did you see how awesome that looked?"

"You're happy about how that went?" I was ready to break. The past hour had not been awesome—far from it. It was almost like he hadn't just experienced the same series of terrifying events as I had.

"Yeah?"

"Dan, we almost died." I resisted the urge to grab his shoulders and shake some sense into him.

"Yeah, but we didn't. I can't wait to see how amazing this segment turns out. This is shaping into the best Hauntastic Haunts yet. Come on." Dan continued to gather his stuff.

I helped him, because hell if I would let him spend one more minute in that barn than we had to. We put the gear away in stony silence. An hour of seething to myself while I broke down and carried the equipment for Dan to stow did nothing to improve my mood.

Dan noted my irritation and kept his mouth shut, but as usual he wore his enthusiasm on his sleeve. A trait I didn't find quite so lovable in this context. He was maddening.

When we'd put everything away we climbed inside the van to drive back down to the farmhouse. No way in hell was I sleeping so close to Frank's ghost. I knew what I had to do.

I wasn't cut out for risking life and limb to get the best camera angle possible. Dan had shown more concern with filming than with the fact Higgs was bearing down on him with a deadly weapon. A weapon he'd already used to put one man in the intensive care unit.

"Want to text Lara about dinner?" Dan asked me with blithe indifference. As though we'd completed a typical day's work. He was grinning at his phone while he scrolled through footage from our confrontation with Frank.

"I can't do this."

Resolute, I gripped the steering wheel and stared straight ahead. I didn't want to see his disappointment.

"Do what, exactly?" Daniel stopped fiddling with his phone. His full attention turned on me.

"I am not cut out to take threats from ghosts in stride. You seem to get off on the thrill, I guess that's something I always knew about you, but I don't. I seriously thought you might die. And I can't handle that."

"Are you quitting?"

"Yeah, Dan. I'm quitting." I forced myself to meet his gaze.

Daniel pressed his lips together in a thin line. "And does that mean you're also breaking up with me?"

"Yeah." I squared my shoulders. "For now. We can try to be friends. But I need time to wrap my head around the fact that ghosts exist before I can accept the fact that my boyfriend is bound and determined to become one."

"I'm not," he protested.

"Well, you sure could have fooled me. The way you acted back there? Like it was no big deal if you died? Not okay. And another thing, you said you insulated the van against ghosts, so why didn't we take any precautions before filming? Did you seriously risk our lives to get a better camera shot?"

"No, I wouldn't put you at risk on purpose, Chad. You've got to believe that. To be honest, I've never communicated with a ghost this powerful before. Or this angry. Never with such clarity, anyway. You've seen the show. This is the strongest spirit I've encountered. I'll take precautions going forward. Salt or whatever. I'll ask Karen what safeguards she recommends. Give me another chance?" he pleaded.

I wanted to. I liked Daniel. More than I should after what he'd just done.

But the past few weeks with him had upended everything I thought I understood about the world and I needed breathing space. Space that I couldn't get if I stayed with him. Stuck in a tiny van without even the distance of the divider between our bunks anymore.

"I'm sorry, but I need space to think about things, Dan. Call Karen to help handle this, please. You're in over your head."

I bit my tongue. Forced myself not to tell him that I didn't want him to die. That would be as much as declaring my feelings for him, something I wasn't about to do in the middle of breaking things off. That would just be cruel.

Daniel looked upset, so I rushed through the rest of what I needed to say. "I'll pack my stuff and go. Don't worry about me. I remember seeing that Greyhound stops at the gas station. I'll get Lara to take me to the bus terminal in town.

"And I'll email you the release forms and stuff I have lined up for the next couple of filming sites we talked about using. You can use whatever footage you have of me, no problem. I've already filed my signed release to that effect and an NDA with the other contracts in the file on your desktop, so you know where to find them."

"Don't go." Daniel's fingers on my arm made it hard to stick to my guns. He sounded so genuine. Like he wanted me as much as I wanted him. But I was making the right choice.

Even accepting this job had been ridiculous. An impulsive decision that could only ever prove a terrible plan. Jumping into a life of following my celebrity crush around the country on a whim had to be the worst idea I'd ever had. I was too young for a mid-life crisis.

I could only blame it on the shock of losing my steady, stable job. But I'd come back to my senses. It was time to put my life back onto the steady, stable track I'd always known I should follow.

I was more than qualified for any number of professional roles and as soon as I could hop a bus back to Connecticut I'd prove it.

Early in our relationship, Daniel had teased me for being too buttoned down. I'd heard that before. I was too serious, too much like a boring middle-aged office drone. Well, maybe that was what I was acting like, but boring office drones didn't get chased by vengeful spirits, so that suited me just fine. I walked away.

# FORTY-THREE

## *Dan*

Vanessa had a vacant air when I got back from dinner with Jane to find all traces of Chad's presence erased. Lara had agreed to take Chad to the bus station in town with no questions asked. They'd left in a hurry to catch the evening bus out of town. That fast, the best thing to ever happen to me, both professionally and personally, ended.

Served me right for putting the show first. I should have taken precautions to protect us once I suspected what we were dealing with. Instead, I'd let the thrill of discovery run away with me.

No amount of sitting around feeling sorry for myself would bring Chad back. The best way to honor my time with him would be to make the episodes he'd helped me create perfect.

Over dinner, Jane had given me verbal approval on the Haunted History webisode I'd sent to her and Lara that morning. As soon as she sent me an email, so I had a written record of their approval, I uploaded the file to my channel and scheduled the release for Saturday.

I worked through the night to piece together the two episodes about the haunting. Over the following days, I buried myself in my work. When I deemed the videos ready, I sent copies of the finished products to the Goodmans to approve. Then I crashed hard.

I received no word from Chad in the week following his abrupt departure. He'd sent me the files he'd promised, and that was that. I spent an inordinate amount of time staring at the bright coloring pages he'd left taped to his cabinets. The reminder of his presence made my heart ache with longing, but I couldn't bring myself to tear them down yet.

Jane and Lara approved the first video describing the haunting. Leon's story, with Chad's flashback scene, came out perfect. It was brilliant. I had expected no trouble with that one. It contained nothing the family might find objectionable.

They raised concerns with the last webisode's content. As well they might, since the ghost had accused their ancestor of cheating with his wife then murdering him and covering it up to steal his farm from him. The only real evidence to support Frank's assertions were the vague journal entries of a child.

The preponderance of evidence inclined me to believe the ghost, he might not be blameless, but his story added up. His desire for vengeance had to be strong for it to keep him tethered here through the decades. Decades of biding his time and growing stronger from the living energy of the agricultural enterprise he'd spent his life nurturing.

When I got the response from the Goodmans requesting I edit out the bits about murder and theft, it was no surprise. I wished Chad was there to negotiate with them.

He excelled at talking people around. A real peacemaker. He'd know just what to say to convince them to let me air the footage.

There was no good way to cut the brilliant footage we'd risked life and limb to capture that cast the family in a positive light. Chad could tell me whether the contract he'd written would allow me to get away with airing the webisode, anyway.

I wouldn't ask him, though. He'd laid out a clear boundary. He needed space.

I refused to push myself on him when he'd made his desires clear. No matter how much I wanted to hear his voice. I put off discussing their concerns with the Goodmans by calling Karen back.

"I was beginning to suspect an angry spirit finally caught up with you," she snarked in greeting.

"Haha," I drawled, not in the mood for her barbed banter. "I'm still alive, no thanks to your advice."

"What advice was that?" she asked.

"Talking the ghost into leaving," I muttered.

"That is not what I advised. I instructed you to communicate with the spirit to determine what was preventing him from moving on."

"He wants revenge on a dead man," I complained.

"Well, that won't be easy to arrange then, will it?"

"No, it won't," I agreed. "What do I do now?"

"Now? The spirit seeks vengeance. Make him believe he has achieved that end, and it will loosen his hold on the place," Karen suggested. "That should render it easy for the spirit to move on with no need for your further intervention."

"How do you propose I accomplish that?"

"You're resourceful, I'm sure you'll think of something." Karen hung up on me before I got another word in. Great. Well, all I had to do now was figure out a way to convince Frank that he'd had his bloody revenge. How hard could that be?

# FORTY-FOUR

## *Chad*

In retrospect, I should never have given notice on my apartment when I took the job with Dan. Another point against ever acting impulsively again. Now I found myself stuck staying on the pullout couch in Kay's finished basement while I searched for a new job.

The situation was uncomfortably similar to being back in my senior year of high school. It was a nice basement, complete with en suite bathroom, and no one bothered me when I was down there, at least.

Kay gave me the space I'd said I needed. I just couldn't shake the feeling I was intruding on them.

Like now, I had my laptop set up at their breakfast bar, perusing job listings in the middle of their morning routine. I got a new email notification.

Around me, Kay and her husband were making breakfast while my nieces complained about having to go to their day camps. Sadie had soccer and basketball, Zoe had swimming, art, and soccer.

"Why can't we stay home with Uncle Chad?" Sadie wheedled. Zoe clung onto my arm, gazing up at me with big round pleading eyes. I didn't know how Kay could bring herself to deny them anything. Those kids played dirty with their puppy-dog eyes.

"Because you made a commitment to your teams, and Uncle Chad is busy. You can play with him tonight."

"But, Mom, Uncle Chad doesn't mind, do you?" both kids chorused. I gave my sister a pleading glance. I hated to be the bad guy, but she was right, I needed to find a new job pronto. If for no other reason, to get my mind off Daniel and be able to afford my own place.

"I said no," Kay repeated.

"Just this once?" Sadie wheedled.

"Your mother said no, now eat your food." Brad turned from where he was cooking to fix the kids with a hard look. They both turned back to their toast, grumbling about how their parents never let them have any fun.

A few minutes later, Brad brought over a skillet full of eggs. He slid some onto each of five plates, including the two covered in Sadie and Zoe's toast crumbs.

He and Kay stood on the other side of the breakfast bar with their food. I skimmed the new email. The request to schedule an interview with a prestigious company shouldn't make my stomach roil.

I should feel thrilled to move forward with my career, not disappointed that it would mean locking the door on my brief foray into spontaneity.

I shut the laptop and slid it off to the side. Without a word, I took the plate Kay offered to me. She must have misinterpreted my expression. "You'll find a job that's the right fit, Chad, give it time," she assured me.

"Yeah, thanks," I mumbled, feeling like an intruder at their family breakfast.

Kay reached across the counter and squeezed my hand. "You're very welcome, we love having you here. Take all the time you need."

I knew that. Kay swore I was no bother. It was nice to see my nieces again. I'd missed them while I was working with Dan, short-lived as that diversion had proven to be.

"Please do. Stay a while—stay forever. It's been great having a live-in babysitter who is too guilty to refuse us or accept pay," Brad joked.

"Whatever, man, my nieces are perfect angels. I enjoy hanging out with them." I pulled Zoe into a side hug and she beamed up at me. The kids were a handful, but now that I wasn't working most evenings, I loved having more time with them.

"I'm so glad you think so, brother dearest, because some friends invited Brad and I to a wedding out of town this weekend. We were hoping you would stay here with the kiddos while we go?"

"Sure, Kay, I'd love to watch your spawnlings all weekend."

Sadie and Zoe giggled at me calling them spawnlings. They liked my humor. Kay flashed me a somewhat guilty expression.

"We'll owe you, and we'll leave pizza money and some cash in case you need anything while we're away."

"No problem, Kaybar, I've got this."

"I'm sure you do, Chadrick."

We stuck our tongues out at each other like we were kids ourselves. Sadie and Zoe giggled again. Brad shook his head at our antics, but he kissed my sister on the temple, his affection for her clear as day.

I didn't mind giving my sister and her husband a break to go on dates. It gave me time to bond with the kids. If there was one certainty in my life anymore, it was that I loved being an uncle.

Time with Kay's kids provided a welcome distraction from the mess I'd made of things. Much as I'd left to have my own space, being surrounded by family eased my heartache. Even if my stuff kept moving when I wasn't looking. I figured it was just Kay tidying up around the house. Or the kids.

Although they all said they enjoyed having me, I couldn't get past the sense I was taking advantage of my sister's hospitality.

We didn't talk much more that morning. Brad and Kay ate fast, then chivied the kids into finishing their food. The house erupted into chaos as they gathered together the stuff they needed for a day at their various camps. By then they were running late, so the morning culminated in a mad rush out the door.

I stayed in my seat, trying not to get in the way.

I listened to the fading sounds of their voices as they piled into their van and drove away. They left me all alone facing another day in a house that loomed around me, huge and empty. A creaking noise upstairs distracted me, just the house settling.

Brad's parents watched the kids between camp and the end of the workday. Kay and Brad spent long hours at their restaurant. They went in early and stayed late. So I'd gotten used to all the sounds the empty house made.

So far, I'd spent the long lonely days putting out job applications and browsing apartment listings. I should be worrying about my stagnating bank balance.

Instead, the gnawing concern that kept me awake at night had nothing to do with my finances. Or even the sudden revelation that ghosts were real, and potentially dangerous. No, my concerns were more vapid and mundane. I was moping about a boy.

I couldn't get my mind off the fact I seemed more underfoot in Kay's spacious suburban mini-mansion surrounded by family, than sharing a tiny van with Daniel. He saw me as useful and competent.

More than that, we'd forged a connection I'd never experienced with anyone else. I missed him. Missed the routine we'd fallen into together, the work we'd done. I even missed the cozy quiet of living in Vanessa.

I stood to go adjust the thermostat on the living room wall above the bookshelf. I took care not to knock Mom's urn from its pride of place among the family photos Kay kept on the top of the shelving unit.

The house was always colder without the family present. I'd taken to wearing sweaters against the chill.

As Dan's assistant, each day was a new adventure. It was a far cry from the staid routine I'd made for myself up to now. Daniel's world didn't have stability, but I was thinking that stability might be overrated.

Would it be so terrible to cut loose, be like Dan, and live a little? Act like a twenty-something pursuing my dreams instead of letting life pass me by.

Besides, Daniel needed someone to keep him from taking giant needless risks. If he planned to face down angry ghosts, I didn't want him to be doing it alone.

His problem was that he didn't think about taking precautions. Sure, I enjoyed his spontaneity as a fan of his show, but as someone who cared about him, it worried me.

I wanted to be with him. But I'd seen this weekend's webisode. The Goodman Dairy Haunted History. He'd postponed the weekly live chat and posted an announcement that I'd quit. I had enough self preservation not to read any of the posts bashing me for leaving him in a lurch and lumping me in with all his other failed PAs.

Part of me wanted a clean break. I even considered deleting my Redherring99 account. With no income, I'd have to cancel my monthly support for the channel.

I didn't want to, though. I wanted to go back to Daniel. Figure out a way forward with him. If only it wasn't already too late.

# FORTY-FIVE

*Dan*

I needed a distraction from feeling lonely and sorry for myself. So I posted that I was doing a livestream to answer fan questions in a few hours. I'd skipped last week's scheduled live chat and postponed the one I should have done last night when the latest Hauntastic Haunts video aired.

It was a Sunday evening, so I expected low turnout. Even though some of my fans were clamoring to know what was up with me after I hadn't been able to gather the motivation to do two live chats in a row.

It had been eleven days since Chad left. Not that I was keeping track. That would be pathetic over a fling that lasted less than a month, no matter how momentous it had seemed at the time.

I lost myself in the final edits the Goodman family had requested. The affair was fine, Frank's violent jealousy could stand as a matter of historical record. Any hint Frank's suicide had covered up a homicide had to go.

That meant cutting and editing the amazing footage Chad and I had captured on our final day together. I cut the footage with a voice-over track to suggest that Frank had killed himself because he imagined his brother-in-law was trying to steal his life.

I implied he'd lost all hope of recovering with the farm failing around him and an unfaithful wife. Defeated, Frank gave up. It was his jealousy of Elmer that had held him here.

That might even be the truth. From what I'd uncovered, Elmer was the more sympathetic character in the story. It wasn't impossible that Frank's jealousy had driven events rather than Elmer taking matters into his own hands.

So, despite my personal attachment to the last scene Chad had filmed, I edited and cut and erased any hint of a smear on the Goodman name. Then I sent the altered file to Lara and Jane with a request to get back to me ASAP.

The first videos had garnered a positive reception so far. Leon's story and Chad's flashback scene came out great. I'd gotten an unprecedented number of requests for the next haunting video to drop.

Loads of comments appeared on the actual video. Some new subscribers. A few messages from my patrons begged to know what I'd found and asked about Chad's sudden departure from Hauntastic Haunts.

My fans liked him as much as I'd expected them to. It had sucked to announce he'd quit. In all likelihood, I would receive questions about him in my live AMA in a few minutes.

It hadn't occurred to me until that moment, as I was logging in to start the live feed, that I'd have to field questions about him. And pretend my heart wasn't breaking. Too late to change that now.

"Hello, hello, to my crew, how is everyone?" I paused as responses scrolled past.

"Glad to hear most of you are doing well. Sorry to hear about your dog, Raf, I hope she's recovering from the surgery."

RadRaf: The prognosis looks good, I swear that dog would eat anything.

"Yeah, good thing you caught it so fast, magnets are nothing to mess around with."

*Drew has logged on.*

Drew: Sorry, I'm late. What did I miss?

"Oh, hey, Drew, glad you made it, I meant to message you, if I don't get back to you tonight, send me a reminder?"

Drew: Will do. How's the new PA working out?

I'd already ignored a barrage of messages in the chat asking about Chad.

No putting off the bad news then, I sighed.

"Seems that some of you missed my announcement. As you can see, I'm down a PA. Again. Chad had to move on to other career opportunities. He's fine. I know the teaser I put out mentioned a serious injury on our set, but it wasn't Chad. His absence is unrelated."

BriBri: Aw, what happened? You two were so cute together.

I resisted the urge to facepalm at her continued interest in my love life. "How many times do I have to tell you, it wouldn't be right for me to get involved with my assistant? Have you seen Vanessa? We live in close quarters. A relationship would be impossible with us living and working together like that."

If nothing else, my fling with Chad had proven that beyond any doubt.

BriBri: Then why so sad?

Drew: Is Chad leaving why you took down the bunk divider?

I glanced over my shoulder and bit off a curse. My recent funk was so all-consuming, I'd forgotten to pull the curtain across the sleep alcove before going live. I reached up to twitch it closed now, but the damage was done. Drew had already drawn Bri's attention to my oversight.

BriBri: OMG, did you sleep with him?

*Redherring99 has logged on.*

Good, it had been a while since my number one superfan had logged in, I'd started to worry that something had happened to him. Or that he'd lost interest in Hauntastic Haunts.

RadRaf: No judgment if you did, that boy was cute.

Drew: Too bad he left, you and Chad were #lifegoals

I was taking too long to reply. That would only fuel their speculation. Thank god Drew had given me a plausible excuse.

"The bed is unrelated to Chad. Just taking advantage of having Vanessa all to myself until I can hire a replacement. Not sure how I will replace Chad, though, he worked magic with the paperwork. If you guys know anyone who wants a minimum wage job following me around the country, send them my way."

I sipped from my empty mug to buy a moment to gauge their response. A few jokes, Drew wishing he was old enough to join me. The usual. I forced a weak laugh in reply as I set aside my cup.

"So, as much as I would love to wax poetic about the best PA to have ever PA'd, let's all respect Chad's privacy, okay, crew? What questions can I answer for you about the Goodman haunting?"

RadRaf: The teaser footage had sirens, was there an actual emergency?

"Good question, Raf, yeah, the spirit of Frank Higgs has a marked violent streak, as will become more obvious in next week's webisode. I won't wander into spoiler territory, but I will say there was no lasting harm done. No one died."

As always, Raf helped me steer the webcast back onto the proper track. I'd arranged this live chat to talk about the haunting, not wallow over Chad.

"This is one of the most active hauntings we've encountered on Hauntastic Haunts. I am so excited to share the final videos in the series with you all. We got some amazing footage, thanks to Chad's ability to keep his head under pressure. Like I said, the guy will be impossible to replace. But I digress, I think the webisode will speak for itself."

Apparently I couldn't get Chad out of my head or stop talking about him.

Drew: Are you calling in expert help?

RadRaf: A case for the professionals?

GhastLee: Medium time?

"Without getting into spoilers, I have called in a colleague to consult with on this one. They appear confident we can help the property owner give the ghost closure and get him to move on. I hope so. After the reception we got from the ghost, I couldn't reconcile leaving him here to do more harm.

"Which brings me to another point. Lara and Jane Goodman, who have been together for over a decade, have shown us amazing hospitality. They have been nothing but cooperative since we arrived. I can't speak well enough of Goodman Dairy.

"They are running quite the enterprise here in Vermont. So if you find yourself in the area, be sure to check out their business. They have amazing homemade ice cream and cheeses. You can tour the farm and get a glimpse behind the scenes of a working dairy. They even have a small petting zoo. You can feed the calves and some other small animals. Plus, they do milking demos so you can see how they used to do things before automation.

"And no, they aren't paying me to advertise, they are just that awesome. I like them. And I always love an opportunity to shout out LGBT+ business owners."

RadRaf: Would you rec the town?

Drew: Official rating?

"So, about the town, everyone acts welcoming everywhere I've been here. I'd recommend this place to anyone looking for a rural getaway. Five out of five rainbows, would visit again."

BriBri: How do you know the local businesses are LGBT+ friendly?

*Shit. Shit shit shit*, that had been a stupid slip up, and of course Bri would pick up on it. Nothing I said now would convince her I hadn't been dating Chad.

Panic made it hard to think of a reply. This whole livestream was a terrible idea. The plan was to distract myself from Chad leaving, not create more reminders of his absence.

Even worse, I couldn't even tell my internet friends how much I missed him. Not without opening a whole can of worms with speculation about any PA I hired going forward.

At the last moment Red threw me a lifeline. I could have kissed them. If they weren't an anonymous person on the internet who I would never meet IRL.

RedHerring99: Lots of rainbow flags in the storefronts?

"Yes, Red, just about everywhere I went had a pride flag or a flag decal. They even did one of the local crosswalks up in rainbow stripes. It was nice to see.

"So like I said, if you're in the area, check it out. And that's about all the time I have today, the next Goodman Dairy video will drop at the usual time next weekend. I can plan to do another live stream an hour after it goes live, if you all want?"

I smiled at the stream of likes and comments saying they would love that.

"Great, so we'll plan on it then. If I forget, I'm counting on you all to poke me with a reminder, okay?"

A few of them agreed, some of them sent laughter emojis because my lack of organization when I was between PAs was notorious.

It was why I always released my weekly webisode at the same time. Having a scheduled reminder was the only way I could stay on top of things. And even then it got dicey early on until my release schedule became ingrained in my routine.

If Chad was still around, he'd be sure to remind me and keep me on track. He'd handled those details with ease. Exactly what I needed in a PA and a partner.

Clearly, this livestream made an awful distraction technique since all I could think about was missing Chad.

"Right, I'll talk to you again next weekend then, hope you all have a hauntastic week!"

I cut the audio, then waited for final comments from everyone, goodbyes and well wishes sprinkled with hype for the next video. When that died down, I ended the stream and logged off.

I had three notifications in my messages. The first hit my inbox halfway through my livestream. Jane and Lara had approved my edits. I shot them a quick thank you.

The video was ready to go, so I marked it approved. I just needed to add in the opening and closing credits and do a final pass on the audio. That, and a final check to make sure everything was perfect before I uploaded it and scheduled the release.

I only had to film myself monologuing for the series wrap-up video now. Chad and I already filmed extra shots of the dairy and the barn to use as wrap video filler material. Then I'd be saying goodbye to Goodman Dairy.

Weird to think I'd be leaving behind the setting for most of my memories of Chad. How had he wormed his way so deep into my heart in so little time? I didn't want to confront that.

I turned back to my inbox. The second message was from Drew.

*Dan,*
*Thanks for your advice. I told the family what I knew about the haunting. You were right. It was the right thing to do.*

*Can I tell you a secret? I think you're the only person who will understand. If I'm overstepping, just ignore the rest of my message.*

*Here goes:*

*Toby was my boyfriend. Is that incredibly weird? I know he was a ghost, but we connected. He wasn't like the ghosts on Hauntastic Haunts.*

*I guess because he got a steady diet of my living energy, he seemed more real.*

*Anyway, I loved him. And now he's gone. It's been a few weeks since he's been at rest, and I'm all alone. I mean. Not all alone, I still have my family. But you're the first person who knows about me.*

*I guess I just wanted to say thanks for being open about who you are. You gave a lonely kid hope everyone isn't just blowing smoke when they say it gets better.*

*Seeing you every week makes me think it really can get better for me too.*

*Drew*

*PS: I know it's none of my business, but maybe we're sort of friends now? You seemed happy with Chad, and I couldn't help but notice how sad you seemed tonight. Misery loves company?*

*Now that he isn't working for you, you could reach out to him? Or not. I hope whatever made him leave, you two can stay in touch.*

*You seemed good together. Or was it just on screen chemistry? He made you smile.*

*Right, you can ignore the dating advice from the awkward teenager. I'm debating deleting this whole message now, so I'm just going to hit send before I chicken out. Bye.*

I smiled to myself. My interactions with Drew were the reason I'd decided early in my vlogging career to be open about my sexuality. Even if he was the only person I reached, he would make all this worthwhile.

And I knew he wasn't. I'd gotten similar messages over the years. It was a welcome reminder of my impact on the world.

I opened a new message to Drew. I found his mention of being in a relationship with the ghost alarming, but it was over if he'd put the spirit to rest. No point chastising the kid over a nonissue. I was there to support him, not judge him.

*Drew,*

*I think we can say we're friends. Solidarity, right? I'm proud of you for letting go of Toby to give him and his family peace. I know that couldn't have been easy for you.*

*There will be other boys. You won't be alone or lonely forever. And you've got me and the rest of the crew in your corner cheering you on, okay? I'm here for you if life gets you down, don't be afraid to reach out.*

*I appreciate your concern about Chad and I. He's a great guy and I wish him well. My career isn't conducive to pursuing a relationship right now.*

*My life is too erratic and nomadic, and that's okay. If I ever try to fit Mr. Right into my life, I will rope him into getting to know the crew, but for now that isn't my priority.*

*Since you mentioned relationships and happiness, I think you might need to hear this? You don't need a relationship to find happiness and fulfillment. There is more to life, okay? Like friendships.*

*I'm glad you reached out to me. Hope to hear from you again soon.*

*Hauntastically your friend,*
*Dan*

I sent the message and opened the last new one. From Redherring99. They rarely sent me direct messages like this. If they did, they kept their correspondence short and to the point. But at a glance, this message was longer.

Unlike most of my top tier supporters, Red divulged almost nothing personal. They were more of a silent lurker. I still didn't know for sure what pronouns they used.

I hoped they weren't messaging to tell me they would no longer be supporting the channel. They had stepped back their involvement of late. Ever since Chad became my PA, come to think of it.

The first word of the message made my heart feel like it might pound right out of my chest, it was addressed to Daniel, not Dan. The only person outside my family who called me by my full name was Chad.

This message had to be from him. Chad was Redherring99.

I wasn't sure whether to be glad he'd messaged me, or hurt that he'd kept the truth from me. I settled on glad. He'd told me he was a fan of Hauntastic Haunts, so it wasn't like he'd hidden anything important.

I braced myself before reading beyond my name at the top. This message might be his final rejection, or a lifeline for our relationship. Either way, I needed to face it head on.

*Daniel,*

*I've got to tell you something. I've missed you. More than I would have thought possible. It's only been days, but it seems so much longer.*

*I've debated whether to tell you this, but let me introduce myself.*

*Hi, Dan, it's me, Chad. I've been cyberstalking you ever since you started calling my direct line at Chorus Insurance to get me to handle your claims.*

*At first, I just followed you because of the novelty of your having a PA to sort out your insurance woes. That's not super common. I thought you must have a huge ego. But then I saw the show, and even though I was a skeptic, it appealed to me.*

*You have an authenticity that's so rare these days. You hooked me from the first grainy amateur video of you taking a dare to stay in a spooky abandoned house overnight.*

*I don't know why I'm writing you this. Or why I'm using my Redherring99 email to tell you. I guess because you deserve to know?*

*If you don't want me to follow you, after everything we shared, I can back off. I'll still keep up my monthly pledge as long as I can afford to, because I believe in what you are doing with Hauntastic Haunts.*

*You've built such a wonderful online community, I don't want to make you feel unsafe there by hanging around spying on you. But I figured I owed you an explanation before Red just ghosted you.*

*Anyway. Take care of yourself. I can't stand thinking about you putting yourself at risk to deal with ghosts all on your own. Please listen to Karen and try not to get yourself killed.*

*So, yeah, TL; DR Red is me, Chad. And we might have only been together IRL for a few weeks, but I'll never forget you or how you made me feel. Be safe.*

*No obligation to reply.*

*Love,*
*Chad*

That was a kick in the balls. He loved me? And this was how he told me? In a goodbye email. Screw that.

Ever since he made his abrupt departure, I'd been giving him the space he said he needed. I still had his number, and he'd contacted me first. I dialed.

The phone rang for so long I expected it to go to voicemail.

"Hello?" Chad's voice, even filled with caution, was music to my ears.

"Chad?" I almost didn't believe it was him on the line.

"Daniel, I, uh, didn't expect you to call. I guess you got my message?"

"Yeah, Red, I got your message."

There was a long silence.

"Why are you calling me?" he asked, was that a note of hope in his voice?

"Because, your message said you love me and you miss me. If I have any sliver of a hope of getting you to change your mind about leaving me, then I had to try. So. Is there?" I asked, heart in my throat at the possibility of rejection.

"Is there what?" he asked.

"Any chance we can make this work?" I swallowed hard.

"I don't know Daniel. It's true that I miss you, but I've got family here. Obligations. I don't know what I was thinking when I ditched them to follow you around like a lovesick teenager."

"You were thinking it would be worth it to follow your heart for once instead of always doing what you think you should," I argued my case, more than willing to fight for us. "That you were ready for an adventure."

"Life with you is that." He sounded so wistful. Like my life was some impossible dream far beyond his reach. This was not going well. How could I make him see that he could have the dream if he would just give himself permission?

"It isn't too late. You can come back."

"Of course it's too late. You already told the crew I left. And I've got a job offer and a lease I just need to sign."

"So, does that mean you haven't signed anything yet? No new apartment to sublet or job to quit?"

Chad sighed.

"Look," I pressed my case, "I get that you have reservations, but we fit together. Can I do anything to convince you to return to the show?"

Chad took a long time to reply. "I can't watch you put yourself in danger like you did that day, Daniel. Higgs could have killed you. Don't forget, I've seen all of your medical claims for all the accidents you have had on sets over the past few years. There are a freaking lot of them. Because you take stupid risks. If you keep running around half-cocked I worry one of these days, you won't walk away from one of these hauntings. I can't get involved with that."

I had no ready defense for that objection. He was right. I didn't always think before I acted. Sometimes I put getting the perfect shot or that bit of extra footage ahead of my safety.

"You're right. I shouldn't ask that of you. What if I make you my production manager?"

"What would that entail?" Chad sounded intrigued. At least, he didn't shoot it down right out of the gate. I might still salvage this situation.

"Whatever we decide it means, I'm making this up as I go along, to be honest."

Chad snorted. "I'd expect nothing else." He sounded amused, and fond.

"For a start, you would have to approve what we film. Help me plan safety precautions so nothing like what happened with Higgs happens to us or anyone on my set ever again. We can go meet with Karen in person for intensive training. Both of us can learn about safety precautions. The woman seems to think I'm her apprentice now, anyway. We might as well take advantage of her knowledge, since she is offering. So? Will you be my boss?"

"Partner," Chad countered.

"Huh?"

"Business partner. So we get equal say in the decision making."

"And equal stakes in the business," I insisted, perhaps prematurely since I'd only known the guy IRL for a month.

This was my livelihood I was offering him. But I'd always believed in going big or going home. And I loved him. Besides, Red was one of my most generous patrons. He'd paid his dues to Hauntastic Haunts.

"No. You keep the majority interest. Let me buy into the company. I have some savings set aside, I can afford to invest in you. I've already seen your accounts, living out of Vanessa means there isn't a ton of overhead for the business. It's a solid investment."

I preened at his praise of my business.

"But Hauntastic Haunts is your baby, you need to protect yourself if things don't work out between us. So, I'll crunch some numbers and make you an offer for a forty percent stake in the company. We can write up a contract as far as how we both get paid."

I cut him off before he could go into any more details. There was only one question I cared about the answer to. "Does that mean you'll come back? Live and work with me again?"

Chad paused, like he was considering. "Someone has to keep you from killing yourself out there, yeah, Daniel, I'll come back."

"I'm still at the dairy. Almost done here, thanks to you, we are ahead of schedule. So, if you can get here soon, we'll brainstorm a plan to put Frank to rest. End this haunting once and for all before we have to travel to the September haunting site. What do you say?"

"I'm watching my sister's kids this weekend, but once she gets home, I'll be on the next Greyhound."

"Promise?"

"Yeah, Daniel, I promise. I'll be there, don't do anything stupid without me."

"Okay. I will hold you to that. It sounds ridiculous, but Vanessa seems empty without you here."

Chad laughed. "I doubt that. But I must have gotten used to the close quarters because I feel like Kay's house is way too freaking big these days. Like there's something behind me, watching me."

That caught my attention. "Like there's another presence there?"

Chad paused, his response was contemplative. "Yeah, like that."

"What if there is? You said you have things you wanted to tell your mom, maybe she needed to hear them?"

"Yeah, I suppose. I should go check on the kids, I'll see you soon, Daniel."

"See you soon." As I hung up, hope fizzed like champagne bubbles under my skin. Chad was giving me another chance. This time I refused to screw things up with him.

# FORTY-SIX

## *Chad*

The end of my conversation with Daniel kept replaying through my mind. What if another presence did inhabit Kay's house? The strange noises, the stuff I kept misplacing. The sensation I wasn't alone when Kay's family left. Even the funky temperature fluctuations I'd noticed.

The door to the basement squeaked open to bump gently against the frame, like a breeze had caught it. The heater was on, and I had the bathroom vent running because I'd just taken a shower. Was it only air circulation causing the movement? It had to be, right?

I'd put the kids to sleep following pizza and a movie marathon. I was the only one on the main level.

"Mom?" I asked. Cold seemed to seep into the room, making me shiver. "If that's you, give me a sign?"

The baby monitor my sister still had set up in Zoe's room crackled on the counter at my elbow. I couldn't interpret the noise into any discernible words, but when I looked at the image, my heart almost climbed out of my chest.

A figure stood in the middle of the night vision image. I ran up the stairs like my life depended on it, terrified that there was someone in Zoe's room. Some threat to her safety.

I threw open her door, only to find my niece sleeping, peaceful in her bed. No sign of anyone else in the room. My heart still pounding with residual terror, I padded across the room to check on her.

Zoe was sound asleep. Her chest rose and fell in a soft, reassuring rhythm. I touched her cheek, to be sure. She snorted, flopped onto her belly and continued to sleep. She was fine.

I checked the room anyway, to be certain no one was hiding under the bed or in the closet. The windows remained locked, the curtains free of interlopers.

Reassured that I'd been imagining things, I went to check on Sadie too. She was also asleep. No monsters lurked in the shadows of her room.

Now I felt silly to have worried. I still checked to make sure Kay and Brad's room was secure, for good measure. Then I checked the main floor, making sure I'd remembered to lock everything tight.

For good measure, I armed the alarm system even though I wasn't going to bed yet. It would alert us if anyone tried to open a door or window.

Now my earlier panic seemed even more foolish. Better safe than sorry, even if I had spent the better part of an hour searching the house for a bogeyman.

At least the kids slept through my paranoia. Before Daniel, I would have dismissed the image on the monitor. Explained it away as radio interference from my laptop being too close or something.

The new me couldn't shake the sense that the kids and I were not alone in the house. I returned to my computer, still trying to shake off my trepidation. I slid back into my seat.

On the screen, my cursor was blinking over a text file I did not recall opening. At the top of the new file, a single line of text had appeared. The laptop was cool to the touch. Strange, since it ran warm most of the time.

Words I didn't remember typing made my heart beat fast again.

*I heard you. I love you, no matter what, Chad. Son or daughter, you'll always be my baby. I'm proud of you.*

Even though I'd investigated the entire house, I looked around as though someone might be playing a trick on me. Did I expect to find Kay hiding behind the counter? My sister would never be so cruel.

"Mom?" I asked, my voice close to breaking. I shivered in the sudden chill. More noise crackled through the monitor. I could have sworn it sounded like a yes.

"Mom, if that's you, I love you. I'm sorry I didn't tell you sooner. If only we'd had more time. I miss you so much. So you know, I'm done playing it safe. I want to do what makes me happy. It's what you wanted for us."

Another burst of monitor static, and this time I was certain it was a yes.

"I've got a boyfriend now. Sort of. I guess you overheard us talking? He's great. I know you'd love him. He gets me out of my comfort zone. He showed me ghosts are real, or we wouldn't be having this conversation.

"Anyway, I don't need you looking out for me anymore. You've waited long enough to find peace. I'm going to be okay, Mom. Kay and Brad have got their crap together and they are doing a fantastic job raising your grandkids. You know we'll always love you, but it's okay if you move on. I know Kay would agree. We'll always miss you, but we've got this."

The cursor on the screen blinked. A few more words appeared.

*Goodbye, Chad. I am proud of you, my son.*

The words I'd never thought I'd get to hear from her. A wash of icy cold moved over me, moving toward the urn on the bookshelf. The lights in the living room glowed too bright, a momentary blinding flash, before the chill dissipated. I saved the word file and waited a long time for anything else to happen. Nothing did. I suspected that nothing would.

My need for her had been what held my mother here and now that we'd gotten the closure I'd so desperately craved, she had left for good. I sent a text to Daniel about it, glad to have someone to talk to about the paranormal.

Kay wouldn't understand how much this had weighed on me. And she was as skeptical about the paranormal as I'd been before working with Daniel. He messaged me back within moments.

We chatted online for a few hours after that. Ages passed before I calmed enough to go to bed. Daniel stayed up with me, late into the night.

I felt lighter with the certainty that my mother accepted me. As though the burden of being a perfect son to make up for never telling mom my truth had lifted. I was free to choose my path now instead of trying to earn approval that had always been mine.

# FORTY-SEVEN

## *Dan*

I was like a kid on Christmas morning waiting for Chad's bus to arrive. It took all my limited self-restraint not to say screw it and drive straight to his sister's house two days ago. Right after he agreed to give me a second chance.

If it weren't for my broken leg still making long drives a problem, I'd have done it anyway. Although, it was just as well I'd held off on that. He was babysitting his nieces, and I wanted to do decidedly not PG things to him when I got him back in my clutches.

Thoughts of those things distracted me enough that I almost didn't notice the giant commercial bus pulling up to the front of the gas station that doubled as a bus stop.

Chad got out along with a handful of other passengers. The driver pulled their bags out from the storage compartment that ran along the length of the bus. I was out of the van and crutching my way toward him before I could think about it.

He met me halfway, dropping his bags and hugging me like we'd been apart for years instead of weeks. I clung to him, reveling in the warmth of his body in my arms. He was here. Really here.

I would not screw this up again. I could act cool, follow his lead. Chad kissed me and it took my breath away. All the passion and pent up longing we'd both felt translated into lips and tongues and hands on bodies. Until a sharp wolf-whistle drew my attention back to the existence of a world outside of his embrace.

We were standing in a gas station parking lot, in full view of an audience. I'd been honest when I said the town seemed accepting, but assholes could be anywhere. I knew better than to get carried away and lose awareness of my surroundings.

Chad came to the same realization. He stepped back to gather his bags. We got him and his stuff inside Vanessa. I relinquished the driver's seat to him, driving with my leg in a cast was a pain.

We headed back toward the Goodman place. We had time to kiss and touch when we reached more private surroundings.

"I missed you," I said, putting a hand on his thigh while he drove. Okay, maybe I couldn't wait to touch him.

"Missed you too. I can't believe I'm doing this. You realize I've never made an impulsive decision in my life, right?"

"I guess I'm just that irresistible."

"You are to me."

"I hope you brought that dick collection you promised me, because as soon as you park Vanessa someplace private I want you to fuck me."

Chad smiled at me. "Is that a fact? And here I thought you wanted me for more than my dick."

"You know I do. I've missed you."

"Right back at you."

Chad didn't waste any time parking Vanessa in our customary spot near the haunted barn. He hit the locks before turning to me. I had my seatbelt off as soon as we stopped moving. In seconds, my lips were on his and we were making our awkward way back toward the bed. I almost forgot to pull the privacy curtain over the cab.

We somehow wrestled our way up onto the bed without breaking our kiss for more than a second. Then we were laying together, kissing and touching. The urgency to get our hands on each other's skin gave way to tender exploration.

He gasped when I kissed his neck. I jerked and shuddered when his fingers brushed my nipples. He thrust his hips against me when I stroked my hand along the small of his back.

"I love you." I pulled back enough to look him in the eyes as I spoke.

We hadn't said it to each other in person yet, and it occurred to me that I needed to put it out there. Make it real.

"Love you too." He gave me a soft sweet smile. I kissed his nose. He laughed and pushed me away. "Okay, enough with the sweetness. Let's ditch the clothes, because I have been dying to get you naked, Daniel."

"Yeah?"

"Yeah."

He didn't have to ask twice. It took a bit of squirming and contorting to manage it without leaving the bed, but soon we were both naked. I'd learned my lesson from our date and worn my loosest sweats so the cast wouldn't be too big an obstacle to getting naked.

If we hadn't gotten distracted with long kisses and lingering touches, stripping might have taken less time.

"I love your ink," I said, tracing the lion that adorned his chest. He had other tattoos too. A spray of rainbow hued stars across his shoulders. The one I'd seen on his hip was a name, Maeve. I traced the script letters.

"Mom's name," Chad answered my unasked question, then changed the subject. "I love your muscles." He ran his finger along my pecs and down my happy trail. Not like I had washboard abs or anything, but I tried to stay toned. I even had a gym membership that came in handy when we were filming near larger population centers. Not so much here.

"Can I touch your, uh, junk?"

"My dick. Yeah, and my chest just not my front hole."

"Okay." I reached between his legs to stroke him. He was bigger than I'd expected, not huge or anything, but he had a noticeable erection. I stroked it. He moaned and bucked his hips into my grip.

"Good?"

"Yeah, stop, I don't want to come until I'm inside you."

"I can get behind that plan."

"I'm the one getting your behind," he teased, slapping my ass cheek. "Now, let me grab my bag."

I rolled over onto my side to let him get out of the bed. I liked the way his ass moved as he walked, and the view when he bent over to rummage through his bags. He returned to the bed with three silicone dicks cradled in his arms and straps dangling from his fingers. He didn't climb back up yet, showing me the options.

"Okay, here we go, we can look into other options to suit your interests, I'm cool with whatever. This one's your old standard, average size and girth. This one is your porn-star size queen option. And for the more adventurous, I've got one right out of tentacle porn. Never hurts to spice things up, right?"

"Right. Which is your favorite? I want you to enjoy it."

"They all feel good. They have a textured bit that stimulates me. And I get to fuck you, so there's that. Which would you prefer?" He bit his lip, like he was nervous about my answer.

"Are you going to judge me if I pick the tentacle one?" I teased.

Chad rolled his eyes. "Dude, have you met you? Of course you'd be the first to pick the tentacle one."

"Hey, I'm an open-minded guy."

"Yeah. You are." Chad leaned in to peck me on the cheek. "To be honest, I've kind of been dying to find someone who would be into it, you sure?"

"Heck, yes."

"Get yourself ready?" he suggested. I pulled the lube out from under my pillow and tried not to look sheepish.

"Um, would it be presumptuous to tell you I prepped before I came to pick you up?"

I watched as he set aside the other two prosthetics and got the neon purple and blue tentacle shaped one strapped into position.

"Nope, the word you are looking for there is hot. It would be super hot to know my schedule-phobic boyfriend thought ahead enough to prep himself for me to fuck him ASAP." He took a moment to roll a condom over his alien dick.

"Cool, now get up here and fuck me." I rolled onto my front, presenting him with my ass.

I recognized the moment he noticed the bejeweled end of the plug I'd optimistically put in before driving over to pick him up. His amusement made the discomfort of sitting with the thing stuffed up my ass for the better part of an hour worthwhile. Chad laughed when he saw the sparkling fake gem. He tapped it then wiggled it from side to side.

"Aw, you got all fancy for me?"

"Hey, not every day I get to use the fancy toys, figured this was a special occasion."

"It is," Chad agreed, he wiggled the plug free, and I heard the thump when it hit the floor behind us. I arched toward him, hoping to entice him to get on with it already. Despite my eagerness, Chad added more lube to the condom before lining the narrow end of his prosthetic up with my hole and sinking in with a low moan. The narrow taper let him slide right in and I pushed back to meet him.

There was a thicker part near the base and it had a bit of a curve that rubbed me just right. He soon had me moaning and riding back against him.

"You okay?" Chad asked when he was all the way inside me.

"Yeah, better than okay." I craned around, seeking his lips and he obliged me with a kiss.

"Fuck me with your big tentacle dick, babe."

With a throaty chuckle, Chad pulled back, gripped my hips and did just that, his hand finding my dick and stroking me in time to his thrusts. I didn't regret my choice of dicks—the prosthetic felt damn good sliding over just the right spot inside me until I couldn't hold back.

"I'm going to come," I gasped a warning.

"Yeah? I'm close too. Do it, come for me." Chad's hips snapped against my ass. He picked up the tempo that last bit more, driving me over the edge. I came in his fist.

He drove in deep and ground against my ass and his muscles tightened where his body pressed against mine as he let out a low cry of pleasure. He'd come too, from the sound of it.

When we'd both recovered from the high of orgasm, Chad withdrew from my body. He tossed the used condom and collapsed beside me in the bed.

"Was that okay?" He sounded so unsure it made me wonder what kind of assholes he'd been with before. But then, he'd already told me.

"More than okay. Incredible." I pulled him into my arms, I wanted to wipe away the insecurity in his voice. "You're incredible."

I kissed him. He kissed me back, desperate and needy. When we broke apart, I searched his expression.

"What about you, was it okay for you?"

Chad's lips curved in a slow smile. "Incredible," he echoed my words back to me, with the teasing edge I loved bringing out in him. We spent a long time losing ourselves in lazy kisses after that. Until he drifted to sleep wrapped in my embrace. Best sleep I'd had in ages.

# FORTY-EIGHT

## *Chad*

I woke the next morning hungry, but content to be pressed naked against Daniel and wrapped in warm blankets. Sex with Daniel was my new favorite activity. He was the first guy in a long time who didn't make me feel weird about my body. I was just a guy he wanted sexual intimacy with. Not a novelty item to try out and set aside.

With him, I didn't get self-conscious about using a prosthetic dick. Not even the tentacle model others had scoffed at. They assumed it was a weird kink, didn't give me a chance to explain that on my bad dysphoria days, wearing something alien felt less bad than the cis-looking models.

Daniel accepted that quirk without demanding an explanation. His easy acceptance of everything else pertaining to my dysphoria gave me a certainty he would understand when I told him why I had it. He didn't make stupid comments implying that he was a real man, and I wasn't. Or act weird about touching my junk. He accepted me.

I didn't worry that he would do anything to make me uncomfortable or touch me in ways I didn't want. I felt safe. That made the whole experience wonderful.

No surprise there. Daniel had always offered acceptance and given me a haven, from our first real conversation as anything other than client and insurance adjuster.

I loved him. We'd said it, in the grips of lust, but the words were no less true for it. They didn't seem big enough to describe my emotions toward him.

"I super freaking love you, you know that?" I mumbled into his chest. Daniel chuckled.

"Yeah?"

"Yeah." I propped myself up on one elbow and shoved his shoulder. "So if you ever pull another dangerous stunt like you did that day in the barn with Higgs again, I'll save the ragey ghost the trouble of murdering you. Got me?"

"Yes, dear." Daniel leaned in close and kissed me. "I promise, no more dangerous stunts. And for the record, I love you too."

"Glad we got that on the record." I gave him another gentle shove.

"Speaking of Higgs, we have a haunting to handle before we can move on to our next location. You up for helping me put our first vengeful spirit to rest?"

"It's a date," I said. "What's the plan?"

"Planning is your department, boss," Daniel teased.

"Oh, about that. Did you find time to read the proposal I put together?"

"I don't think we need a formal contract, babe. I'll give you half of Haunted Holdings, or like since you're stubborn 49%. Uncle Kurt helped me set it up as an LLC back when we were working on Vanessa."

"We are doing this right. I am not letting you sign away half of everything to me, like an impulsive love-struck dupe. Have your uncle review the contract. Then if you agree with the terms, sign. Otherwise I'm not taking a position as anything more than your lowly PA."

"Fine, I'll forward everything to Uncle Kurt. Where did you learn to write that lawyer shit, anyway?"

"It's hardly complicated legalese. I know some stuff about running a business from getting my MBA. And I worked with contracts at Chorus. They are big on making sure their policy contracts are airtight, you know? I picked up a thing or two." I shrugged it off.

"Well, Haunted Holdings is lucky to have you on board. I might make you like, the CEO. Maybe the President." He hugged me tight. "That'd be hot to say I'm fucking a CEO, right?"

I laughed at him. "Sure, boss, whatever you say."

Daniel made a face. "Seriously?"

"Don't worry, I hear it on good authority the future CEO of Haunted Holdings doesn't mind if employees conduct consensual relationships."

"Is that a fact?"

"Yeah. So, we're in the clear. Now, let's get ready and call Karen. It's time to end this haunting."

# FORTY-NINE

## *Dan*

Karen was as cryptic with her help as ever. But after we hung up, Tabitha forwarded me PDFs of relevant books and resources. Chad and I spent the rest of the week reading up on how to cleanse a place of lingering spirits. I focused on the details of putting Frank to rest.

Chad hit the books about protection. He drew up a spreadsheet covering ways to protect ourselves. He compiled a list of possible dangerous scenarios that might unfold. Then priced out a shopping list of paranormal gear to keep us safe on our adventures.

"I'm not sure all that junk will fit in Vanessa. We only have so much space, you know," I observed while reading over his shoulder. He gave me his best 'don't fuck with me' look.

"I'll make it fit. Don't you worry."

"You are the expert at making things fit into other things." I leered at him. He shoved me away, but he was laughing.

"Pervert, get back to work."

"Yes, boss." I grinned as I turned back to my current reading material.

It made for dry reading—I wasn't sure how someone made a book of rituals to put the dead to rest boring, but they'd managed it. I preferred the one earlier that had been a compilation of first-person accounts.

It didn't contain much in the way of instructional material. But the ways others had handled hauntings painted a broad picture that left me feeling confident that if they could do it, so could I.

Hours passed with me not getting through very many more chapters. I turned off my e-reader. Times like these, I missed physical books and the satisfaction of slamming a heavy tome shut. But traveling light was essential with Vanessa, so no physical books.

The library would have to do to get my fix of their aged vanilla scent and the soft whisper of turning pages. And the ability to express my pique with dramatic gestures.

I set aside the device and stretched. Chad arched a brow at me. "Done already?"

I debated telling him I was only taking a break. But I was already sick of planning. I itched with the need to act before anything else happened with Frank.

"Yep," I said.

"Really? You have a plan?" Chad looked skeptical.

"I promised I would, didn't I?"

"Okay, let's hear it."

Well, he wasn't beating around the bush, was he? Put on the spot, I drew from what I'd read and my experience with the paranormal over the years, to bullshit a plan. It wasn't as painful as I'd expected it to be, Chad even nodded along and suggested ways to make it safer.

To my surprise, within the hour we were walking into the haunted barn to execute my plan, such as it was. It was only then that I realized I still had no practical clue what I was doing, and we would probably die. At least Frank would be there to keep our spirits company.

# FIFTY

## *Chad*

D aniel's plan sounded decent. He seemed confident it would work. We were both eager to stop Frank before he hurt anyone else. So armed with the stuff I'd been able to gather on short notice—salt, blessed water and some calming incense to soothe the angry spirit—we made our move.

That might have been hasty, in retrospect. Our hearts were in the right place. It was evening. Since the ghost only seemed to appear later in the day and overnight, I didn't expect we would have much luck in the light of day. Much as that would have felt safer.

We went inside, cameras rolling at Daniel's insistence. At my insistence, the camera we were using was his GoPro— hands free, for the win—even if the footage might come out shaky. We left the IR camera set up by the barn door to capture a second angle, and those were the only concessions I allowed for recording equipment.

We stood near the entrance to the loft, the place where we'd seen the ghost the most. I sprinkled a line of salt around us, prepared a spritzer of the certified fancy water, and nodded to Daniel.

Daniel finished what he was doing, arranging his notes at our feet. Then he stood and squared his shoulders to address Frank.

"Mr. Higgs?"

We waited. At first nothing happened, then dust and bits of straw blew across the floor in a breeze I didn't feel. The hairs on the back of my neck stood on end. We weren't alone here anymore.

"Dan?"

Daniel nodded. "Frank, can I call you Frank? I have exposed the Goodmans for their crimes against you. See?"

Daniel held up the altered newspaper announcement he'd photoshopped. The headline screamed that the Goodman family had orchestrated Higgs' death to take over the farm.

The surrounding straw flew up higher, disturbing the line of salt. It made me wish we'd waited for the protective stones and herbs I'd ordered online to arrive.

The lights we'd brought with us dimmed, as though something drained their batteries. Then a powerful gust of wind ripped through the barn. The door near Vanessa slammed shut.

The flashlight guttered out, leaving us with only the LED indicator on Daniel's GoPro and whatever light seeped in through gaps in the rundown roof and walls.

"They shall pay!" Frank's deep bass voice boomed through the structure.

"They paid, see?" Dan held up the doctored headline. Higgs' ghost materialized in front of him and snatched the paper, skimming it.

"Higgs Dairy?" the gruff voice demanded, seeming to come from all around us.

"Yes, I promise. We will tell anyone who will listen about what happened here," Dan swore. His sincerity and earnestness sounded utterly genuine. Frank gave him an appraising look. The fierce gale slackened, the temperature warmed a degree.

I harbored a brief hope we might be in for an anticlimactic confrontation.

Then Frank turned to me, his spectral pitchfork appeared, he leveled the prongs inches from my chest. I froze.

"Blood for blood," the ghost bellowed, his voice was clearer now as it fed on our fear.

"What are you doing?" Dan yelled over the noise of doors slamming and wind roaring through the central aisle carrying eddies of dust and debris.

"Take back what's mine!"

I was still holding the blessed water, so I spritzed it toward the weapon aimed at my heart. The solid tines took on an ethereal appearance, like I could pass my hand through them if I tried. Instead, I took a few prudent strides backward.

The ghost followed, stalking after me with slow deliberate steps. When he stepped over the area where Dan had left his notes, he stopped. The ethereal wind died away. The din of objects moving gave way to eerie silence.

We started at Frank's ghost.

It reminded me of watching a bug trying to crawl out of an overturned glass. He scrabbled at the air in front of him as though it were an impenetrable field.

I glanced down at the sigils Daniel had chalked onto the floor from his notes. He breathed a sigh of relief.

I listened as he spoke ritual words. Frank faded with each line Daniel recited, his figure growing fainter and fainter until he dissolved in a violent flash of blinding white light.

Our flashlight beams brightened back to life.

The sensation of being unwelcome I'd barely registered anymore lifted. The barn no longer seemed like hostile territory. My perpetual urge to flee the building, present since I first stepped foot inside, dissipated.

The place still had an air of disuse about it, but it no longer gave me the oppressive sense of something ominous lying in wait.

"I think we did it," Daniel said, with a hopeful smile.
"Yeah," I grinned at him, "I think we did."

# EPILOGUE

## *Chad*

"Hey, Crew! So how did you enjoy the wrap-up episode for Goodman Dairy?" Dan grinned into the camera.

As always, his smile made me want him, but I could keep it in my pants for the length of the livestream. There would be plenty of time to jump his bones afterward. It would be our first sex in New Hampshire en route to Hawk Lake for the September haunting.

That made me think we should start a map of every state we'd fucked in. With our line of work, I figured we could check off all of them, maybe minus Alaska, Hawaii, and the outlying territories I made a mental note to mention the plan to Daniel after the live chat and find a map to print out for marking our progress.

Daniel nudged me with his elbow to get my attention. I tried to cover my distraction by waving for the camera. "Hey, crew, did you miss me?"

"Surprise! Chad took me back. How was that twist to this week's video? Did you like it?"

I didn't read the comments. I didn't care what they thought, Daniel chuckled at whatever they were saying though.

"Yeah, he made me grovel, didn't you, Chad?" Daniel bumped my arm again. I looked at him, unable to hide my affection as I took his hand in mine.

"Just a little groveling."

"And you'll all be glad to hear I am not banging my PA."

Daniel held up his hands, like he was quelling a protest. I glanced at the comments, surprised to see most of them seemed disappointed at the implication we weren't a couple.

"It's true," I said, playing along.

"I know, I know—we are super cute together, thanks Bri. But we've discussed it and Chad will continue with Hauntastic Haunts as my partner, not my assistant. He's got some fantastic ideas to improve the channel, and I think you guys will appreciate his organizational skills. Case in point, we will now have a regular scheduled live stream each week after the new video drops. Instead of just doing it whenever the fancy strikes me. That should make it easier for everyone to tune it.

"We are throwing around having a live watch party for the big Hauntoween haunting coming up in October. It will be epic. Chad is already working out the permits for us to film at the site we have planned. The next full webisode will be the unboxing for a gadget that improves on our current EVP recorder. The maker had some impressive claims, which we will test for your edification. I can't wait to give you the first sneak peek at the latest gear and our newest haunting."

"Can we give them a hint about where we're headed?" I asked.

We paused, letting them comment begging for details. Then Daniel grinned at me. "Yeah, babe, give them a teeny hint."

"We're headed to a location that has shown up in regional fiction. And since Dan is still on medical orders not to drive long hours with his leg healing, we are staying in the Northeast next month. So we'll start a post with your guesses as to the haunted site later tonight. Once we have front-runners, we'll set up a poll so you can vote on where you think our next Hauntastic Haunt might be."

"See? I told you this guy is way more organized than me, he will bring you all kinds of interactive goodies going forward, so monitor the channel for announcements. This fall will be a blast."

"Do we have time for some questions, Dan?" I delivered my line.

"We have a few minutes, who has questions for us?"

A few rolled in and Daniel snorted.

"Questions that aren't about Chad and I dating?"

A glance at the comments showed that was a big negative.

"Okay, I know when to give the people what they want, Chad, you want to field the first one?"

Daniel pointed to a comment from RadRaf.

"I made the first move, Raf. Dan was too worried I'd perceive any move on his part as workplace harassment. But the chemistry between us was undeniable, so I took a chance on him, and I'm so glad that I did."

We answered a few more questions. Where was our first date? What pet names did we use? Who was the blanket hog? Silly couple stuff.

We ignored the sprinkling of questions about what we did in bed. That was none of their business, though a small childish part of me wanted to reply with a link to tentacle porn. I thought better of it though. Too on the nose. When the questions slowed, Daniel wrapped up the chat.

"Thanks for tuning in, everyone, it's nice to introduce my boyfriend to you knowing you'll all show support. I am so proud of the community we've built here. You can't know how much each of your support means to me. Thanks for making me a part of your lives and I hope that our videos continue to bring entertainment to your lives for a long time."

"You guys are making him all mushy," I teased. It was true Daniel was getting emotional, so I wrapped my arm around him and hugged him. "Let's end it on that note. Watch for the teaser trailer for the September unboxing later this week. Until next time," I paused, glancing at Daniel in a prompt for him to join me in saying his catchphrase. He picked up on my cue and we spoke in unison, "Have a hauntastic day!"

Daniel ended the livestream, and I kissed him.

"You are so hot when you get in front of a camera."

Daniel chuckled. "Is that a request to dabble in amateur porn with me? I could get on board with that."

I gave all his high-tech gear a significant stare. "I mean, tempting as that sounds, nope. Not interested in showing the world my junk. Or sharing your alien fetish with anyone."

"Fair enough. But we should totally practice, you know, in case you ever change your mind."

"You don't think I look good fucking you already?" I batted my lashes at him, moving to straddle his lap.

I could feel how hard he was, his dick jutting against my ass through his jeans. To be honest, I was rock hard too. We'd been busy since Frank's departure.

First getting the final Goodman Dairy wrap up video out on time. Then working with local law enforcement about the accident that put Ben in the hospital. It helped that the man was conscious and talking. He confirmed that we'd had nothing to do with his injuries. No one was pressing any charges, which worked out for us.

A few days of getting the runaround about how to get our camera back from evidence and I was ready to call it a lost cause. It was a stroke of luck that Leon had a buddy on the force and he put in a friendly word for us.

With no case, they released the camera back into Daniel's custody. Then we'd spent a day completing the paperwork with Daniel's uncle for me to buy into Haunted Holdings LLC.

I liked his Uncle Kurt. He seemed to have Daniel's best interest at heart and it showed in the negotiations. Daniel was ready to sign whatever I put in front of him from the start. His uncle made him slow down and consider the potential consequences. The process took longer over video chat than it would have in person, but we'd come to an agreement.

On top of all that, I had to make the final arrangements for next month's haunting. It had been a busy few days. I was excited to take on our next challenge. With Daniel, it felt like every day held the promise of adventure.

"I'm sure you look fantastic, which is why I'm thinking of installing a mirror above the bed. Then I can see you fucking me without having to record it."

"Or we could rig up a projector and you can play tentacle porn on it while we fuck, get you in the mood. And terrify or confuse anyone who stands too close to Vanessa when we get going."

Daniel laughed. "Oh, man, don't tempt me. How hilarious would it be to play that shit when we get nosy neighbors?"

"Does that happen often?"

Daniel shrugged. "More in the summer. When more people are camping."

I snuggled against his warm chest, dropping my head to his shoulder. His arms wrapped around me to hold me close. I wriggled in response, teasing us both with the slide of friction between our groins.

"Or we can just leave the ceiling a blank slate."

"Or that." Daniel pressed a kiss to the top of my head. I intended for the evening to end in our cozy custom bed with both of us sexed up and sated. For now though, I was content being close to Daniel.

\*\*\*

If you enjoyed this book, I'd love it if you left a review at www.amzn.com/B07YSV2ZNQ. Dan and Chad's next adventure takes place in Dan's Hauntastic Haunts Investigates: Hawk Lake available at www.amzn.com/B081LM3WXP

For a free short story, sign up for my newsletter at http://eepurl.com/dNcScQ. And be sure to check out my urban fantasy series, Psions of SPIRE, starting with the novella Shelter available at www.amzn.com/B07NM9XL8K. Thanks for reading!

# About the Author

Alex Silver grew up mostly in Northern Maine and is now living in Canada with one spouse, two kids, and three birds. Alex is a trans guy who started writing fiction as a child and never stopped. Although there were detours through assisting on a farm and being a pharmacist along the way.

Visit Alex online at:

http://alexsilverauthor.wordpress.com/

Join my Facebook group at:

https://www.facebook.com/groups/AlexsAlcove/

Follow me on BookBub at:

https://www.bookbub.com/profile/alex-silver

Sign up for my newsletter for a free short story at:

http://eepurl.com/dNcScQ


And as always, consider leaving a review on Amazon or Goodreads if you enjoyed this book, reviews are of vital importance to independent authors, thanks!

# Hauntastic Haunts Series

## Novels:
Dan's Hauntastic Haunts Investigates: Goodman Dairy (*Book 1*)
Dan's Hauntastic Haunts Investigates: Hawk Lake (*Book 2*)
Dan's Hauntastic Haunts Investigates: Ivarsson School (*Book 3*)

## Shorts:
Drew's Haunted Hangout (*A Hauntastic Haunts Short Story 1*)
Rafael's Haunted Halloween (*A Hauntastic Haunts Short Story 2*)
Lee's Haunted Holiday (*A Hauntastic Haunts Short Story 3*)

### *Drew's Haunted Hangout*

*What if your imaginary boyfriend wasn't so imaginary?*

Drew was no stranger to feeling ostracized from his peers. His obsession with the paranormal began young. When he befriended Toby, the dead boy who lives in his garage.

Drew was the weird unathletic kid everyone avoided on the playground. As a teen, he found understanding in an online community created by a paranormal investigations vlogger.

Falling in love with Toby only made Drew's interest in ghosts more intense. But when he discovered Toby's striking resemblance to an unresolved missing person report, he didn't know how to help his ghost boyfriend.

At a loss, Drew turned to his online idol for help. The truth could set Drew and Toby both free, or destroy everything between them.

This is a young adult paranormal MM short story.
http://eepurl.com/dNcScQ

## *Dan's Hauntastic Haunts Investigates: Goodman Dairy*

*When ghosts reach across the veil, Daniel Collins is there to tell their stories.*

Dan is a vlogging ghost hunter. He has devoted his life to documenting paranormal activity. In his converted van, he travels around the country exploring haunted sites. He loves the thrill of filming restless spirits.

Chad Brewer, skeptic, works for an insurance company. He doesn't believe in ghosts, but watching Dan's vlog is his guilty pleasure. The cute vlogger is accident prone. He has Chad's work extension on speed-dial. The two talk whenever Dan gets hurt during an investigation, a frequent occurrence.

When Chad loses his job for approving too many claims, Dan offers him a position as his personal assistant. The pair sets out to investigate a haunted dairy barn for the vlog's next video series. The catch is that they must live and work together in Dan's tiny traveling home.

As the paranormal activity at the haunted dairy ramps up, so does the romantic tension between the two men. Can the love between a skeptic and a social media sensation conquer a vengeful ghost?

Dan's Hauntastic Haunts is a paranormal MM romance between a gay vlogger and his trans personal assistant. Buckle up for a hauntastic good time. www.amzn.com/B07YSV2ZNQ

## *Dan's Hauntastic Haunts Investigates: Hawk Lake*

*When ghosts cry out, Dan and Chad heed their call.*

Daniel and Chad are on the road to Hawk Lake, Maine, to investigate rumors of a haunting. With his new role in Daniel's life, Chad feels like he has something to prove. He is determined to make the Hawk Lake haunting videos the best Hauntastic Haunts has ever aired.

Daniel gets sidetracked when he realizes that he might have gotten in over his head with his long distance apprenticeship to a genuine medium. Old insecurities rear their heads and threaten the budding relationship between Dan and Chad.

Neither member of the Hauntastic Haunts crew is ready for what they uncover when they discover the truth behind the ghost ship haunting Hawk Lake. Secrets and lies that threaten to tear apart a community that is still healing from their grief might be better left buried. Daniel and Chad have to decide which is more important, telling the stories of the living or preserving the memories of a handful of ghosts.

Get ready for a hauntastic time with this paranormal trans MM romance. www.amzn.com/B081LM3WXP

## *Dan's Hauntastic Haunts Investigates: Ivarsson School*

*When a curse comes calling, Dan and Chad confront their greatest challenge yet.*

Hauntastic Haunts is investigating the historic Ivarsson School. With Halloween right around the corner, the vlog is in peak season. Dan and Chad are eager to explore the decades-long string of strange deaths among the school's young scholars. While they delve into the mystery, both men must come to grips with Chad's newfound talents as a medium.

Dan and Chad's efforts to uncover the haunting's truth meet with mixed messages from both the living and the dead. They're left wondering if this month's site is full of tricks, or if there's a treat awaiting discovery. The locals blame a curse for all the misfortune at the one-room schoolhouse, and if the pattern holds, the guys are at risk of becoming the latest victims.

Join ghost hunters Dan and Chad on their third hauntastic adventure in this trans M/M paranormal romance. www.amzn.com/B087QPR6TD

# Psions of SPIRE Series

| | | | |
|---|---|---|---|
| Shelter | Novella 0.5 | February 2019 | www.amzn.com/B07NM9XL8K |
| Bright Spark | Book 1 | February 2019 | www.amzn.com/B07NZ8KPS6 |
| Bold Move | Novella 1.5 | February 2019 | www.amzn.com/B07YVGZXDM |
| Keen Sense | Book 2 | April 2019 | www.amzn.com/B07R6L8W91 |
| Weak Link | Novella 2.5 | June 2019 | www.amzn.com/B07T4J2LJZ |
| Quick Fire | Book 3 | July 2019 | www.amzn.com/B07VGTF3NB |

| | | | |
|---|---|---|---|
| Clear Sight | Book 4 | March 2020 | www.amzn.com/ B07ZQP7BDS |
| New Look | Novella 4.5 | August 2020 | www.amzn.com/ B08F4GBK63 |

# *Shelter*

*Family is what you make it.*

Former foster kid and abuse survivor, Elliott Sheffield, lost everything when he developed telepathy at twelve years old. He's used to not relying on anyone. There are worse things than being lonely and alone, even for a psion who craves closeness. He has plans for his life and nothing can distract him from proving that he can succeed. That will show everyone who cast him aside. Especially his former best friend Caleb Gaetz.

Pansexual, poly, psion, Caleb is comfortable with all of those labels. Life seems easy for Caleb. He has a supportive family and a vibrant social life. The future will figure itself out. For the present he plans to enjoy his university years to the fullest extent possible. He knows his hedonistic tendencies irritate his former best friend, Elliott, to no end. He just doesn't understand why Elliott takes Caleb's sex life so personally.

When life throws them both curve balls, they must adjust their visions for the future to one that will give them both a happily ever after, or risk their plans falling apart.

This urban fantasy romance contains an open M/M relationship, mention of past abuse, and positive HIV status. www.amzn.com/B07NM9XL8K

## *Bright Spark*

*Sometimes growing up means giving up your preconceptions.*

Aaron Anderson and Jake Matthews were childhood sweethearts until Aaron developed psionic abilities that turned both of their worlds upside down and tore them apart.

Six years later they reconnect when Aaron returns home to work with a youth summer camp affiliated with SPIRE. Jake is at the same camp, along with his current partners, to protest the organization funding it. Sparks fly when the couple reunites and Aaron discovers hidden abilities that bring him to the attention of SPIRE.

Aaron and Jake have every intention of seizing their second chance at love. But once more, forces outside their control are at play. And the organization Aaron believes in is at the center of events targeting vulnerable youth.

This urban fantasy romance contains M/M and an open M/M/M relationship. www.amzn.com/B07NZ8KPS6

Made in United States
North Haven, CT
23 July 2023

39301156R00171